VICE BOUND

D1519183

Mathieu Crowley

ISBN: 9798841215257 (paperback)

PROLOGUE

Talons scraped on cracked cobblestones, unseen by the eyes of the innocent. A darkness of no natural cause draped the grounds of Capital Vice in a shroud that comforted demons of death. At the center of the secretive commune, a ceremony of high delirium was taking place.

To the common Zealots of Capital Vice, this celebration signified the culmination of an era of depthless selfishness. The Zealots were learning that their self-centeredness must be spurned in favor of unity, solidarity, and indivisibility.

Exceeding them all sat A'devios, the Zenith Authority of Capital Vice. He held a scepter made of exquisite jewel, and he was perched in a wooden throne that was presently engulfed in a roaring blaze of black flames. A'devios had assumed the throne boastfully, in order to illustrate his power to his followers: the sweltering heat licked at his limbs, yet his skin remained unblistered. The searing fire assaulted his clothes, yet his garments remained unburnt.

A'devios addressed the congregation mightily. "Question not the power of Zephiscestra, especially as you intoxicate yourself on her Glory. Is it not She who hath given all of you all your greatest desires? When you first invoked Zephiscestra's name, She granted you Zealots the Entrusted Offerings that are gathered among us, today. Let them be an ever-present reminder of her boundless ability! Remember, now, that your Entrusted Offerings protect you! They must surpass you, because your bodies are weak!"

A'devios clutched his scepter to his heart. Suddenly, a drunken Zealot threw himself into the merciless wildfire. The Zealot's soul was instantly transported to The Ultimate Plane, where Zephiscestra awaited them all. The body's demise was followed by a discrete shower of glittering light, which was met with fervent applause from the surviving members of Capital Vice.

A'devios, the Zenith Authority, bellowed with mirth. "You must all see! Individually, you are weak. A lonesome Zealot could not withstand the flames that I myself have created, by my own power!" Again, A'devios clutched his scepter to his chest.

A sc'ermin of Wrath, coiled by the edge of the fire, disentangled itself and slithered gravely towards the throne. The Zealot who had created the sc'ermin, a man who rippled with muscle, screamed in protest; his sc'ermin paid no heed to his cries. The sc'ermin was able to wrap itself once around the Zenith Authority's throne before succumbing to the flame, erupting in a shower of light.

The affected Zealot forgot himself and crumpled to the cobblestones in a daze. A'devios arms raised above his head, bellowed in arrogant triumph. "Do not pity this Zealot, for his Entrusted Offering was not sufficiently cultivated! Alone, he is lost, as you all will be if you do not follow my rule. Truly I tell you, the members of Capital Vice are lost without my guidance! Only under the rule of A'devios, the Zenith Authority, shall you prepare sufficiently for the Preeminent Offering. Only by following the Zenith Authority may you reach The Ultimate Plane with Entrusted Offerings worthy to serve Zephiscestra forever!"

A'devios clutched at his scepter, keeping his hands raised above his head. An utter silence ensued in the minds of the Zealots of Capital Vice, allowing for A'devios' sermon to fill their heads without obstruction.

"Capital Vice! For too long have you laid drunk in Zephiscestra's boundless Glory. You have grown stagnant, basking on the plateaus of your Pride and spending every opportunity for Envy on your virtue of Sloth. You have grown so fond of your Entrusted Offerings that you forget that they are to be returned to Zephiscestra at the Preeminent Offering, so that they may serve her in battle forever. But, fear not! For I have enacted a plan that will save your souls from Boundless Humiliation!"

A'devios' followers rejoiced, their own mouths forming words that they themselves could not hear. A sc'ermin with a massive jaw snorted soundlessly in gratitude, causing droplets of Glory to sputter from her cavernous nostrils. An insatiable sc'ermin of Gluttony was quick to lap up the wet specks that steamed on the ground.

A'devios' continued, saying, "Zealots, heed my word! The only directive that you have is to properly cultivate your Entrusted Offerings by nourishing them with lesser sc'ermin who are not within the ranks of Capital Vice. I have determined that it is time to deliver a boundless bounty upon you!"

"Zephiscestra has tilled the fields, and indeed I tell you, the fields have been ready for years. In Her infinite power, Zephiscestra has ensured that each human being on Earth, each member of the Ignorant Mass, now carries a device that will allow me to deliver a series of perfectly constructed, ingeniously fabricated messages directly into their hands. Using my own intelligence, granted to me by Zephiscestra Herself, I have determined that the time is now to plant the seeds in the fields that Zephiscestra has tilled!"

A'devios raised his scepter above his head, and before he could speak, the black flames around his throne intensified greatly. He raised his eyebrows and screamed his proclamation, the decree that he had planned to deliver, as the oppressive heat began to sink into his limbs.

"Zephiscestra, I now prompt you to sow the fields that you have tilled for us!"

As the Zealots of Capital Vice watched in fierce ecstasy, A'devios leapt from his fiery throne and landed heavily amongst his followers.

He began to walk in their midst, saying, "Just now, messages that contain the Binding Ritual were sent all over the globe. We shall monitor the emergence of lesser sc'ermin with great interest. Soon, we shall reap the yields of the fields, and your Entrusted Offerings will consume enough nourishment to rival the power of the goddess Herself! Soon, you will harvest the bounty so gracefully bestowed upon you!"

A'devios clutched his scepter, and the voices of Capital Vice collectively sent shockwaves in all directions towards The Ultimate Plane. Some cultists wept with what they called joy, while others gnashed their teeth in anticipation of fulfillment. Zephiscestra smiled on them all.

CHAPTER 1

CASEY BENTON WIPED his forehead and found that it was slick with sweat, despite the air conditioner blasting in his one of his workplace's many break rooms. He and Charlie Falk sat at the same table that they used every day, at a time that was too early for most of their coworkers to justify spending their lunch hour. Although the break room was empty, Casey silently begged Charlie's headphones to remain as quiet as possible, on the off chance that any of the other employees decided to use this time to leave their desk and make a purchase at the vending machine.

Casey didn't usually wish to hide from his coworkers, but he presently desired the utmost privacy while he allowed Charlie to listen to a song that Casey had just finished producing in his bedroom. Casey considered himself fortunate to have someone to personally entrust with his music, especially someone as nice as Charlie.

Casey had appreciated Charlie since they day they met. When Casey was placed into Charlie's department, they instantly forged a working friendship based on two main factors: division of workload, and memes.

During Casey's first day at the company, Charlie informed him that Bill Desta, the other employee at their station, spent nearly all of him time at the office browsing unrelated material on the internet. Noticing Casey's confusion, Charlie explained that there was only enough work for one person in the department, but there was plenty of internet to go around. Because of this, Casey was able to receive a steady paycheck and a pair of friends who supported him, while Charlie was able to stay focused on performing a job that he loved, in addition to receiving a steady stream of content curated personally by his in-house internet professionals.

Once the song finished playing, Charlie waited a few moments to remove his headphones. He wanted to absorb every bit of Casey's creation, so he unconsciously treated his headphones like a gas station nozzle that liked to hold on to the last few cents of his purchase. Once he was satisfied that the music had been poured completely into his ears, he removed his headphones and readied himself to give his review.

"So, what do you think?," Casey asked, apprehensively. "Give me your first impressions."

Filtered sunlight glittered between them as Charlie locked eyes with Casey. Charlie believed that, if he could look directly into someone's eyes, he could determine what that person was feeling with a high degree of accuracy. At that moment, Charlie sensed a conflicted person in front of him. On the surface, Casey was terrified of showing his work to anyone at all. But, Charlie surmised that Casey believed in what he did, deep down into his core. Charlie determined that the outward fear was caused by an underlying belief that Casey's work wouldn't be accepted by anyone else, so he would be left on an island of his own support.

Charlie brought his gaze back to the computer screen where Casey's video had just ended. The screen displayed an image of Casey's smiling face, free from the doubt that plagued him in life. The image of Casey showed his true feelings: that he was a talented artist who got lost in his creation.

Charlie knew that Casey needed support, and that support came out of him easily. "It's good. Actually, it's really good. Did you show it to anyone else?"

"I sent Bill the link last night," Casey said, the relief clear on his face. "I don't trust anyone else in my life enough to tell them." Charlie swelled with pride. "There are twenty-two views. Do you know else could have watched it?"

"Well, I watched it three times to check how it sounded... one is yours," Casey flashed a sheepish grin, "and at least one is Bill's, but who knows how many times he played it. The rest are random people from LitMille."

"You should definitely show this to other people. The lyrics are a little silly, but that's where the charm comes from. And, your voice sounds incredible."

"Yeah, maybe I should," Casey said. "There are a lot of things that I want to do with this platform. I'm deathly afraid of talking about it, but, for some reason, I still want people to watch it... Am I conceited?"

"Ugh, I wish you were," Charlie said. Casey looked at him in mock disgust.

"Maybe then you would take a chance on *Peter*." As he said it, Charlie's heart skipped a beat, and he wondered why he even mentioned Peter at all.

"Peter?" Casey looked around nervously. "Don't tell me he's here already."

Charlie shook his head with a sigh.

The employees at their multimedia company were allowed to take their lunch breaks at any time they chose. This led to a constant struggle of gauging how hungry Peter Adams was going to be on any given day. After initially noticing him, Casey still hadn't worked up the nerve to break the ice, even after a few weeks of what some would consider light stalking.

"Oh, okay," Casey said. "Anyway, I'm just saying that—since you're my best friend—I don't know if you really think it's good or if you just want me to feel good."

"Trust me. It's good. And, if you want to hint at your sexuality, I think that singing about rainbows is a good way to start."

"Yeah, and maybe *Trevor* will see it," Casey said. He imagined his celebrity crush sitting rapt at a computer, replaying the video over and over.

Charlie frowned. "Why would he see your video out of the millions of others out there?"

"Come on, don't be like that," Casey said. "He's on LitMille all the time. My video is on LitMille. That way, he could hypothetically see it."

It wasn't likely, given their current situation. Casey and Trevor Greenbrook couldn't have been more different. While Casey was a bit tightly wound at times, Trevor was a free spirit. Casey wore muted colors while Trevor dressed extravagantly. Casey shied away from parties, whereas Trevor was the life of them. However, the starkest difference between them was that Trevor was notably famous. Casey, on the other hand...

Charlie put a hand over his own aching heart. "You two truly are star crossed lovers."

"Okay, I know it's a stretch," Casey said, backtracking for a moment. He then pushed on, saying, "But what a tale it would be if I, lowly bedroom singer Casey Benton, could meet up with the illustrious Trevor Greenbrook?"

Charlie counted himself among the few who could coax the energy out of Casey. Charlie felt pride in the fact that Casey was comfortable enough around him to shed his nervous demeanor in place of more personable behavior. He was a bit disheartened, however, to realize that he could never inspire Casey to create such a public display of creativity, especially when Trevor Greenbrook did so without ever speaking a word to him.

"More like a fairy tale," Charlie said, bitterly hearing the jealousy in his own voice. He decided to save face, saying, "Don't let me put down your dreams. Next time, maybe you should give him a shout out?"

"Good idea," Casey said tentatively.

Thousands of Trevor's fans tagged him in their own videos every day, hoping to be noticed. They mentioned him in social media posts, wishing to spark a conversation. Almost every night, Casey browsed their posts for hours, analyzing Trevor's sporadic responses to glean any hint that the influencer was having sex with any of them. Would it hurt Casey to know that Trevor was flying around the world to hook up with horny admirers? Or, would it give him hope that he could be next on the itinerary?

Suddenly, Charlie nudged him and said, "Look who *is* here."

Bob Sutter walked slowly by their table, holding a brown lunch bag. As he passed, he said, sourly, "My niece isn't as obsessed with rainbows as you are." Bob flicked a bit of food that landed with a *splat* near Casey's computer, laughed, and sauntered away.

"Ugh," Casey said. "Maybe he's right. Twenty-seven might be too old to write stupid songs about colors."

"Listen to me," Charlie said, reaching out to rub Casey's back, then thinking better of it. "Grown men can like rainbows, too. Especially gay ones. It's not some nursery rhyme, it's a symbol for equality and love. Remember Trevor's bathing suit from Guadalajara?"

Casey nodded. Indeed, he would never forget.

"Bob is a toxic prick," Charlie said. "You want your videos to be happy and fun, something for us to take our minds off of the darkness of the world. That's why I loved it. Trust me, it's really good."

"But I only have twenty-two views," Casey said, his face suddenly parallel with the table's surface. "I can't put myself out there so publicly for that little attention. Plus, now I know that the other views came from Bob and his friends making fun of me. Why would I want to expose myself to people who would only want to make me sad?"

"That's the thing," Charlie said. "That was only, what, your third video? You won't get noticed by anyone special with only three posts. You need to keep putting yourself out there. Don't worry about the haters. Isn't that what Trevor always says?"

"Trevor's haters are different. His only exist in the comments section. Mine can beat me up after work."

Casey knew that his workplace adversary had never touched him, but sometimes it felt like Bob would want nothing more than to punch him in the face. Contacting Human Resources had always crossed his mind, but Casey worried about the consequences that might ensue if Bob found out that he reported him.

Casey continued, "Maybe I should take my channel down, now that they found it."

"Oh my god, don't be so dramatic," Charlie said. "If you like doing it, then keep doing it. I'm here to support you."

"I'm here for you, too, and don't you forget it!" Bill Desta, the third member of their trio, suddenly appeared behind his usual chair. "Casey, I loved your video. It was fabulous, and I mean that in every sense of the word."

Bill dropped his lunch bag carelessly onto the table, then gently placed his laptop next to it. The laptop was Bill's prized possession. It was an ordinary portable computer, the same model owned by both Casey and Charlie, but Bill put his laptop to much greater use than his friends did with theirs.

Casey had scrolled through digital miles of Trevor Greenbrook's social media feeds, but his daily screen time paled in comparison to the relentless browsing that Bill was able to sustain.

"Thanks, Bill," Casey said, eyes cast down. "I'm glad you liked it."

Bill couldn't help but notice Casey's palpable anxiety. "Hey, what the matter?"

"Casey is upset because he got one bad review," Charlie said. "From a literal troll of a man."

"I just want more people to view the things that I put out, people who aren't Bob Sutter," Casey said.

Bill pouted as hard as he could. Such an expression could usually make Casey laugh, but his present effort did not receive the effect he hoped for.

"Casey, don't take your songs down. I've listened to your previous one every day, and you look so happy in them. Who cares if you aren't famous for them?"

"It's not even that he wants to be famous," Charlie said. "He wants Trevor to see them." Bill gave Charlie a sideways glance, then put his hand up in exasperation. "Ugh, you keep talking about Trevor. What about the friends that you have right here?"

Charlie nodded—a little too vigorously for his own liking. "I don't know, he's kind of my celebrity inspiration. I really want to impress him," Casey said.

"More like he's your celebrity crush and you want to kiss him," Bill said.

He and Charlie laughed as kindly as they could.

Casey managed a giggle. He said, "If only there was a foolproof way to meet him. I could tag his username in in my next video. But, I would be so embarrassed if he didn't notice it."

At Casey's admission, Bill recognized a perfect avenue in the conversation, one that would allow him to unveil his most recent, fleeting obsession. Bill straightened his face, trying to make his appearance as serious as possible. He knew how ridiculous his next statement would be, and he didn't think his friends would believe him. However, even though Casey was going through a rough patch, Bill couldn't help but play a harmless prank.

"If you really want to meet him, I might know a way to do it."

"You do?" Casey, still disheartened, didn't sound convinced. Bill had anticipated this, but he decided to push on with his shenanigans.

Bill said, "A couple of days ago, I stumbled across a post on my favorite message board about a mysterious…well…process. I've been following the thread closely ever since I discovered it. Basically, if you take some certain steps, you can get anything that you want. Even your *deepest* desire."

Bill paused for dramatic effect. His friends waited attentively. Charlie's lip started to curl into a subtle smirk.

"A bunch of people on the boards are commenting on it. It has 40 pages of comments so far."

"Well, what is it?" Charlie asked. "And how many pictures of his feet will Casey have to sell?"

"I mean, it's nothing," Bill said, teasing out the information to sustain his gratification. "I just thought that it would be a good story."

"I'm listening," Casey said halfheartedly. He was understandably doubtful, but Bill's stories were usually good for some quick amusement. Casey figured that if his spirit could be lightened, he should just go along with it.

Bill laughed again, although he understood that he was only holding a fragment of their attention. He attempted to reel out the line, so to speak, so that he could pull them back in. "I shouldn't have brought it up. You two are too pure for this kind of garbage."

"Why not try to entertain us?" Casey asked. Bill dropped the charade, yet held on to the gratification that came from holding an audience. "If it's entertainment you want, then strap in, honey. There's this devil ritual, and—"

"You're right, I didn't want to know," Charlie said, cutting him off midsentence.

"Okay, so it's definitely not a real option," Casey said. "For the sake of the conversation, however, do care to elaborate."

Bill pressed on, galvanized by Casey's appeal. "So, apparently, there's this ancient, religious incantation. You can enter into a contract with this random goddess that I've never even heard of before. Allegedly, rulers and high-priests would do it in the early days of civilization. They would say a magic spell, then take certain…actions. Then, whoever invoked the goddess' favor could achieve miraculous accomplishments. Apparently, after making the deal, a small tribe of hunter-gathers immediately discovered how to make cities out of stone and cultivate the land for agriculture. Even if they were incredibly outnumbered, warriors who prayed to the goddess could win a battle against full armies of enemies. As the centuries went on, sick and inbred royals could even recover from genetic defects overnight, just by entering into this divine contract."

"You've finally lost it," Charlie said giddily.

"I agree," Casey said. "Thanks for the tip, but I'd rather do my usual thing of trying to telepathically talk to Trevor in my sleep."

"It's all obviously fake," Bill continued, undeterred. "But, some of these crackpot theories are admittedly interesting. Don't get me wrong, the people attempting to further this hoax are indisputable trolls, but they are going to extreme lengths to make it look authentic. There are full pages of vague, pseudo-historical claims that are being linked together in impressive ways. The message board's members are posting grainy photos of cave paintings and associating them with ancient prophecies that are, in all likelihood, entirely fabricated. The whole mess is highly contrived, but it's kept me entertained for a good while."

"Wait, you said it was a goddess," Casey said, his finger on his chin. "Why did you start by calling it a devil ritual?"

"Well, the original post alleges that the deity connected with the ritual can grant your wishes. I guess I kind of latched on to that. But someone else in the thread posted photos of small idols made of jewels that are supposed to be related. The carvings depict demons with horns and wings. Stuff like that. You know, claws and fangs?" He bent his fingers to demonstrate. "Based on that evidence, some people in the thread think that they were tokens from a deal with the devil."

Casey and Charlie scoffed in unison. Bill wasn't known for superstition, but he did enjoy researching all kinds of outlandish topics.

"Oh, come on," Bill said. "Do you want to look at it, or what?"

"Oh, whatever, pass it here," Casey said. Bill clapped his hands together in glee. "I have it saved on my laptop."

"I don't want to get anywhere near that kind of crap," Charlie said. "That stuff really freaks me out."

"Well, then, avert your eyes, babe," Bill said, passing the computer to Casey. Charlie groaned and looked away.

Casey took the computer and tried to glean any sort of knowledge from the screen. He skimmed the pages, his focus drawn to the photographs and hyperlinks. There really were hundreds of comments in the thread, some linking to places like the National Library and credible news outlets. A few of the subthreads were articulate, yet profanity littered the page. Casey's eyes glazed over as he tried to avoid the harsh language.

"I hate that you always visit that site," Charlie said. "It's full of misinformation."

"That's the fun of it," Bill said.

Casey wasn't paying attention to either of them at that point. He was back at the top of the first page, engrossed in the original post. There was a picture of a wall in what looked like an ancient tomb. Hieroglyphics and symbols were engraved into the dusty bricks, which were illuminated by floodlights.

Casey couldn't read anything that was written on the wall.

However, the caption to the post read: "Presider of the Zenith, raise my offering so that I may ever perfect it in your Glory. Set for me a contest of strength, that I may demonstrate my worth in the fruits of your eternal fields. Behold my dowry into your everlasting service and take it unto your ranks for the day when the universe fades and your divinity can be seen behind the stars."

The ancient words, which had given fortune to some, pain and suffering for others, tumbled out of Casey's lips, unbidden by free will.

The lights in the break room remained undimmed. There was no crash to be heard in the hallway. The tables and chairs stood still, unaffected by any earth-shattering revelation.

Bill shrieked in nervous glee.

Casey jumped in his seat, startled by Bill's outburst. "What was that for?"

"Did you not read the comments?" Bill asked. Casey shook his head. "If you read the incantation out loud, you've entered into a contract with the goddess. Now, you have to appease her before the night is over. Otherwise, you're toast."

Charlie's eyes widened in fear.

"Why didn't you tell me that first, Bill?" Casey asked.

"I was getting to it, but I didn't think you were going to read it out loud," Bill said. "Also, I think I might have said that it starts with a magic spell, which, of course, is what you just read."

"I don't even remember saying anything," Casey said. "Are you messing with me?"

Bill and Charlie looked at Casey with confusion. "No, you really did recite it," Bill said. "Are you messing with me? I don't remember reading anything about memory loss in the thread..."

"I don't care who messed with who," Charlie said, "You could have stopped him."

"Sorry, guys," Bill said. "It was just a little prank. Nothing is really going to happen."

"Well, you were pretty convincing earlier," Charlie said, rearing into a defensive. "See? That's why I don't touch those things. Remember those chain emails in high school?"

"About the ghost girl who would kill your family if you didn't forward a picture of a spooky pickle to five of your friends?"

"That's the one."

"What, you never sent them?"

"What do you mean? I sent those things along to everyone I knew," Charlie said. "I wasn't gonna have my family murdered by ghosts!"

"Well, whatever," Casey said. "You're the expert here, Bill. If you don't even think that this is real, then I'm not worried," Casey said.

"Yeah, well, I don't want to lose you, Casey," said Bill. "Do you want me to tell you how to escape the chains of Zephiscestra?"

"Who?" Charlie asked.

"The goddess from the ritual," Bill said.

"Yeah, tell me what to do," Casey said with a dismissive wave of his hand. He was still unconvinced that he even read the words aloud. His nonchalance put both Bill and Charlie at ease.

"Do I have to pray over some dark beads? Or, should I go to the supermarket to buy a steak that I can throw into a bonfire?"

At Charlie's horrified expression, Casey said, "What? I'm not actually going to do anything."

"Little worse than that…" Bill said. His companions looked at him expectantly. "You have to sacrifice… a *human*!" Bill flung back in his chair and laughed. Charlie frowned. Casey smirked.

"Well, that shouldn't be too hard. There are plenty of humans around," Casey said.

"You can't be serious," Charlie said.

"Hey, all you need to do is kill one person, and you can get whatever you wished for," Bill said.

Charlie remained unamused.

"I'm kidding! Sheesh!"

"You better be," Charlie said.

"What did you wish for, by the way," Bill asked. "Not that it really matters within the context of ancient rituals."

"I didn't wish for anything. I just read it," Casey said. "Allegedly."

"Well, what were you thinking of, in your head?" Charlie asked hesitantly.

"But wait, what if it's like a birthday cake, and if you tell people your wish then it won't come true?"

"That's a pretty macabre birthday if you have to kill someone before you get your presents," Casey said. "But I guess I was thinking of my LitMille videos, and how I want a lot of people to view them?"

"I bet you wished to be boyfriends with Trevor Greenbrook," Bill said. Casey brushed him off.

"If this is the thing that finally brings us together, you can be my best man," Casey said. "But, whatever, it's not going to come true anyway. It was a good way to kill some time, though." He crossed his arms in defiance of everlasting subjugation.

"Glad I could help," Bill said, satisfied with his presentation of another intriguing oddity.

"Well, I need to get back to my desk," Casey said, standing. He thought that the hoax was very well done, and, even though he believed that the ritual was bogus, it captured his attention long enough to forget about Bob.

"I'll go, too," Charlie said, rising from his chair and picking up his briefcase. "Let's not kill anyone on the way."

"You don't need to worry about that, Charlie," Casey said. "I'm a lover, not a fighter."

"But watch out, because he's also a fighter for what he loves," Bill said. He blew Casey a kiss, and Casey reached out and caught it gently.

Charlie groaned and started to walk towards the door. Casey lingered at the table to gather his things.

"Are we hanging out after work?" Bill asked, opening his lunch. "No, I have to stay after hours to prepare a report," Casey said. "Charlie has been bombarded with work these past two weeks."

"I know," Bill said casually. "He's been ignoring some of the memes I've been sending. Doesn't even have time to look."

"That's how you know it's bad," Casey agreed. "I'm going to be here 'til 7:00."

"Well, good luck with that," Bill said. "I'm sure you'll be bright and chipper tomorrow morning."

"Unless I'm snapped up in the jaws of Zephiscestra," Casey said.

"I love you, Casey. Don't be getting yourself dragged to hell now."

"Don't even joke about that!" Charlie yelled from across the room.

"How did he even hear that?" Casey asked.

"It's because he loves you even more than me." Bill said.

"If you say so," Casey said. He turned to leave, and at that moment Peter Adams entered the break room.

"What I really should have wished for was to be hungry at the same time he was," Casey said.

Bill smiled knowingly and said, "You'll get him next time."

CHAPTER 2

CASEY LEFT THE office at 7:13 PM. He could see the sun hanging, sleepy, in the distance, but there would still be just enough light to walk home. He adjusted his grip on his briefcase and started the journey back to his apartment.

The route was simple. He would follow one of the many roads of the town through the Business District, over a bridge that crossed the river, and then follow the same road until he reached his place.

On the north side of the river, the town was all concrete and bricks. Once he was able to cross the bridge, the landscape would shift to hills, homes, and gardens.

He usually walked home with Bill. Now that Casey was alone, he had no other company than the thoughts in his head. His mind fell into its usual solitary pattern: LitMille and Trevor.

Trevor had commanded much more of his attention since Casey started uploading his own videos. Trevor's channel featured all sorts videos, and Casey was infatuated with everything about him. At thirty-two years old, Trevor was a successful fitness guru. He documented all types of exercise, from weightlifting to yoga. He was training for a marathon, and Casey had watched his every step in his training videos. Trevor offered tips about men's fashion and created tutorials on personal hygiene. His most popular series detailed how to grow and maintain a beard. Casey kept his face clean shaven, but he relished every opportunity to witness Trevor trim his scruff into impressive shapes and contours.

Trevor was a famous proponent of LGBT rights and was seen as an activist in various online communities. He was one of the first gay "Millers" to reach over a million followers. He had already established a strong base for himself as an authority on the male lifestyle before ever talking about his sexuality.

His coming out video only increased his viewership, bridging the gap between health-conscious hobbyists and hunk-obsessed voyeurs.

Trevor was comfortable with all sexualities, which allowed him reach a wider fan base. He spoke openly about being gay, and he brought guests onto his channel to discuss the struggles and achievements of people in the community. He delved into research that could disprove a stigma or shed light on supposedly queer members of history.

Some early adopters of Trevor's videos claimed that the fame had warped him into a caricature of who he once was. In truth, his earlier videos were simply more subdued. Casey considered the change an evolution. He thought that Trevor grew all the more irresistible with each post on his page. He was an inspiration, someone that deserved all of the platitudes he received.

Casey sighed. He knew that their chances of meeting each other were negligible. They lived on opposite coasts and had vastly different lifestyles. Casey lived in a town that he considered ordinary and plain. There were no attractions to entice Trevor to visit, and Casey couldn't convince himself to take a vacation to Trevor's city.

Deep down, Trevor was one of the main reasons that Casey started to make LitMille videos. Casey did have a passion for singing and songwriting, so his interest in becoming a creator wasn't completely co-dependent. However, he held onto the secret desire to get famous enough to meet his idol on even ground. Then, Trevor might ask him on a date…

Could I really get famous enough to meet Trevor?

What if fame was just a means to an end, something that he didn't really want? The thought of popularity certainly seemed appealing to many people, but it would mean the end of a private life. He could hardly imagine having his face plastered over the internet, let alone the whole country.

Such exposure would be the ultimate goal of the pursuit of fame, but Casey felt as if that destination were a train to a certain type of hell. Even if he did cross the threshold of fame, what if the Trevor he met was vastly different than the Trevor that he envisioned?

That was the problem with celebrity crushes. They create an alluring persona, but these personality traits were manufactured; you never really know what they will be like in real life.

The paradox gave him a momentary bout of anxiety. He couldn't understand how he could know a persona of someone so well online, yet never be able to converse face-to-face.

Or, mouth to mouth.

Casey smiled absentmindedly as he reached the river. The banks of the river were strengthened with smooth concrete that met the water at a ninety-degree angle. The suspension bridge that spanned the river stretched high over the crevasse. It was the most common means of transport between the north and south sides of the town, separating businesses from the residential areas. A walkway on each side allowed pedestrians to cross. Railings stood on either side to protect from the motorway on one side and the sheer drop on the other.

Coming from the north, Casey would cross the west side of the bridge, otherwise known as "the business" side. The south side of the bridge was safe to jump off of, to splash harmlessly into the water below. Looking over the west side, however, one could see jagged rocks protruding from the water.

There was no one else visible on the bridge, which was normal for the 7:00 hour. Most people in town were eating dinner at that time, either in their homes or already seated at a restaurant from whence he came.

The air was still a bit warm, but the sun was nestling itself into the horizon. As Casey started to cross the bridge, he tried to remember if he had leftovers in the refrigerator. When he was halfway across, he noticed something that he had overlooked, something that didn't register when he first scanned the bridge.

A man stood on the outside of the barrier, looking down into the water below. His arms were spread out wide, gripping the railing behind him. The tips of his boots jutted over the edge of the concrete. There was a sudden, palpable sense of death and depression that muddled Casey's mood. He immediately understood that the man had resolved to commit suicide.

Casey approached him slowly. Normally, he would never speak to someone that he passed on the street, but this situation was clearly different. However, Casey had no idea how to broach the issue of this man's mental state and what immediate action he was willing to take.

Just say something… anything to get him to know that you're here.

"It's a little late to go swimming," Casey said. He cringed at himself for starting their conversation in such a way, but his brain was fizzling with anxiety. Casey tried to remain calm, but the possibilities flooded his awareness. He had never been in a life or death situation, and Casey wasn't sure that he could convince this man to preserve his life.

The rushing sound of the water beneath them conveyed evil and uncertainty. It was as if they were transported from their town and deposited into a splinter reality where fears were incarnate. The gentle breeze, usually a source of comfort, brought forth the imagery of napkins being blown from a table, and of a hat being carried away by the wind. Any sunlight that filled the eye provoked visions of being blinded while speeding on the highway. Any sudden sound in the distance harkened memories of jumping after a startling noise. All of these small, nontangible things that were experienced from day to day suddenly took on an heir of ludicrous disaster.

The man said nothing.

"I was just trying to lighten the mood," Casey said. "I know you don't want to go swimming."

The man remained silent.

"Can I help you with anything? What are you doing up here?"

The man didn't reply, and Casey noticed that his face was wet with tears.

"What's the matter?" Casey asked, his chest tight with dread. "You can talk to me."

Casey understood that no one on Earth owed him any explanation of their actions. However, the man finally spoke.

"Have you ever heard the phrase, 'If you don't have anything nice to say, then don't say anything at all?' I don't have anything to say that won't make you want to kill yourself."

Casey's throat constricted, and he felt a gaping hole in his abdomen. This stranger was going to kill himself. Casey considered his role in the situation. He had no experience with crisis negotiation, but there was no one else around to help.

Casey felt as if tight ropes constricted his stomach as he took his place next to the man's right hand. Still standing on the walkway, Casey grasped the railing for support, took a deep breath, and looked into the sky.

The brilliant orange, red, and pink of the atmosphere did nothing to calm him. In fact, the strong colors gave Casey the sense that he was hallucinating. Casey exhaled. "I'll still listen to you. I'm safe over here, why don't you join me?"

The man scowled, turning his head to look at Casey. When they made eye contact, Casey sensed the stranger's desperation. He almost shrank away from tangible despair that filled the space between them.

The man shook his head. "No, I don't think you would understand. Nobody would, not even my..."

Casey looked down into the water as the man lost himself in thought. He remembered times when, during the summer, he and Charlie and Bill would jump off of the bridge into the water below. However, they would leap from the other side. The other side was safe. Below the tips of the stranger's boots were an array of jagged rocks.

The surrounding air wrapped tightly around Casey's head when the gravity of the situation hit him. In that moment, he felt responsible for the stranger's wellbeing. He strained for the words that would make the man move to safety. The balance was delicate, and Casey feared disrupting the man further.

The man continued, "No, I've been quiet lately because I have nothing good to say about myself. A lot of people want me to talk, so they ask me questions. They ask me what I'm thinking about. They ask me how I'm feeling. They ask me if I have any hope for the future."

"What do you say?" Casey whispered. Sounds of water lapping against the rocks drifted up from below. Casey imagined hungry dogs licking their lips before devouring a bone.

"I don't say anything. I don't want to tell them the truth: that I feel awful all the time. I don't have the energy to lie. So, I just don't tell people anything. It's easier that way."

Casey looked up from the water and fixed his gaze on the man. "Then... why are you talking to me?" Casey asked. The man turned his head ever so slightly to look down at Casey out of the corner of his eye. He heaved a sob, and Casey was ensnared by the immediate fear that he would suddenly jump. After a moment, when the man was still standing on the bridge, Casey took a breath and realized that he didn't recall any sensory information from the previous two seconds.

The man composed himself as much as he could and said, "I guess it's because this is finally the end. Here I am, about to end it all, and who shows up to see me go? I don't know who you are, and you don't know me. I can say anything I want to you, and it won't mean anything at all. There is absolutely no connection between us, so there isn't any reason to protect you."

"You're really making me scared," Casey said. Beads of sweat rolled down his forehead, and his body felt drenched and sticky. Their conversation had done nothing but verify his fears. This man was going to attempt to take his own life. "Are you really going to do what I think you are?"

The stranger became silent, but he was still looking at Casey out of the corner of his eye.

Casey said, "Think about what you're going to do. Things seem bad now, but the nature of the universe is to change. If you kill yourself, you won't be able to see the good times when they come. Think about your family, the people that love you. Think of your friends who would be lost without you. Talk to me, please. I want to know how to help you."

The man appeared to wrestle with Casey's reasoning. He sighed, a bitter exhalation of defeat. Casey, himself, couldn't breathe. The man adjusted himself on the ledge and let his left hand off of the rail. He pivoted on his right foot, still holding the rail with his right hand, the one that was next to Casey. His left arm swung deftly over the water, and his left foot did the same below it. Casey's heart felt like it was drowning in its own blood. He envisioned the man slipping, falling, plummeting into the darkness below. The man finished shifting his body. He was still on the other side of the railing, but his back now faced the water, and he was directly in front of Casey.

Casey took a step backwards to give the stranger more space. For a moment, he thought that he had reached a deeper part of the man, a part that would keep him alive. The man stooped so their faces were level. His shirt collar flapped slightly in the wind. With a furrowed brow, the man said, "The thing is, I don't owe you anything. I was here, just minding my own business, and then you came out of nowhere into my little world. I was fine here, and then out of nowhere comes this random person trying to guilt trip me into living. You know what? I'm finished thinking about others. I'm finished thinking about everything. I've already decided what I want to do. If you want to be with me when it happens, then that's on you. I never asked you to reach out to me."

Casey felt tears bite at his eyes. His face bore naked confusion and remorse.

The stranger's face was that of a man determined in his despair. He leaned over the railing towards Casey. The man's face blocked out the setting sun so that he was haloed by deep red. An even deeper purple seemed to manifest out of the air like a supernatural aura.

"I'm just trying to help you," Casey said, his face burning with frustration. "But I don't know how to save you."

Casey suddenly remembered the incantation that he had invoked earlier in the day. The skin on his back rippled with goosebumps. The intense stress of the interaction with the stranger instilled a deep paranoia in Casey's psyche. At that moment, he was struck with unambiguous belief of the goddess Zephiscestra. The doubt was stricken from his mind, and Casey wholeheartedly understood that there was a goddess presiding over him, one that called for blood.

When he first heard of the ritual, he believed that it was an internet hoax. He couldn't have considered anything else. Set within the banality of the office, the mythical ritual was as mundane as a budget report. On the bridge, on the very cusp of mortality, Casey's actions were undeniable. He had recited the ancient words.

Now, the day was almost over. Unless he made an offering to Zephiscestra, he was going to die. Casey's instinct of self-preservation pointed out that the stranger's suicide could be used for his own gains.

Casey realized that he had the opportunity to push the man from the bridge. Alternatively, in the case that the stranger somehow wasn't fully committed to death, Casey could further convince the man to jump from the bridge.

Casey couldn't decide which action was more horrific. He experienced a sense of disgust at his own mental processes that would try to convince him to perform such acts of evil. He felt a deep pang of guilt, and he felt as if a shroud of shame enveloped his head.

Despite his personality, the goddess seemed to call to him. She offered herself to him in the shape of a suicidal man on the edge of total destruction. To the goddess, the man was nothing more than a coin, a bartering chip to exchange for all of the happiness in the world.

Evil temptation coiled its way around Casey's arms, snaked its way into his mouth. A few words, or a simple exertion of force; Casey had the option to snatch away the stranger's ultimate choice, his terminal decision. Terror roiled in Casey's intestines when this unholy enlightenment manifested in his mind. He found himself at a nexus, where sensibility halted at the border of reality and cast a deformed shadow on the path that led to the void.

The water rushed and spluttered below like enemy horses on a blood-soaked battlefield. Casey wrestled with his conditioning, the lifelong lessons he had gathered to develop himself into what he believed was a good person. Through the lens of integrity, he struggled to behold the man for what he really was.

The man was not a sacrificial goat, nor a pawn in the game of human sin. The man was a lost soul whom Casey could deliver unto relative safety by simply letting go. This was not an opportunity to hijack a sinking ship. It was a chance to reject the seduction of domination over the life of another.

He understood that, without an offering, Zephiscestra would strike him down that very night. With that knowledge, Casey resolved to die.

"Just... come back to solid ground. We can go to my apartment and talk it out. Even if it sounds excruciating, anything is better than what you're about to do."

The wind tried its best to bite into his jacket. He kept staring into the man's eyes as the sun finally set, plunging them into a decisive darkness. The man closed his eyes. With a dour sigh, he pushed off of the railing, backwards into oblivion. Casey gasped and lunged forward, reaching out instinctively.

Just don't push him just don't push him just don't—

He tried to clutch at the man's gray shirt, but the fabric was too tight against his chest. Tears stung Casey's eyes as he understood the futility of his attempt to save a life. The man fell back, further and further, until his body was parallel with the concrete surface of the bridge.

His boots lost their contact with the pavement, and then the stranger was lost from sight.

CHAPTER 3

CASEY WAS MET with blinding light.

He reached into his pea-coat pocket and procured a pair of horn-rimmed sunglasses. Casey put them on and began to wave at the crowd of fans that surrounded him on either side of the walkway.

"Right this way, Casey." Marcus, the giant bodyguard, led Casey away from the studio and through the delighted crowd.

Journalists held out their fingers for "one question, please." Reporters repeated Casey's name in front of their cameras. Paparazzi jostled each other for a better view of their favorite obsession.

Casey continued to wave, smiling broadly. Red carpets had become a constant in his life. The love and adoration of his fans was expected; The ensuing satisfaction was always fresh. Each encounter with a new crowd that adored him brought him back to his first premier. Even with the countless albums, the endless hits, Casey remained grateful of his fortune.

"Vanessa, how are you?" Casey shook hands with a writer who was almost entirely devoted to crafting articles expounding upon his life.

"Casey, how is the new album coming along? How is your professional relationship with Jennet?"

Casey laughed as he signed a fan's tee-shirt. James Jennet was a constant talking point in the industry, especially since his infamous meltdown in a recording studio the summer. News outlets wanted to assure their readers that Casey was being treated with respect by the producer, who was a juggernaut in every sense of the word.

"Jimmy? He's a dream to work with. I almost can't wait to wrap up with this album with him so that we can keep making more." Casey, ever the professional, knew better to bring up Jennet's overt displeasure with a certain caterer's spread.

"David, good to see you." Casey shook the photographer's hand and then posed for a picture with two other fans.

"Casey, looking good. As always." David snapped a few more shots, the crowd roiling with delight in the background.

"Don't let your wife hear that. She might get jealous." The sunlight was so bright that it was almost tangible; it seemed to hang in the air like a mist, and Casey could feel it enter his lungs as he took a breath.

"Casey, right this way." Marcus was edging Casey along again. He was over-protective, but Casey never could complain. Marcus was the best. That's why they hired him.

The day seemed so perfect that Casey was certain that nothing could go wrong. He was on top of the world. Casey and his entourage kept moving to-wards a massive tour bus emblazoned with his own face on the side. Johnny was already inside, making lunch. Casey could see Arnold at the wheel, smiling and waving at Casey through the windshield. Casey waved back as Sydney climbed the bus's steps to open the door for him.

Casey was presently realizing the intrinsic meaning of "marvelous." He wit-nessed his own actions as if he were an ardent observer, the object of his own subjectivity. He felt what it meant to be his own admirer, to be swept up in his own mythology, enraptured by his own machinations. He beheld his own image and reveled in the thrill of his own gratification.

It was true, what they said about him.

He was perfection.

That's when Casey saw the man from the bridge.

He sat atop the bus, his left leg crossed under him and his right leg dangling over the door. He lifted his drooping limb to allow Sydney to swing the door open. Then, he settled it back in front of the open frame. Sydney didn't seem to notice.

The stranger gazed down at him, and Casey saw that his eyes contained all that was outside of reality.

Casey felt fear entomb his stomach. He hastily nudged his bodyguard.

"Hey, Marcus. What is he doing up there? Should he be there?"

Marcus shrugged. "Who? Arnold?"

"No. That guy on the roof of the bus," Casey said. He removed his sun-glasses to get a better look.

The brilliant light had faded, while the dry heat remained. The man kept looking down at him, swinging his leg back and forth, in and out of the doorframe. Red and purple light radiated from behind him.

"What are you doing? Get down from there," Casey shouted.

The man simply smiled.

Casey covered his mouth when he saw the man's teeth. All of them were broad and pointed as if they belonged to a wild, apex predator. The stranger continued to nonchalantly swing his leg.

"Casey, right this way," Marcus said. Casey checked over his shoulder and saw that the studio had disappeared. In its place was a sea of faces. A massive crowd was moving towards him.

Casey turned back to the man. "What do you want?" Panic took hold of Casey's voice as the crowd closed in on him.

Wings made of jet-black feathers unfurled behind the man on the bus. He extended them to their full span. Their tips flittered as he stretched out his arms above his head.

"Only to serve you until you meet your demise, then fight for you in the afterlife," the man said.

He smiled again, baring his sharp teeth as a crowd as far as the eye could see collapsed onto Casey.

Marcus was nowhere to be found.

As the crowd assaulted him, Casey fell to his knees, then kept falling. As he dropped through the Earth, he looked down to see vicious waves churning miles below him. Their crests took the form of hands that reached up to grab him before breaking into each other, sending foamy fingers crashing into chaos. Casey looked up to see thousands of ravenous fans plummeting towards him. They shared an agitated, hungry expression, their hands plying greedily. Bewildered animals thrashed in the midst of the floundering humans. Dogs, pigs, and lions flailed their legs as they tried in vain to gain a foothold. Snakes twisted and writhed as they descended. Birds flew freely amongst the tumbling wretches.

The man appeared beside him, wings folded in a nosedive.

"Hold on, this is gonna be tight," he said, enveloping Casey in a bear hug. Casey wrapped his arms around the man and craned his neck to look down at the waves.

Black water swelled until a gigantic reptilian head exploded from the depths. The beast crawled up through the air at ludicrous speed. Casey screamed as its head split in two, revealing rows of menacing teeth. He held the man even tighter as they fell into the mouth. The man jerked his head back and spread his wings out to their full length, just as the jaws slammed shut.

Casey snapped his eyes open at the same moment that his bedroom light turned on. His roommate stood with her finger still on the light switch. Casey wiped cold sweat from his face with moist palms. His drenched shirt clung to his chest as he took a few deep breaths.

"Casey, are you ok? You were shouting in your sleep," Lynette sat down on the edge of the bed and rubbed his back. "You're soaked in sweat," she said.

"Sorry, Lynette, I'm fine," Casey said.

She felt him shudder.

"Just a bad dream, is all."

"It's okay, it's all over now." Lynette hesitated before saying, "Did you dream about that man?"

Casey started to nod, but his body suddenly froze.

Unseen, unheard, from within the cracks of reality, Zephiscestra exerted her power over her new ward. This one, this man who said the ancient words on accident... this one was different. He possessed as much passion in his heart as the most fervent zealot, yet his soul was malleable and his mind was unaccustomed to torment. Yes, he would be perfect for Zephiscestra's own machinations...

Now that the Offering was being prepared, Zephiscestra would strip Casey of his knowledge of Her and her incantation. He would come to learn of Her and Her actions on Earth... gradually. If all went according to Zephiscestra's plan, Casey would eventually accept Her. No, more than accept Her. He would beg Her to take his life in Her own hands.

Casey's brow furrowed in confusion, and he left Lynette's question unanswered while he ruminated over what had occurred just a few hours ago. He had come home the night before and immediately called Bill and Charlie on the phone. With Lynette by his side, Casey had described the suicide that he had witnessed minutes before the call. He neglected to tell Lynette about the incantation from work, as well as the seemingly psychotic belief that a goddess tempted him to sacrifice the man for his own gain.

Neither Bill nor Charlie mentioned the incantation, either, although they were fully aware of what a coincidence it was. The trio still had the knowledge of Zephiscestra before they went to sleep. Presently, though, the shadow of ignorance cast dark holes in their memories.

Lynette swept her short bangs off of her forehead and whimpered. "Do you want to talk about it some more?" The night before, once they all processed what had happened, Lynette had suggested that Casey file a police report.

"No, I'm just really tired right now. The had me at the station for a while," Casey said.

"I know. I picked you up." Lynette smiled warmly and wrapped her arms around him. She continued, saying, "Do you want to skip work today? I think you could take the day off."

"No, I don't want to get behind," Casey said, spurned on unconsciously by the goddess. "Really, I feel fine. I'm still a little freaked out, but the biggest problem right now is that—" Casey yawned, "I'm utterly exhausted."

"Well, I'll fix you a big cup of coffee. Lots of cream and sugar, right?"

"Thanks," Casey said. Then, he was left alone in his room. He laid his head back on his pillow and closed his eyes, hoping to get some adequate rest before he prepared for work. Unfortunately, Casey could easily conjure an image of the man's face. They had looked into each other's eyes in his last moment on Earth.

He feared that the memory of those eyes would haunt him forever. The man jumped. Or, more accurately, he fell backwards. Casey had tried to save him, but he only managed to nudge him in the direction he was headed.

Casey wondered if the man would have regained balance if he didn't try to grab on to his shirt. Did he really push him away, in the end?

Either way, the man was surely dead.

Casey still saw those eyes in his mind, full of anguish and defeat. Casey wouldn't have wished such a state on anyone, not even Bob Sutter. Casey had watched in horror until the man was out of sight. He remembered the stranger plummeting headfirst, his feet up in the air. There was a sickening thud and a terrible splash, and then he was gone. The black water below swallowed him up, and with the sun having set, there was no way for Casey to see anything at the bottom.

After that, he just ran home. He didn't stop until he reached his front door, burst in, and told his friends what he saw.

The next couple of hours were all questions from the police. Who was he? What were you doing on the bridge? Did he say anything? Did you push him?

That last one hurt. Casey struggled with the answer in his mind, but he vehemently denied blame to the police. Surely, the man would have fallen if Casey hadn't done anything. However, the guilt chewed at the corners of his consciousness like a rat. He couldn't help but imagine that the man could have reached out to take hold of the railing again. The thought of his culpability made Casey sick to his stomach.

When he finally got back home, Casey collapsed onto his bed and immediately went to sleep. Of course, he didn't sleep soundly, not with that awful dream.

Although he couldn't remember the specifics of the dream, Casey understood that the dream troubled him when he was experiencing it. Did he already have PTSD? He hoped not.

Casey was thinking about all of the psychological problems that could come with this experience when he felt something push on his belly and caress his cheek.

Casey flung his covers off and sat bolt upright in his bed. There was no one else in the room. His bones felt like they were encrusted in ice.

Maybe he was going to have some serious issues after all. Maybe he would hallucinate when his eyes were closed. If that were the case, every nap would be a nightmare.

Casey decided to get out of bed, fearful of sleep. He made his way towards the bathroom and locked the door behind him. He stripped off his shirt before turning on the shower, twisting the knob to ensure that the water would be extra hot. Casey slid out of his pajama pants and let them pool around his ankles. He walked over to the mirror and looked at himself.

His eyes were droopy, complete with dark circles. He stared at his face for several minutes. He could hardly recognize himself, and he figured that he was a changed man. He could lie to everyone and say that he was fine, but he could never be the same, not after witnessing something so horrid.

He splashed some cold water on his face from the sink. A chill ran through his body, and Casey shivered despite the thick steam that was already billowing from the shower. Casey pulled back the curtain and stepped into the basin. Reaching through the scalding water, attempting to detach his experience of pain from his physical body, he adjusted the temperature until the water was as hot as he could bear.

Casey stood under the stream of the shower for a moment before reaching for the shampoo. He lathered his hair first, then rubbed soap on his chest, arms, and legs. Casey turned back around and held his face under the stream, envisioning the water cracking the skin from his face.

He let the water wash the soap off of him. When his skin glowed red and tender, Casey turned his back to the water and pressed the heels of his palms against his eyes. He took his hands away and opened his eyes. Then, he rubbed them again to make sure that he was seeing correctly.

Towards the back of the basin, a phantom stood a few inches taller than Casey. There was no body to be seen, but the steam shifted around the form of a human, outlining its shape and dimensions. The vapor swirled towards Casey as a ghostly arm reached out to touch his face. The hand was made of infinite daggers whose multitude rounded their surface, making it appear as a single construct. Its aura was unmistakably evil. The steam itself seemed to take on an essence of madness, a screaming train whistle signaling impending doom.

Casey howled and fell out of the shower, through the curtain, and onto the bathroom tile. Sputtering for air, he peered apprehensively into the boiling miasma.

The form was gone.

CHAPTER 4

"IT WAS SURREAL. There was someone there, but there wasn't. It was like looking into... a void. *The* void. As if everything that didn't exist was contained in a single point, right here on Earth."

Laptops had already taken the places of their finished sandwiches and chips. Bill was typing furiously on his keyboard, while Casey had Charlie's undivided attention.

"There has to be an explanation," Charlie said. "Maybe..."

"Oh, you don't really believe that Casey saw a ghost," Bill said, a bead of sweat forming at his temple. He had his own reasons to be paranoid: overnight, all of Bill's browsing history was inexplicably deleted, much to Bill's own surprise. Years of data was wiped out in an instant, and, with it, Bill's memory of the incantation.

"But what if it was... you know." Charlie didn't want to mention the man that jumped from the bridge the night before. He was able to remember that the man committed suicide, but, like Casey and Bill, he had no recollection of the incantation.

Concerning the man on the bridge, neither of Casey's friends desired to open such a fresh wound, but it was all that the three of them could think about.

The others immediately understood what he implied. Bill held a finger up to his lips, but Casey just shook his head.

"I don't think I really saw anything, but it must have had something to do with... him."

"Casey, are you sure that you want to talk about it? I mean, you are obviously really shaken up. Maybe you should talk to a therapist."

Indeed, neither of Casey's friends wanted to discuss what Casey had seen the night before. They wanted to support him by directing him to a professional who was trained to handle such situations.

Charlie nodded in agreement. "Yeah, definitely talk to a counselor." He hesitated for a moment, thinking about how to proceed. "My therapist helped me out a lot. I'm sure someone could help you, too."

"You have a therapist?"

"This is the first time I heard of that," Bill said.

Charlie said, "Yeah, he's given me a lot of good advice. We talk about things that effect my everyday life, and how I can start becoming myself by taking the right actions."

Casey and Bill both wanted to inquire further, but they chose to respect his privacy. If he wanted to speak more about his private sessions, they would give him space to do it by his own free will.

"I'll think about it," Casey said. "If my problems persist, I'll go to a therapist."

"Then, what are you going to do in the meantime?" Bill asked.

Unseen and forgotten by the trio, Zephiscestra played Her hand. With the incantation recited and the sacrifice complete, Casey's wish was bound by blood to come to fruition.

"I'm just going to edit an instrumental that I saved to my computer," Casey said, offhandedly. "It's for another song that I'm writing. It will take my mind off of things. Hopefully." Bill sighed his relief. Despite the fact that he had no knowledge of sharing the most deadly secret of humanity with Casey, unwittingly setting off a chain of events that would change Casey's life forever, he still felt a sense of guilt. He perceived it as a personal failure for not being strong enough to work through trauma that he believed Casey was burying deep within himself.

"Well, if anything will take your mind off of that guy, it's one of your cute songs," Charlie said. His face glowed red when he realized which adjective he had selected.

"Thanks, buddy." Casey delivered a light punch to Charlie's arm. Zephiscestra had worked Her charm, and things would start to look up for Casey.

"Hey Casey, I loved your video."

Casey felt his own face turn red when he heard the unmistakable voice of

Allie Thatcher behind him. He quickly turned. "Uh, Allie. Haven't spoken to you in while." Casey said.

He and Allie were friends in elementary school, in the same town where they now lived. They used to go to each other's houses almost every day after school, finding one another's company enough to keep them occupied exclusively for hours on end. Once they got to high school, though, Allie found that she was outgoing and sociable, and strived to make as many new friends as possible. Casey, on the other hand, retreated to his room after losing his best friend. He found solace in the internet, which was where he first discovered Trevor.

"I just found your channel last night. I was feeling kind of lonely in my empty house, and your face cheered me right up!"

Although they were both employed at the same company, Allie and Casey only spoke once during the time since Casey had started working there. He didn't even know that she had a desk on the other side of the building until after months of coming into the office, when they bumped into each other by chance.

"Thanks, I worked really hard on it, so I truly appreciate that."

"I shared it on my page, as well. I hope you don't mind," Allie said.

Casey's heart skipped a beat.

"Oh, you didn't have to do that," Casey said. "Thank you so much. Really."

Allie laughed. Then, she noticed the editing software on his computer screen. "Hey, is that a new song that you're editing?"

Casey shut his laptop as quickly as he could without breaking it. He didn't like to let anyone see his work until he was fully satisfied with it. Allie laughed again, not unkindly. She was always in a good mood, no matter what happened around her.

"I get it. I can't see it until it's done."

Casey nodded.

"Well, maybe you could give me a sneak peek on Friday? Marissa is having a party, and maybe we could get ready together."

Casey hadn't attended a party with more than two other people in years. But, even with the previous night's trauma, he couldn't deny a request from Allie.

"Yeah, sure, what time?" Casey said.

"We can just text about it later," Allie said. "You still have my number, right?"

"Yeah, I have it," Casey said, "as long as you haven't changed it since the summer before high school."

Allie didn't so much as flinch. "That's the one!"

"Can Bill and Charlie come, too?"

"To the party, or to my house beforehand?"

He looked around to his friends, and then turned back to Allie. "Both?"

"Well, you two can both come to the party," Allie said, addressing Charlie and Bill. "But, I want some time to be alone with Casey before we go. Do you mind if you just come over when the party starts?"

"I don't mind," Charlie said, tentatively. "All of my things are at home, anyway. It's just easier that way."

"Well if that's the case, then I'll just hang back with Charlie," Bill said. "We're his only friends, and I can't have him going to the party unescorted."

Charlie glowered at Bill.

"Cool," Allie said. "Well, Casey? Would you still want to come over to my house, the day of?" Casey looked at both of his friends, who gave him nods of approval.

"Sure, I can't wait," Casey said.

"Perfect," Allie said. "Don't forget. I'll text you all the details later."

"Okay, see you." Casey said.

Without even knowing it, Casey was beginning to Indulge. As Allie turned and left the room, Casey felt warmth flood through his body, and the edges of his vision softened dramatically.

"Oh. My. God. This is crazy. This has never happened before," Casey said. "Why would she suddenly invite us to a party? We've never been invited to a party before."

"It's because she saw your video and really liked it. You're basically famous now, Casey," Bill said.

Casey smiled broadly and ran his fingers through his hair.

"Yeah, well, don't forget us little guys," Charlie said. "And, Bill, thanks for hanging back with me."

"You know I would never leave you, babe," Bill said.

"Yeah, I bet you would love to see Allie getting ready to go to a party, though," Casey said. "Isn't that like every straight guy's dream?"

"Yeah… she's so… hot," Charlie said. He kicked at something near his loafers.

"Well, I should count myself lucky she found it, although I guess Bob told her about it," Casey said.

"Right, they're dating," Bill said. "The only flaw to that beautiful soul is her romantic counterpart."

"Yeah, that must be it," Charlie said. "Although, how *he* found it I will never know."

"I don't know," Casey said. He opened his laptop to check on his channel. He wasn't expecting much more than thirty views on his newest song, a few more than the previous day. When Casey opened up his account, his heart nearly stopped. "Oh…"

"Or maybe she heard one of us talking about it at work?"

"My…"

"I don't know. I never really talk to her anymore. Do you?"

"Guys…"

"I don't either. Casey—Whoa, what's the matter?"

Casey's face looked similar to when he had seen a ghost earlier that day. "Holy… god… guys…" Casey couldn't get his voice above a whisper. He just pointed at his computer screen. Charlie and Bill got up from their chairs to look. The next few moments were a blur. Bill was jumping up and down. Charlie was fanning his face with his hand. Casey just stared at his computer screen, his jaw in his lap and his heart in his throat. He saw a certain number, one that wasn't that big in the grand, cosmic scheme of things. However, the digits left him awestruck. He tried in vain to communicate what he was seeing.

Charlie was the first to speak. "10,000 followers?" He could barely contain his excitement. He felt a sense of relief that can only accompany accomplishment. Charlie shed the strenuous hours he sat and watched his best friend struggle with creating content for people around the world. He obviously had a passion for it, and he was really good at it, but Casey felt like a failure without recognition. Now that all of his hard work paid off, Charlie felt just as excited as Casey—maybe even more so.

Casey's body stayed stiff as a board as he turned his head slowly towards Charlie. He wore an expression somewhere between disbelief and horror. He slowly began to process what happened, and then sat back in his chair, with the biggest grin that his friends had seen in a long time.

"Casey? This is awesome. How did this happen?" Charlie moved closer to Casey and touched his arm. Casey shrugged, oblivious.

"I don't know." He was at a loss for words. "Yesterday, I had 10 followers. Today, I have 10,000. How it that even frigging possible?"

"I don't know, but it's just what you wanted, right? This is a dream come true!" Bill had stopped dancing by then, and he sat there breathing heavily in excitement.

Casey shook the surprise out of his hands. It felt like butterflies were still swirling around inside of him. With an army of 10,000 followers rallying Casey's emotions out of him, he stood up and clenched his hands into tight fists. He said whatever came to his mind, one thought after the other. Maybe, by saying it out loud, the whole thing would make more sense.

"Charlie, I don't know what to think right now. This is honestly the craziest thing I have ever seen. 10,000 followers in one night? I think I'm shocked. Like, I cannot possibly even fathom what is going on anymore. Is this real life? Am I in a simulation or something?"

No matter what he said, the truth had fled from their awareness. Zephiscestra moved in darkness, and ignorance was Her shadow. Only those who gained Her favor could glimpse reality… when the time was right.

Casey cupped both of Charlie's cheeks in his hands. "Pinch me! Am I dreaming?" "You're not dreaming, Casey," Bill said from across the table. Just then, an alarm went off in Charlie's pocket.

"Unless that's my alarm clock," Casey said.

"Well then you better wake up, because you're late for work," Charlie said.

"Very funny," Casey said.

"Actually, *I'm* the one who has to get back to their desk," Charlie said. "I'm still swamped, but this makes it better."

He embraced Casey and put his head on his shoulder. "But, I'm so proud of you. I'll talk to you later." With a wink, he was off. The other two friends packed up their things to go, too, and left the break room with endless possibilities running wild in their minds.

Casey went through the rest of the day in a haze. He kept pinching himself to make sure that he wasn't dreaming. Coworkers whom he had never spoken to before commented on his post. About a dozen people in the large company personally complimented Casey on his work.

Casey nodded along or said, 'thank you.' He couldn't believe that he was really getting recognition for his work.

"Hey, Casey! That cover you did was really good."

"Oh my god, Casey, I couldn't stop blasting your song. My roommate came downstairs at midnight and started freaking out!"

"Bro, I know we've never talked before, but that way that you sang? Shit was cash, man."

Casey smiled and thanked all of them. He had never ingested any sort of illicit substance before, but he felt like this is what it must be like to be high. When he sat at his desk, people would whisper and point at him, smiling. Usually, whenever that happened, Casey would feel self-conscious because he would assume that people were making fun of him. After his influx of followers, he was under the impression that those people were admiring him from afar.

His heart skipped a beat when he heard himself being compared to his hero, Trevor Greenbrook.

CHAPTER 5

CHARLIE DECIDED TO walk with Casey after work ended.

The 5:00 PM sun was hanging in the sky, the birds were singing, and flowers were swaying in the breeze. The pair left the office building and began their journey home.

Bill, for once, didn't take his usual path with them; he had to go right to his mother's house to help her unpack her bags from a trip she took. Bill's mother was always taking long trips, and she took numerous bags with her. For some reason, she always refused to carry her bags between the car and the house. It's not that she had a tantrum about it or anything. The bags would simply sit there until Bill took care of them. Casey was saying all of this out loud.

"I know why he isn't here right now," Charlie said. "Are you not totally excited? Why aren't you talking about it with me?" The pair talked about nearly everything together. Two twins conjoined by a corpus callosum didn't share as many thoughts as Casey and Charlie.

Casey was still a bit shocked and couldn't really believe that he had somehow amassed 10,000 followers in one night. "I just don't believe it," he told Charlie. "Like, I was miserable yesterday after Bob bullied me in the break room, but now I'm just on top of the world. It's like I feel numb or something, like nothing can touch me."

"Hey, fag." Bob seemed to come out of nowhere, and he planted his hand firmly against Casey's chest. Surprisingly, the larger man was alone. "What are you doing talking to my girlfriend?"

"She just asked me if I was going to the party tomorrow," Casey said.

"And you're not, right?" Bob's narrowing eyes acted completely opposite of Charlie's.

"Yeah, I am, actually," Casey said. "Charlie is going, too."

Charlie rubbed the back of his neck and smiled sheepishly.

Bob curled his fingers into Casey's shirt so that he had a balled-up wad of it in his hand. "What is this about you going over to my girl's house before? You trying to fuck her or something?"

Casey tried to back away, but found that Bob's grip was even less lenient than Bob's own father's. "Um, you called me a fag, and you still think I'm going to try to have sex with your girlfriend?"

Casey looked at Bob right in the eyes. Zephiscestra's influence gave him confidence that he had never experienced before.

"Look, man. All I know is that when my girlfriend comes around saying that she's gonna have some guy over when she's taking a shower and stuff, that guy is always me. You hear? So, when she tells me that you, of all people, are coming over to help her get dressed. . . you can understand that I'm going to be a little concerned."

"Bob, I'm gay. You know this. Allie knows this. All I'm going to do is help her pick out a top that matches her mascara."

Bob chuckled. Casey realized that Bob wasn't angry. In fact, it was quite obvious that Bob was enjoying this whole thing. Charlie, in the background, silently feared what Bob's good mood, coupled with his intimidating hand placement, might mean for Casey.

"Okay, kid, so here's what's what," Bob said. "I'm not a bad guy, so I'll let Allie keep her little play date. Err, *gay* date." He put his face closer to Casey's. "But, if I hear that you're getting frisky or whatever you people call it, I'm gonna grab your dick, rip it off, and feed it to my iguana. Okay?"

The threat sounded like it was straight out of a movie. Casey, veins thick with Indulgence, wasn't intimidated by such cartoony line such as that. "You know you'd have to touch it, then."

The color drained from Bob's face and he moved his head as far back as it could go while still keeping his hand firmly curled up in Casey's shirt. "What the fuck did you just say?" Bob's face twisted into a disgusted sneer and he looked over his shoulder as if to make sure that none of his friends or relatives had heard the slander that had slithered from between Casey's teeth.

Bob didn't want to touch any other man's business, and he decided to prove it. He did this, ironically, by making contact with Casey's crotch.

"Fuuuuuuuuuhhhh." Casey's eyes squeezed shut and his mouth formed an "O" as he sank to his knees. Bob, of course, didn't touch Casey's genitals with his hands, but with his right kneecap, and with 3 layers of clothes between them.

"Don't you ever fucking talk to me like that again," Bob said. "Okay, *gay boy?*"

Bob walked away, leaving Casey on the ground, nauseous with pain. Charlie knelt to rub his back and help him stand.

"Are you okay? Oh my god, Bob is such a dick," Charlie said.

Casey didn't speak for a few minutes. He had to catch his breath. When he finally spoke, he said: "Please, don't even mention the word 'dick' for a while." As the pair started to walk on towards home, Charlie whimpered, "But, I thought you loved dick."

Casey's mouth dropped open. "When did you get so bold?" If there was a category for it, Charlie would be the one voted "Most G Rated" in his high school yearbook. He didn't usually curse, and he wasn't fond of dirty jokes.

"This whole day just has my adrenaline pumping," Charlie said. "Like, first you get like 10,000 followers, and then you get into a fight with Bob?" He fanned his face and pretended to swoon. "I swear I might just pass out from all the excitement."

"Talk to me about passing out why don't you," Casey said. "I've never been hit in the balls before. It hurts so badly." He gingerly cupped his crotch with his hand. The area was still tender.

"Well, put some ice on it when you get home," Charlie said.

"Yeah, I guess so. I can't believe Bob would do something like that."

"You don't believe that? He is the biggest jerk in the world. I knew he was going to do something like that when he first grabbed your shirt."

"Then, why didn't you do anything?" He instantly regretted his question when he saw Charlie look down in shame. "Hey, I'm just kidding," Casey said. "I didn't expect you to do anything, really. Who would want to mess with Bob?"

Charlie wiped his eyes. "I'm sorry, Casey. I would have done something, but I was just... scared."

Casey managed a painful smile. "Hey, it could have been worse. You're right, he's terrible. Makes me start to rethink going over to Allie's."

Charlie looked off into the distance. "Will you forgive me?"

Casey said, "Of course I will. How could I not? You're my best friend. I could never be mad at you." Then, he added, "It's not like you kicked me in the balls yourself."

Charlie thanked him, then suddenly said that he forgot something at the office. Casey saw through the lie, but he allowed Charlie to part ways without protest.

Bob had assaulted Casey's body, and at the same time hurt Charlie's pride. Yet, through Zephiscestra's influence, neither of them thought to contact any authority. The goddess possessed no inkling of corporate Human Resources.

Casey gritted his teeth and continued his journey, alone. Gathering his energy, and for the second time that day, he tried to remove his concept of pain from his physical body. Removing his sense of feeling from himself, Casey tried to focus on the external world, the things that he never paid attention to.

Casey realized that he never really appreciated the place that he lived. The air was always clear, the sky was often bright. Casey spent a lot of his time online, especially on LitMille, and he ruminated on digital dopamine during his ventures outdoors. Walking through the warm climate, he could forget about his pain for a moment. The grass was green and there were birds and squirrels, as well as trees to house them.

The beautiful weather lent its hand to aid his rising mood. With the pain gone, Casey's mind began to drift towards his creative endeavors.

Casey had always dreamed of having his art being received positively over the Internet. Since he perused the net so often, he had grown to love the people that put content online. Of course, his favorite online personality was Trevor Greenbrook, by far. Trevor had kept Casey company for a few years now.

Years ago, when Casey had just come out of the closet, he felt alone and nervous, even though his family was incredibly supportive. There was something about being exposed that was new to Casey, who had spent more than twenty years of his life living a lie. When he found Trevor, he found someone he could relate to. He found someone who spoke with the voice of the LGBT people who found themselves marginalized. He found a role model. He found a friend.

It wasn't long before Casey found himself obsessing over Trevor. He checked his idol's social media channels almost compulsively. After years of lurking, Casey decided that he would follow in his hero's footsteps and start to make LitMille videos. Casey hoped that Trevor would acknowledge his accomplishments, but it was considered to be more of a delusion than a true goal.

But, now that he had 10,000 followers, his vision had the chance to become a reality. Casey knew that, while it was hard to get started, fame could start to compound quickly once it got some momentum. Maybe meeting Trevor was actually feasible...

But, how did he get so many followers? How was it possible that he could gain thousands of interactions in one night? Could his song have been that good? Was it the pinnacle of rainbow-based entertainment? While Casey had enjoyed making his song and thought that it turned out great, he didn't think that it could have netted him 10,000 followers alone. But then... what could it have been?

Allie had reblogged it, but not even she was connected enough to amass such a crowd so quickly. Casey reckoned that she had around 2,000 followers on her microblog. Even if all of them followed him back, where did the other 8,000 come from?

Casey was approaching the bridge. What he saw made him stop, because it was even crazier than what had happened the night before.

The sun was still bright in the sky. People walked casually down the street without jumping aside or shielding their eyes. Cars drove over the bridge without honking their horns. A couple of men sat across the street, and they weren't filming anything with their phones. Some women in bikinis were standing on the safe side of the bridge, about to jump in. They were laughing and looking down at the water.

None of that would have been strange on its own. What was strange was that there was a tall man with dark hair standing stark naked on the sidewalk. His clothes were balled up on the sidewalk next to him. He was staring up at the girls on the edge of the bridge.

"Hey ladies, how about you turn around and take your tops off?" The man stood straight up, with one hand on his hip and the other doing something unspeakable. Casey heard a faint slapping sound that might have been the currents of the river.

Casey looked around in surprise, but no one seemed to be doing anything about the man. He debated crossing the street to avoid the commotion, but then decided against it. An otherworldly force compelled him to confront the man. For some reason, he felt as if they were connected.

The women jumped into the water below. Casey heard the splashes. When people jumped from the "fun side" of the bridge, they had to swim underneath it to reach a ladder that climbed back to street level. The men on the other side of the street peered over the railing to watch the women emerge on the other side.

"Hey, where did you go?" The man put both hands on the railing and leaned over the edge. Casey walked up right behind him. He resisted the urge to look at the firm buttocks that were presented before him.

"Um, hey, what do you think you're doing?" Casey asked. The man didn't turn around. Casey furrowed his brow and tried again, louder. "Hey, what in god's name are you doing?"

The man stopped looking into the water below. He straightened up and turned slowly around until he was facing with Casey, who was shocked to see a dead man.

"Well, I'll be fucked," the man said. "You can see me?"

CHAPTER 6

CASEY COULDN'T BELIEVE his eyes.

Standing erect in the sunlight was the man who leapt from the bridge during the previous night. Casey thought that he had witnessed a suicide. Now, the man's nudity made a lot more sense; He was clearly insane. That explained why he wanted to kill himself with a recreational bridge, and that was why he was standing naked on that same bridge twenty-two hours later.

Casey immediately felt remorse for him, since the man couldn't help the fact that he was plagued by deep-seated mental issues. Casey considered it a tragedy that someone so young could have already lost their mind, and he decided that he wanted to get this man to a treatment center as soon as possible.

Casey was on the verge of offering to walk him home. Before he could do that, the man reached out and gripped the hem of Casey's shirt.

"So, are we doing this or what?" The man lifted up Casey's shirt and exposed his torso.

Casey yelped and flailed his arms. The man let go of his shirt. Casey took a few steps back, panting.

"What do you think you're doing?" He thought the stranger had lost his mind, and Casey wanted nothing less than to feed into his insanity.

"What? I was going to try to bang those chicks, but they didn't respond to my pick-up lines. Plus, they're gone, now," The man flicked his thumb behind him to point at the now empty railing. "But, *you'll* do, too. You're really cute, you know."

The man made another advance, his bare feet plopping against the concrete of the sidewalk. Casey jumped back again and held his arms out to keep the nameless stranger at bay.

"We aren't doing anything like that, you freak," Casey said. His face was burning. He didn't intend to call the man names, but he was caught off guard. The man seemed like a completely different person from when they had their first encounter. Whereas before, the stranger was withdrawn and overtly depressed, he was now energetic, , aggressive, and almost swaggering.

"You need help. Let's get your clothes on and get you to a hospital." Casey checked behind him to see if the people across the street were going to come to his aid. The others were still looking out over the railing on the opposite side. Casey heard the faint sounds of laughter and splashing from below.

"A hospital? Fuck that. I don't need a hospital. That would be a waste of dream time. Let's just do this already. You're the only one that has been able to see me all day. It's my dream, the least you could do is make it a pleasant one for me."

"You must have suffered a concussion when you tried to kill yourself last night," Casey said, shocked at his bluntness. "This is real life."

"Kill myself?" The man seemed even more confused at the idea. "Why would I do that? I feel great! In fact, I really have no idea what you're talking about. The only things that I remember are a few things that happened today."

Casey continued to backing away, his hands outstretched. "Look, man, you're not dreaming. This is real life. You are really naked in the middle of town right now. Look."

Casey reached out and slapped the man in the face. He didn't strike him too hard, and the contact sounded like a halfhearted high-five. The feeling, though, was electric. Pure awareness spread through the man's face and into his psyche, allowing him to understand, if only for a moment.

The man stopped in his tracks and felt his cheek with his fingers. There was already a red mark above the man's rigid jaw. He looked at Casey dead in the eyes. Then, he looked over at the other people who were still leaning over the railing. No one else was on the street, and not even a car had passed by since Casey and the man had started talking. The man raised one finger, as if he were about to bring up an important point. Then he did something that Casey didn't expect.

The man stomped his foot on the ground and slapped his hands against his bare thighs, the way that a toddler would whilst throwing a tantrum. "This dream sucks. I can't talk to anyone, I can't fly, I can't spawn things, and I can't even have sex." He sat down against the railing so that his knees were up near his ears. He rested his arms on his kneecaps and sunk his head down between his legs. "What's the point of having a lucid dream if I can't have sex with people?" At that angle, Casey didn't have a problem seeing what else was between his legs, but he blushed and jerked his head away when he found himself peeking.

When Casey did have a chance to examine the man, he noticed even more differences than the change in personality. First, the man looked as if he had put on thirty pounds of muscle overnight. His jaw seemed squarer, and his hair appeared much thicker. A fleeting fantasy entered Casey's mind, one he tried his best to ignore.

Casey squatted until he was at the same level as the man, fighting the urge to look anywhere other than his eyes. He mentally kicked himself at even thinking about this poor man in such a sexually explicit way.

"Hey, this isn't a dream, okay?" Casey spoke calmly and tried to make his voice sound soothing. He didn't want to disturb him, but he did want to tell the man the exact situation that they were in. He figured that if he told the man the truth, maybe it would knock some sense into him. "You are standing. Naked. On a bridge. On a bright afternoon." Casey segmented his phrases so that they could be easily digested. "This is real life. I am real. I can help you get dressed if you want. I can also take you to a hospital if you think you need it."

Casey held out his hand. The man took it, rising with Casey's assistance. Again, the electric awareness spread through the stranger's body.

"So, this isn't a dream?" The man stared into Casey's eyes as if he were challenging him. The way the man had asked it, the question could have come from hour three of an intense interrogation.

Casey met his gaze, tried to appear as sincere as possible, and shook his head 'no.'

"So then, what you're saying is..." the man continued, "That... that..." Casey waited for the man to finish. The man closed his eyes, as if he were trying to remember something. An inadvertent glance revealed to Casey that the man was bloodless. "That my unwilling solipsistic delusions were correct, and this universe and all that inhabit it are merely figments of my subconscious memory that have somehow seeped partially into my conscious mind, allowing me passive control over time, space, and other's free will, based on my various automatic emotional states?" The man opened his eyes again and looked back at Casey, expectantly.

"Um. No?" Casey didn't really understand what the man had said, but he had learned years ago to answer 'no' to any question that he did not fully hear.

The man turned red from his face all the way down to his torso. He jogged over to his clothes, bent down, and shuffled them around until he found his boxers. Still bent over, he stepped into them and then stood upright, pulling on his underwear and assuming a semblance of dignity. His baggy boxers were decorated with little cartoons of brawlers, each one wearing red gloves and shorts.

The seemingly insane stranger dressed himself in silence. Casey stood some distance away, motionless. He didn't know what to do; the situation was too bizarre. He watched the man's back muscles stretch as he bent over to pull on his khaki pants, then drop to his knee to put on his socks and shoes. Casey noticed that the man put on the sock and boot of one foot before he started on the other. The man solemnly buttoned up his shirt, avoiding Casey's gaze. Casey approached him as he fixed his collar.

"Are you ready to go?" Casey said. "We can go back to my apartment to get my car, then we can go to a hospital."

The man said nothing for a minute.

"If this isn't a dream, then why can't anyone see me?" The stranger looked earnestly at Casey. He wasn't asking a loaded question. He wanted an honest answer.

"Well, that's not true. I can see you," Casey said.

"Right, but no one else can," the man said. "Look. I'll show you." He turned towards the street and looked to his left and right to check for cars. Then, he walked across the bridge to where the others had finally lost interest in the women down below.

The three men were sitting on the railing, conversing with one another.

The stranger walked right in front of them, but they didn't acknowledge him. He started to yell at them and wave his hands around, but, still, no one looked up from the conversation. The man jumped up and down, did jumping jacks, push-ups, and even started to dance the Macarena. He pretended to punch each of them in turn, swinging his fist and stopping it only an inch in front of their faces, screaming 'Ah!' each time he swung.

None of them even flinched.

At this point, Casey decided to step in and stop him. He figured that the others were ignoring him because he was acting so strangely. Casey looked both ways and jogged across the street. The others saw Casey coming and they looked up to stare at him. The stranger was waving his open palms in front of two of their faces.

"Hey guys, I'm sorry for my friend. I'm going get him out of here," Casey said.

The other men said nothing and gave Casey quizzical looks.

"Come on, bud. Let's get you home," Casey said.

"Uh, are you talking to me," one of the men asked.

A couple of thin grins spread across the other two men's faces.

"No, sorry, I'm talking to him," Casey said, pointing towards the man.

"Who the fuck are you talking about?" Another man looked at Casey like he was the one who had just performed the most embarrassing dance of the 90s.

"My friend, right here," Casey said. He put his arm around the broad shoulders of the man who was otherwise being ignored.

One of the others hopped off the railing and pretended to put him arm around an invisible person, mimicking Casey. "Hey guys, I think he's here to take his girlfriend back." His two cohorts jeered.

"Yeah, that's the best he can do, huh?"

"She's just so skinny that you can't see her when she turns sideways."

"But that means that she's flat as a board."

"No ass. No tits. Shit, it doesn't look like she has any body parts at all."

Casey, through wide eyes, looked at the man he was holding.

"Hey, let's get out of here," one of them said. With that, they walked away, laughing. "Good luck, bro."

"You really don't see him?" Casey shouted after the pack. They ignored him.

"See? I told you I was dreaming," the man said. He showed Casey a broad smile that exposed his teeth.

Casey gasped and dropped his arm from around the man's shoulder.

For some reason, Casey hadn't noticed his teeth while they were talking earlier. Now that he was so close, it was obvious: The man's mouth was filled with broad, sharp teeth that looked like they belonged to a wild animal.

CHAPTER 7

CASEY WINCED AS a piece of grilled chicken was picked off of his grandmother's plate.

The invisible stranger examined it for a moment before popping it into his mouth, chewing thoughtfully. He looked over at Casey and shook his head.

"Fuckin' nothing. This chicken has absolutely no flavor," the man said. He had already sampled the cheesy scalloped potatoes, the creamy tomato soup, and the buttery broccoli that were set on the table. Each time he ate another piece of food, he complained to Casey how bland it all was.

"Food's delicious, Grandma," Casey's brother, Kyle, said. Casey's grandmother took no notice of her pilfered chicken. The rest of the family who were gathered at Casey's apartment for dinner didn't see the man hovering around their periphery, either.

"Thank you, darling," Grandma said. "I had it marinating in the kitchen all day. I put a lot of work into it."

"As always, dear," Grandpa agreed, chewing on a piece of the succulent chicken.

Casey hadn't touched his food. He couldn't believe that no one else could see the hulk of a man standing in front of them. A few hours had passed since Casey had met the man on the bridge, yet no one even acknowledged the bulky intruder as he had sat on the couch, walked around the house, and raided the fridge. Even on the walk back to his apartment, Casey had received nothing but incredulous looks from a few pedestrians when he asked them if they could help his "friend."

"I don't know what the fuck they're talking about, Casey. This dinner tastes like paper," the man said loudly. "Have you ever eaten paper before?"

Casey just stared at him. "Me neither, but this is what I imagine it tastes like."

Kyle noticed that Casey was staring into the distance and gave him a quizzical look.

"Casey, why aren't you eating?" His mother looked concerned. Casey was broken from his reverie for a moment. He picked at his food with his fork.

"I'm just not hungry, is all," Casey said.

He was a lot more confused at his current situation than the rest of his family was confused at his lack of appetite. Things had started off strangely since Casey had picked up the man from his naked frenzy, and not many questions had been answered since. Casey had tried to get some information from the man and ended up with nothing.

The man didn't know his own name, where he came from, or where he lived. He didn't have any memory at all about his own identity. Interestingly, the man was familiar to the world around him. He could still speak fluent English and he could recall various celebrities and well-known historical events. As for personal information, the stranger knew as much about himself as Casey knew about him. Which is, to say, nothing at all.

"Well, I hope that you can find an appetite," his mother said. "When you called us in such distress to come to your apartment, we wrapped up all of this food to share with you."

"The food tastes great," Casey said.

"Speak for yourself," the stranger said.

"I just don't feel like eating. I appreciate that you brought the dinner, but I appreciate the fact that you came to comfort me even more."

His family had already spoken to him on the phone about the suicide he had witnessed. His father asked him if he had any thoughts of doing that to himself, and Casey had answered 'no.' His father told him to appreciate the life that he had and to use the perspective that, while bad things happen in the world, he didn't have to take it onto himself to feel the pain of others that could put his life in danger.

His mother had enveloped him in a hug when she had arrived that night. Other than that, she didn't mention anything directly about the suicide.

As for what had happened to him the night before, the man had nothing to say. He claimed that he woke up underneath the bridge at around noon with no knowledge of how he got there. After that, the man had wandered around town for a while, quickly realizing that he was effectively invisible to everyone that he encountered.

While he had found it strange, the man had dismissed his situation as being part of some Kafkaesque dream. He quickly took advantage of his condition, taking whatever food he wanted from restaurants and diners (which immediately lost its appeal when he realized he couldn't taste) and infiltrating women's locker rooms (which he found far more enthralling).

After a while, he made his way back to the bridge, where he ran into the first person to see him.

After his initial outburst, the man didn't seem to get concerned about his fate. He had a lightheartedness to him that one wouldn't expect him to possess after waking up with amnesia and apparently existing on some different plane of reality.

Casey put a piece of broccoli in his mouth and chewed unenthusiastically. The delicious juices burst in his mouth without notice.

"Oh, don't worry dear," Grandma said. "I won't take it personally if you're not hungry. That's what grandmothers are for, anyway."

"Maybe your stomach is just too full of butterflies, since your channel just exploded." Kyle said. He was one of Casey's original subscribers on LitMille and was just as surprised as Casey was when he saw the channel that day.

"Yeah, that must be it," Casey said quietly. The secret he was keeping from his family was making him feel nauseous. He usually told them everything, which was the reason he called them to his apartment. For some reason, he couldn't bring himself to tell his parents that he might be hallucinating. It was just too unnerving. He decided that if the problem persisted for more than a few days, he would bring it up. For the time being, he didn't want to upset anyone.

"Well, you don't seem too excited," Casey's father said. "When I closed my first deal as a realtor, I was ecstatic. I think success should make you happy." Casey's dad was successful in his field, but never let his accomplishments get to his head. It made sharing problems with him easy, which was why Casey's unwillingness to confess was all the more unsettling.

"Well, artists are different," Grandma said. "A lot of famous painters still regard their art to be awful, even if it is widely celebrated. Don't be too hard on yourself, Casey. You are a very brilliant man."

His Grandpa agreed.

"I just don't feel well. Mind if I go to my room?" Casey pushed his plate away and removed his napkin from his lap before he got an answer.

"Sure, honey. Do you want us to leave?"

"If you don't mind," Casey said. "Thanks for coming, I just need some alone time." He got up and started for his room. The imperceptible figure set Grandpa's milk back down on the table and wiped away a white mustache.

"Is this skim? Grandma, next time, remember that I don't fuck with anything below 2%," the man said. Then, he followed Casey out of the kitchen.

Casey's room was far away enough from the kitchen that he could talk freely until his family had fully cleared out. His roommate had left for a planned, months-long visit to relatives in Europe, so Casey had all of the time in the world to figure out what was going on.

It all would have been clear, had it not been for the influence of Zephiscestra, pulling the strings on their minds and making them both ignorant to information that was accessible to other people who had committed use of the ritual.

Paranoia set in, and Casey was sharply cognizant of the fact that he didn't want anyone to overhear his conversation with the stranger from the bridge. Casey decided he would keep his volume to a minimum, as well as play some music from his laptop so that his voice couldn't be distinguished. He sat down at his desk, opened his computer, and played a song by one of his favorite singers on LitMille.

"Okay, so first of all—"

"Ew, what the fuck is this?" The man snarled, disgusted. His fang was visible from beneath his curled lip.

"What?"

"This indie crap music. You listen to this?"

"It's good," Casey said. He found that, with his success on LitMille, he was unconsciously willing to talk back to a dead man.

"This is some hipster crap. Put on some fuckin' horror core."

"You seem pretty energetic," Casey said. He added, as delicately as he could, "Which is strange considering you might very well be dead."

"I seem to have boundless energy," the man said, "But, I don't really have anything to do."

The man sat down on the edge of Casey's bed, facing him. "I mean, did you see me at dinner? I could take whatever I wanted, but it wasn't satisfying in the least bit."

Casey furrowed his brow. "That's what I wanted to talk about. I called my family here for support. Then, you stole their food from their plates. You can't go around messing with my family. I love them more than anything, and if you try to hurt them…" Casey realized the futility of his words. The man could do whatever he wanted; literally no one else could see or touch him. His newly bulging muscles and sharp teeth pointed more towards the fact that the stranger would put up a hell of a fight even if someone did oppose him. "I don't know what I'll do," Casey finished.

The man put his hands up defensively. "Relax, Casey. I didn't want to hurt them. I was just… experimenting. You see, I seem to have lost all sense of taste, as well as smell. My hearing is incredible, though. But, I had to taste that food, because even though it was delicious to you mere mortals, I had absolutely no sensation whatsoever."

"Seriously? You don't you even… wait? Mere mortals? What are you calling yourself? A god?"

"I'm not saying I'm all-powerful or anything, but I'm definitely not a human. Look at my fucking teeth, for starters. And no one but you can see me? That's not something that happens to normal people."

"Okay, let's not get ahead of ourselves. We have no idea what is going on. For all we know, I could just be hallucinating this whole thing. In fact, that is what I believe."

"You can't seriously fuckin' believe that," the man said.

Casey swiveled around to face his computer.

"Hey," the stranger said. "What in the fuck are you doing?"

"I'm ignoring you," Casey said, cringing. "If you're not real, then all I should have to do is just keep in mind that you're not real, and then you will disappear. I'm insane, but I'm not insane enough to not know that I'm insane." Casey glanced up and to the right, trying to think if he said that correctly. The man did the same.

"I'm realer than a rash on your fuckin' nutsack. How can I prove it to you?"

Casey tried to think of some ways. He couldn't come up with any, so he just didn't answer. Instead, he searched online for "Schizophrenia symptoms." He thought he was experiencing hallucinations and delusions, but he didn't have apathy or emotional flatness. If anything, Casey was becoming even more emotional because of all of the strange occurrences.

Casey was just beginning to notice how quiet the man was being when the stranger came up from behind him and put a dinner plate on his desk.

"Fuck, yeah. That proves it. If I wasn't real, then how would I be able to put this very real plate in here? You dumb idiot."

Casey looked at the plate.

"The plate isn't real," he said.

"Touch it," the man said. Casey touched it. It was real.

"I walked out of the room and got it, but my delusions made me forget about that and made me think that you did it," Casey said.

"You're a real piece of fuckin' work," the man said.

Casey sighed and considered his options. While it was definitely strange that this plate had appeared on his desk, it was highly possible that he had just placed it there without remembering. His mind was occupied with a lot of different things that had happened that day. It was alarming that he might be losing his mind, but all of the unnatural things that were occurring could have just stemmed from a mixture of A: the excitement of both his recent influx of LitMille subscribers and the invitation to his first impressive party, and B: the fear from the events that he witnessed last night, the late hours at the police station, and the altercation with Bob after work.

Casey reflected that he had started hallucinating that morning in the shower, but his visions weren't hyper-real until he was on his way home.

The man looked at Casey expectantly, waiting for him to go into the kitchen. Casey turned back to his computer and opened up LitMille.

"You aren't going to go investigate this utterly bizarre occurrence?" The man seemed disappointed.

"Nope, I'm just going to ignore it," Casey said.

"Sounds dumb," the man said. "But, hey. *Your* life."

"Also, if you are a hallucination, but I actively recognize you as such, then you will probably disappear soon. If not, then I will tell my parents."

Mental illnesses are tricky for those who have to endure them. Such diseases are still mysterious, even in the scientific community, so people who suffer from them don't have a lot of precedent to work with. If someone breaks an arm, they will go to the hospital right away. If someone starts hallucinating, but feels no physical pain, they might try to push through it; this may be because they don't want to seem crazy.

"Well, I guess that's a sound plan," the man said. "But, trust me on this. I know for a fuck-ING fact that I am not a hallucination. I don't think I'll be going anywhere anytime soon."

"That's just what a hallucination would say," Casey said. They both pondered the statement for a moment. The man laid back on Casey's bed.

"But a hallucination would only say that if you genuinely believed that you weren't hallucinating. Since, of course, a hallucination is just a projection within your own mind that you perceive as real. A hallucination can only know what you know."

The man sat up straight. "Oh, fuck, I got it!"

He rushed over to Casey's desk and picked up his laptop.

"Hey!" Casey jumped out of his chair, but the man held his hand up, open palm, in the universal symbol of 'stop.'

"Hear me the fuck out. If I'm not a hallucination, then I can know things that you don't know."

Casey swiped at his laptop, but the man ducked and spun around the room. Incredibly, he was able to balance the open laptop on one flat hand while he danced away from Casey's attempts to retrieve the device.

"Don't drop it," Casey said in an angry whisper. He wasn't sure if his family had left, yet, but he didn't anyone to hear him fighting with himself.

"Then stop harassing me," the man said. He held Casey away at arm's length, with the laptop another arm's length away. "Listen. I will look something up online that you don't know, and then you can look at it to see if I'm right."

Casey admitted defeat to the man's arm and backed away.

"Alright, thank fucking you," the man said. Facing Casey so that he couldn't see the screen, the man clicked around for a second before saying, "Okay, how many LitMille subscribers do you have? Wait. Never mind. You would already know that, this was the last screen that you were looking at."

"I know. I have 10,000 subscribers. I just looked at it today," Casey said. "Now give me back my laptop."

"Heh. Nope."

"Nope?" Casey was getting angry, which was exacerbated by his belief that he was getting angry at himself.

The man smiled. "Nope. I thought you would know that," he laughed. "You do not have 10,000 subscribers. Not even fucking close."

Casey's heart sank into the pit of his stomach. Maybe a lot of his subscribers unsubscribed when they found out how silly his videos were. Maybe his burst of fame was like an explosion: it expanded very quickly, but soon was reduced back to nothing. Casey had heard of the expression "15 minutes of fame," but he hadn't expected his run to be finished in just one day.

"Whoa, don't look so sad. This is good news," the man said. "You're have 20,000 subscribers. Fuck, that's a lot."

"What?!" Casey's heart rocketed back up into his chest so fast that he thought it might burst. "That's impossible... it was at 10,000 this morning."

"Well, it's twice that now," the man said. "I didn't know you were so popular. Also, looking at you, I don't know why that would be the case."

Despite the insult, Casey couldn't hide his grin. Sure, he might have been talking to a physical manifestation of an imaginary projection of a man who Casey had witnessed committing suicide the night before. But, his subscriber count had doubled in only a few hours.

Under the influence of Zephiscestra, the boon made everything seem somewhat okay.

"Well, you're right," Casey said. "You knew something that I didn't. Now give me back my laptop." He still wasn't convinced, but he wanted his computer back in his own real hands.

"Not so fast, bitch. Let me ask you a few more questions," the man said.

Casey regained control of his computer only after incorrectly guessing the price of several blue chip stocks, the current temperature of a city halfway across the globe, a famous rapper's real name, and the total runtime of a cult classic film produced three decades before that day.

The man sat back down on Casey's bed, satisfied. "See? I must be fuckin' real if I could know things that you don't," he said.

Casey, sitting at his computer, simply shook his head. "Well, for all I know, I was just sitting here the whole time looking up facts and then imagining that I was asking them to myself."

The man groaned. "Do you fuckin' believe that?"

"No," Casey said. "But is it really less believable than you being a ghost or something?"

"I don't know. You tell me," the man said. "I don't know what you're thinking."

"I'm thinking that maybe we should find out your identity," Casey said. "Sound good?"

Casey, despite the incredible turbulence of his situation, experienced a moment of elation because of his success. He decided that if he could amass such a large amount of followers, then he could surely get to the bottom of this haunting ailment of his.

The man smiled. "Yeah, find out who I am. Because if I'm not you, then who the hell am I?"

CHAPTER 8

FRIDAY CAME QUICKLY.

The day of the party was only two days after Casey had received the invitation from Allie, and the rotation of the Earth brought Casey steadily towards his destination. He and the invisible man didn't sit idly to pass the time.

Casey took to the internet, researching mental illness with the fervency of an acute schizophrenic who had discovered his destiny to save the world from an inevitable, supernatural onslaught. He discovered that hallucinatory voices experienced by Americans tended to be hostile and disturbing. The man pulled pranks on random people around town, and the words that spewed from his mouth were definitely disturbing. He also embodied the form of a man who had committed suicide in front of Casey. However, Casey didn't deem him to be exceptionally violent.

Casey also found that the type of hallucination he may have been experiencing was classified as a Complex Visual Hallucination. These hallucinations were characterized by seeing animals, humans, or scenes that didn't exist in reality. When patients recounted their hallucinations, they described the people or animals they saw as being very bright, ringed with light, and dramatic. The man wasn't very bright, at least not in the literal sense, although Casey had to admit (chuckling to himself) that his practical jokes were quite clever.

The stranger's most complex prank involved the loosening of every screw in a local college class. The screws were left in place so that everything would seem normal, but every piece of furniture fell to pieces at the slightest touch. The genius here was that the professor kept her door locked until the start of her first class, and no one could sit down until reciting the Pledge of Allegiance. After the decree of "God Bless America," 20 students found themselves on the ground covered with pieces of their desks and chairs.

Although Casey concluded that this was definitely dramatic, it decreased his belief that he was truly hallucinating. There was no way that Casey could have gotten into the building while he was at work. However, the pranks did create a fear that Casey was beginning to black out and not remember what he was doing.

He made it a habit to send frequent and periodic texts to his friends so that there wouldn't be an extended period of time where his location wasn't documented. He also kept his phone with him at all times and checked his routes using his navigator. His phone hadn't traveled to the school during the night, which meant that Casey probably didn't go, either. So, if Casey wasn't the cause of these pranks, then it could be logical to assume that the man was actually the mastermind behind them. Or—and Casey highly suspected that this was the case—some other prankster was on the rise and Casey's subconscious was simply taking responsibility.

While it was still frightening that Casey was losing touch with reality, it was reassuring to think that he was still in control of his actions.

Even then, the possibility that the man wasn't a hallucination pulled at the edges of Casey's nerves. As much as Casey fought himself from believing it, there was a chance that what Casey was seeing was real: there was a man who had tried to kill himself, may or may not have survived, and was now accompanying Casey on his day-to-day activities because Casey was the only one that could see or hear him.

Casey kept trying to push the idea away, but it was still possible, although highly unlikely. The problem was that there was no logical cause to this scenario.

The men were back in the break room, the respective laptops already open in front of them. Joining them was their "friend" Harry Schiest. Schiest's name used to be infamous throughout the campus where Casey had attended college. "Shiest" had effectively replaced the words "creep" in its adjectival forms, essentially becoming the university's term for "sketchy." "Greasy" could also apply, but no one used it except to explain the expression that was constantly plastered on Schiest's face. He was too disconnected with reality to understand that this was a bad thing, and he often used the phrase with a demented pride.

While Casey and Schiest were never friends in school, the outcast clung to him when he realized that they worked at the same company. Sometimes, when he wasn't busy doing other schiesty things, Schiest joined them at their break table.

"We have a new project today," Charlie said. "Shouldn't be too hard, but we will all have to put in some work. Honestly, I think—"

"Hey, did you guys see Rebecca today? Her ass is looking FIRE!" Schiest spoke up for, remarkably, the first time that day. Apparently, Schiest could only communicate in an extremely specific way, which Casey, Charlie, and Bill had already mapped out with surprising scientific efficiency:

1: Someone has to already be speaking.
2: The topic that Schiest brings up will be in no way even remotely related to the prevalent surrounding conversation.
3: Schiest will almost always start off by asking a question.
4: Schiest will add his own little schiesty answer to his question.
   Charlie choked on his sandwich. As the only recognized straight person at the table, other than Shiest, the question was almost assuredly addressed to him.
   "No, I didn't see her today," Bill said, clearly forgetting the last rule:
5: Schiest does not require acknowledgement. If he doesn't receive a response, he will simply laugh to himself, smile, and then presumably take the next ten minutes to think of another stupid question.

Shiest laughed his shiesty laugh that was close to being a snort, but not quite. He looked back down at his computer. The others silently lamented their being with Schiest. They concluded that they didn't really hang out with him, so much as he hung out with them. However, none of them were brave enough to tell him to never to approach them again.

The stranger appeared suddenly and sat down in an empty seat. No one looked at him except for Casey, who quickly remembered that he would seem strange for looking over at nothing.

"Sup, fuck. Guess where I've been?" The man was beaming. Casey didn't answer vocally, but instead gave him a slight nod. Although the man remained a mystery, Casey was had come to accept that he was a part of his life.

The other two were engrossed with whatever was on their screens at the time and didn't notice the acknowledgement. Bill was on the fan page of a muscular movie star. Across from Casey, Charlie wore a dreamy expression while browsing Casey's social media pages. Schiest was shifting through pornography thumbnails.

"I just filled up fuckin' Bob's car with ping pong balls," the man said. Casey stifled a laugh. "Like, all the way to the brim. It's gonna be awesome when he has to drive home." The man looked around at the other three. He took a swig from a bottle of hot sauce. Casey grimaced in disgust.

"What? Oh, the hot sauce?" The man took another gulp. The bottle read 'Texas Cletus eXXXtra Hot' with a picture of an exploding thermometer on the side. "I got it at the store when I picked up the Ping-Pong balls. It's seriously the only thing that I can taste right now. And this still seems pretty fuckin' mild."

Casey turned back to his computer. He pulled up Trevor's personal blog. Trevor smiled back at him with the corner of his mouth. His green hair was styled up into a wave. Casey felt himself drooling. He had never seen such a beautiful selfie before.

Trevor always posted selfies, but Casey figured that this one was the most attractive. Such a thought always accompanied a new selfie from Trevor. Casey saved the picture on his computer. He already had a folder with a few other pictures of Trevor. Casey had taken these pictures for granted for a while now, but they suddenly seemed all the more important to him. Even the fuzziest, worst quality photo of Trevor seemed to jump off the screen at him.

Casey imagined himself in Trevor's apartment, the one that was featured in all of his vlogs. He imagined Trevor fixing them each cup of tea, then sitting next to him. Trevor put his hand on Casey's thigh. Casey inhaled with a sudden passion, both in the fantasy and in real life. Trevor leaned in for a kiss and Casey consented. Trevor reached around the back of Casey's head, simultaneously pulling him closer and running his fingers through Casey's hair. Casey was pursing his lips when he was broken from his reverie by a loud outburst from beside him.

"HAHAHAHA! THIS GUY IS WATCHING PORN!" The stranger's face was distorted in pure glee and he was rocking back and forth in his chair. Casey blushed when he discovered the roll of quarters that had appeared in his lap under the table.

The man slapped Schiest on the back. Schiest didn't seem to notice, but his face was now considerably closer to the screen.

"I like you, kid," the man said. "You got spunk. And by that, I mean you're a fucking freak and it's entertaining to watch." He chuckled but got over himself. "Actually, with what you're watching, you probably do have some spunk right now."

"Your office is weird, Casey," the man said. "Actually, it was kind of the same thing in the store." He shuddered. "I didn't need to know the intricacies of senior citizen's pickup lines in grocery stores. Maybe the elderly have this unwritten code where they just wait till the middle of the day when all of their children and grandkids are at school or work…"

He turned back to Casey. "But, everyone in here is horny as hell. Seriously. You should have seen the amount of people making out in the bathrooms and the hallways when I was walking around. Everyone's got their tongue's down each other's throats."

The man got up from his chair and rounded the table. "That guy is watching porn," he said, pointing to Shiest. "This guy is looking at hot guys," he said when he passed behind Bill. He walked behind Charlie, saying, "This guy is looking at… Oh!" He glanced at Casey. "What a fuckin' surprise…" The man stroked his chin.

Casey shot him a quizzical look.

Just then, Allie Thatcher walked by the table.

"Oh, and you should have seen this one in action!" The man said happily. "I don't know why no one can see me, but let me tell you it's been a blessing, 'cus I got to see this girl's--"

Allie's greeting disrupted the man right before he was going to something that would have been heinous.

"You're still coming over before the party, right?"

Casey closed out of Trevor's page and said "Yeah, thanks again for asking me, Allie. Um, I was just wondering—"

"Any of you guys ever jerked off with a banana peel? Shit is so cash." Schiest was looking around haphazardly.

Allie showed the slightest hint of disgust: one of her nostrils flared and an eyebrow pricked up. Bill was a lot less conservative with his emotions. Charlie looked at Schiest in pure disbelief. Casey blushed. Hot sauce erupted unseen from the man's nose.

"Well, just text me, okay?" Allie walked briskly away.

Schiest laughed and flashed his shiesty smile.

"What. A fucking nut," the man said. "He's coming to this party, right? Guy looks like an animal." He took another gulp of Texas Cletus eXXXtra Hot and looked around expectantly, finding no audience. Casey, meanwhile, wondered when his life had gone to complete hell.

CHAPTER 9

CASEY COULDN'T FIND any more information on the dead man, no matter how much he scoured the internet.

The man didn't seem too interested in his identity, anyway. He was content with his new freedom that was unlike anything he had ever experienced before. The man still didn't have any recollection of what it was like to be bound by the normal laws of physics, but he often mused that such a normal life could only pale in comparison to the one that he was presently living. He said that wouldn't trade anything to live like normal people do; he was having too much fun. The power to do whatever you wanted with no consequences was as intoxicating as it was liberating.

Casey would have been more concerned about the man's presence if it brought bad omens along. Instead, Casey started to regard the man as more of a crude-tongued guardian angel. On Wednesday, two days before, Casey had amassed 20,000 subscribers. At a rate of around 20,000 per day, Casey's LitMille channel had climbed up to 60,000 subscribers.

Although the stranger remained nameless, "Casey Benton" could be heard all throughout the streets of his town. People both whispered and shouted his name, and his new fans came up to him to pat him on the back and ask him when his next video was going to come out. A few men told him that he should post on other social media sites more. A group of women said that they wanted to see more of his selfies. He put his phone number in dozens of devices and soon received an influx of text messages asking to hang out, to eat lunch, or if he was going to Marissa's party.

By Friday, Casey was exhausted after another day of talking to people that he had only met once. Unfortunately, the invisible man took Casey's exhaustion as a chance to answer fan mail in between gulps of increasingly spicy hot sauce.

That night, Casey, Charlie, and Bill got ready at Charlie's house shortly before Casey left his friends to go to Allie's. Charlie donned a white button down with khakis. Bill wore a violet cardigan and was deciding whether to add a purple or black cap. Casey wore a gray and black crewneck sweatshirt that was a size too big, adorned with the logo of a professional sports team that he could not name. His hair was styled (by Bill) into loose curls that spilled over his forehead.

Casey made the quick trek to Allie's and, after being let in, found himself sitting on her bed. The man stood unseen, fiddling with the collar of his shirt, which neither of which seemed to get dirty no matter how much hot sauce he spilled on them. Soon, he was doubled over in laughter at what Allie was saying.

"Bob totally freaked out when he found his car like that," she explained. "I've never seen him so angry. It took us 15 minutes to drain the balls from the car, and then we ended up just leaving them in the parking lot. So, he might be a little on edge tonight," Allie said. "But, then, he's always got a short fuse."

"Then why the fuck are you dating that jerk?" The man had learned very quickly that he could speak freely now that only one person in the world could hear him.

"If you don't mind me asking, why do you date him if he gets angry all of the time?" Casey said.

Allie sighed as she compared two different tops. Her two final options were a loose gray crop top and a red shawl. She wore a tight white tank top while she was making her decision. Casey thought that it was strange seeing Allie Thatcher getting ready like a normal person. Casey had always assumed that when she woke up, flawless, she rolled out of bed in perfectly ironed sun dresses.

"What do you think, Casey? Gray or red?"

"How about you just leave them on the floor," the man said.

Allie didn't hear him. There was a bottle of vodka on the table next to her. Allie had already taken a couple of shots. When Casey had asked why she was drinking before the party, Allie asked if he had ever heard of a 'pregame'. Casey had not. He had also refused to take a pure shot of alcohol. Since he hated the taste of the stuff, Allie suggested that he wait for the jungle juice—vodka prepared with water, powdered drink mix, and soda—that would be at the party.

Casey shrugged. "I like the red, I think. I don't really know that much about girl's fashion, though. I am a man, you know."

"Right, but aren't all gay guys supposed to be really hip and fashionable?"

"Well, not everyone," Casey said. The man laughed.

"You know, Casey, I never thought that you were gay before the word got around," Allie said, "And even then, I didn't believe it."

"Believe it." Casey flashed a smile and made a 'peace' sign.

"But you don't have that gay lisp, or any earrings, or dyed hair or anything. I don't see you wearing rainbows or scarfs, besides your video," Allie said. "Is that just an act?"

Casey bit back the frustration that he felt in his forehead. He would rather have a culture that had moved past stereotypes, but he didn't want to ruin Allie's night. He shrugged again. "Well, I don't think that those are bad things. And, not every gay person has those things. That's just a generalization," Casey said. He pictured Trevor, with his neon hair and the obvious camp in his voice. Casey thought that Trevor was the sexiest man alive, but he never thought to dress like him. Casey had his own preferences when it came to clothing.

He told Allie all of this.

"But, anyway," Casey continued, "Why do you still date Bob if you don't like him?"

"I never said I didn't like him," Allie said. She took a swig from the bottle, then chased it with a sports drink. She looked serene when she drank alcohol. She didn't frown or scrunch up her face at the taste. Allie drank the stuff like water. "I just said he has a short fuse. And that's only when it comes to other people. He never gets mad at me."

Allie dabbed a droplet of sugary liquid from her lips. "Plus, he has a cock like nothing I've ever seen."

Casey gulped.

Allie laughed, just a touch unhinged. She hung the gray crop top back in her closet and held the red shawl to her chest. She put her other hand on her hip and shot Casey a look.

"Why do you keep asking all these questions about Bob?"

The man looked back and forth between Casey and Allie. He rubbed his hands together.

"I'm just making conversation," Casey said. He wondered how someone so angelic could end up with a brute like Bob. The two made a real Beauty and the Beast type pairing.

"You know," Allie said, laying the shawl out over the bed, "Bob was a little nervous about you coming over. He thinks that I asked you over here to have sex." She licked her lips and moved towards him.

The Indulgence that followed the invisible man like a fog had crept throughout the house, whether Casey wanted it or not.

Casey blushed. "He said the same thing to me. I told him that I was gay, so there was nothing to worry about."

Allie pouted. "*Is* there nothing to worry about?"

Casey looked at her blankly.

"I mean, you are super cute, so I guess I could believe that you were gay," she said, "but I don't think you could be fully gay. I mean, no one is, right?"

"I really am gay," Casey said. "Uh, let's see. I would walk barefoot for a thousand miles just to tie Trevor Greenbrook's shoes." He was getting increasingly uncomfortable with the conversation, and he found himself using hyperbole to try to escape.

"Hmmm," Allie said. "I don't know..."

"Well, how can I prove it?" Casey asked. He expected her to ask for his phone, so she could see the pictures of shirtless actors that he had saved. Instead, Allie crossed her arms, grabbed the hem of her tank top at the waist, and pulled it inside out over her head. Allie's breasts bounced out of her top.

Casey stared slightly openmouthed at her pink nipples. She put her hands on her hips and looked at Casey.

The unseen man almost did a back flip.

While Allie had never felt a romantic connection to Casey before, the past few days had been eye opening for her. She saw Casey in a new light, one where they could be together forever. There was a sort of dark, animalistic instinct that had awoken inside of her, and, since Allie was extroverted and honest with her friends, she had shared these feelings with a few others. Everyone she spoke to revealed that they shared her sentiment, although they couldn't explain why. People who had never even thought about talking to Casey suddenly found themselves obsessed with him.

To Allie, that was an invitation to strike first, without giving Casey a chance to choose anyone other than her.

"So, you don't like this?"

Casey, unwilling to further subject himself to unwanted advances, shook his head 'no' while averting his eyes.

"You don't want to feel them, then?"

The man floated towards her with his tongue out.

"I can touch those puppies if you don't want to, Casey." The man reached for Allie's breasts.

She didn't notice. Casey yelped and hopped up off of the bed in alarm.

"Oh, so you do want to play," Allie said. She ran her tongue over her teeth. "Grab on." She took Casey's hands and placed them on her breasts, overtop of the man's hands.

Casey appeared as neutral as possible. There was absolutely no question in Casey's mind about his sexuality, though. Allie Thatcher had the type of body that ancient wars could have been fought over, but she couldn't get Casey to even lift his sword.

Casey held his hands in place for a few moments before dropping them to his side.

"Yup, I'm totally gay," he said.

Allie frowned. Suddenly, she reached out and grabbed Casey's crotch.

Casey yelped, but was too surprised to back away.

"Yup, you're totally gay," Allie said, frowning. She turned away and pulled on a black tank top.

The man went down to his knees in anguish.

"Look I'm really sorry. I swear that I'm never like this." She slurred her words in only the slightest sense. "But hey, at least I know now. I thought that maybe I could turn you straight."

Casey had never in a million years imagined Allie Thatcher touching him in that way.

"I know," Allie said. "I know. I don't know what came over me, though. I'm not going to lie, Casey, I've been feeling so horny around you lately. The worst part is that I know our orientations just don't match up. And, before you, every guy I've wanted has always agreed to do whatever I want. So, now that I want you... I'm just not used to unrequited love, is all." She draped her shawl over her tank top. "And I want you so badly that I have a hard time giving you up."

"Okay dude, here's your chance," the man said. "Tell her that you two can fuck once and get it over with, and if she seriously can't convert you to hetero-sexuality then you just part ways."

Casey tried to patch up what was left of Allie's pride. "Allie, you're the type of girl that makes me wish I was straight," Casey said. "You're perfect. You really are. But you're right. Our orientations just don't spin the same way. Don't take it personally or anything."

It turned out that she didn't need him to try to save her. "Oh, don't worry. I won't take it personally," Allie said. "I'm just gonna have to take out my aggres-sion on Bob." She giggled. "I'm going to put some makeup on in the bathroom. Do you want to help me?"

Casey shook his head. "Like I said, I don't know anything about women's fashion, and I know even less about makeup."

"You don't look like you would need it, anyway," Allie said, and she went into her bathroom and closed the door.

"You fucking pussy," the man said, playfully punching Casey's arm.

"What? I didn't want to have sex with her from the start. You know that I'm gay."

"Right, but who could be *that gay* to not want to bang her?"

Casey was getting frustrated with the man and wished that he had never come back from the dead.

"What do you mean *that gay*? Think about it the other way. It's like if Trevor Greenbrook asked a straight guy to have sex, the straight guy would say no, even though Trevor is the dreamiest person to walk the earth."

The man made a face. "That was the gayest thing I've ever heard anyone say."

Casey shrugged and smiled sheepishly. "What can I say? You've noticed how everyone has been so horny lately."

"Right, but they all want to fuck you, apparently." The man thought back to Charlie, but, for some reason he didn't say his name. "So how about you go fuck yourself? I would kill to be in your position."

Casey gulped. A shadow of awareness of the ritual invaded his mind, not enough to be recognized, but enough to constrict the muscles in his stomach.

"Okay, who's ready to party?" Allie emerged from her bathroom looking even more stunning than before. Her makeup had erased any possible feature that the mainstream media could claim was a flaw.

"I am," Casey said, meekly, as the awareness left him.

"A little more enthusiasm for this goddess would be appropriate," the man laughed. Allie's mind was apparently elsewhere, because she didn't skip a beat.

"One more drink, then let's hit the road," Allie said.

Allie went and poured herself another shot. The man filled a shot glass up with hot sauce and clinked it against Allie's. Casey pictured how his first party would go, hoping that things could possibly get more surreal.

CHAPTER 10

CASEY DIDN'T SPEAK on the way to Marissa's house.

Too many thoughts were running through his mind as he drove Allie's car. The world that he now lived in was suddenly bizarre, too alienated from the one that he grew up in. His rising fame was one marker of this new life that he lived. And the other; an anonymous, invisible stranger.

In the car, the man decided to call himself Anon. Short for "Anonymous," the moniker served a couple of purposes. First, Anon couldn't remember his real name. Also, the members of a few edgy online message boards that Anon had recently discovered used that term to address each other while sharing pictures of gore and chemical warfare. Anon said that he was a superhero with the power of invisibility. Casey couldn't tell if he was serious, since Anon certainly didn't act like a hero. However, he couldn't deny that his presence had helped him in ways that no normal person could.

Casey felt that the achievement of an identity carried a counterbalance: a sense of defeat. He still could not discover any information on Anon's real identity. He had the entire internet, all of the information in the world, one massive encyclopedia encapsulating the entirety of human knowledge. Still, the real Anon was nowhere to be found. Casey was unsettled by the fact that Anon, the real, living man, was missing from the world's database.

Casey pouted absentmindedly.

"Oh, come off it," Anon told Casey. "Just enjoy yourself. You're going to a party. These things are legendary for their debauchery, aren't they?"

Casey wasn't as excited as he thought he should be. He knew almost nothing of parties except for what he saw in movies. And from what little knowledge of parties he possessed, this night would be a horrific disaster. Casey imagined himself getting thrown up on or getting arrested. And that was just the way high school parties were portrayed in movies. There were other party scenes that were much more terrifying than getting jostled around by drunken juveniles.

As a child, Casey had seen scenes of night clubs in a few movies. They scared the living shit out of him. Bright, flashing lights; people dressed in tight, freaky outfits; loud noises and frightening crowds. Casey feared those types of images when he saw them in the rated-R sci-fi films that he wasn't supposed to watch. Casey was actually very afraid of what he was about to walk in to, and he had the sinking feeling that he was literally going to die at the party, where his screams would be drowned out by the music.

Anon was less than phased. While Casey barely said a word the whole way, Anon acted as a sort of demonic hype-man. No matter Allie's attempts to stop her imperceptible foe, Anon rolled down the windows and turned up the volume of the car's radio.

Soon enough, they arrived.

The houses on the street were far apart enough that the party would go undisturbed by the neighbors. Allie flitted up the front steps to the porch, almost tripping on the way up. Anon reached out to grab her before he realized that she wouldn't even feel him. It wouldn't have mattered, though: she was already too drunk to notice a phantom touching her side.

She greeted three people that were vaping out front. Casey wondered where Charlie and Bill were. Allie met her friends loudly and warmly. Casey didn't know two of the people that were on the porch, but he knew the third one all too well.

At least, in his head.

Peter Adams had medium length blonde hair that would naturally wave on its own. He was taller than Casey, in better shape, and...

Much cuter, Casey thought. Casey hid his crush on Peter since the first day that he had realized that he existed. Casey often saw him around the office but was always too shy to ask for his name. He only learned it in happenstance when he saw Peter on one of his social media pages. Casey and Peter passed each other in the hallways. They often looked into each other's eyes but never acknowledged one another further. Casey didn't think that Peter knew his name, and he was too nervous to introduce himself.

"But you know Casey already, right?" Allie was motioning behind her.

Casey's eyes widened painfully when he heard his name mentioned in Peter's presence.

"Of course, I know Casey!" Peter exhaled a cloud of vapor when he answered Allie. He broke into a wide grin and put his hand around Casey's shoulder. Casey felt his eyes widen even further, and he almost recoiled at the touch, but Peter didn't mean any harm. Casey let the arm loiter.

"You're gay, right?" Peter asked.

Casey was taken aback. With other people, he didn't think twice but answer truthfully. To Peter, though, the question meant so much more. A simple 'yes' could change his entire life. Tension filled the void between them.

Casey blinked.

"Uh, yeah," Casey said.

"Oh, good. Same," Peter said, and Casey's heart started racing.

Casey could smell the vodka on Peter's breath underneath the strawberry scent that the vapor left behind. The alcohol instantly explained the straightforwardness.

"Do you want a drag?" Peter's vaporizer hovered in front of Casey's mouth.

Casey harbored a distinct distaste for cigarettes, but didn't know how he felt about vaping. A long time ago, cigarettes were considered cool, but those days were from high school. Now, most people thought that cigarettes were scummy, and vaping was a new favorite pastime.

Casey's perception instantly changed when he saw Peter doing it. His face was a sun peeking out from behind the clouds, and Casey decided that it was time to grow wings.

Maybe it was the fact that Peter was talking to him for the first time. Maybe it was the adrenaline from Casey's first party or from all of the attention that he was receiving online. Maybe it was because Anon was lurking behind them all on the porch, unseen, checking out both Allie and the people that she was talking to. Whatever the reason, Casey parted his lips and let Peter slide the vaporizer between them. Casey sucked in his cheeks as he inhaled the vapor.

"AHEHEHECHU-CHUEHAA!"

Casey coughed violently and swatted the device from his mouth, swirling vapor around the tips of his fingers.

"OW," Casey said, shaking his hand wildly as if to dry it in the air. "That was hot." Vapor was still coming out of his mouth, and Casey had a sullen look on his face. Head down, he slowly raised his doe eyes towards Peter's face.

"I'll say so." Peter was swooning. He looked at Casey through slightly droopy eyes, but his smile made Casey's knees go weak. "Let's go inside," Peter said. He took Casey lightly by the hand. "You don't mind if I kidnap your friend, do you Allie?"

Allie laughed. She had gotten her hands on a cigarette from one of the men, who had gotten his hand on Allie's rear end. "I don't mind, Peter. Take care of him." She slapped Peter a low-five. "But, hey, don't keep him from me too long. Casey and I need to get to know each other, right Casey?" She exhaled as she met Casey's eyes.

Casey gulped and nodded. He was suddenly afraid of his situation, even though it should have been perfect. Hanging out with Peter and Allie at the same time had been a secret dream of his. Casey hoped that he wouldn't screw it up. He eyed Anon warily.

"Okay, then. Let's go Casey," Peter said. He knocked on the front door. A few seconds later, the sound of a latch opening could be heard from inside, and then a woman's face appeared. It was Marissa, the homeowner.

"Hey, Peter, you have a friend with you? Did he pay five?" She poked her head out of the door and looked at the people on her porch. Loud dance music spilled out of the house from behind her.

"Hey, Allie, I'm going to need five dollars from you for the alcohol."

Allie waved her off.

"I've already paid you," Peter said. "And I've got Casey with me… he doesn't need to pay, does he?" Peter smiled prettily. Casey smiled, too.

"Oh my god," Marissa exclaimed. "Casey Benton is here?" She stepped out and embraced him in a hug. "Sorry, my eyes were still adjusting to the dark and I didn't see your face. Oh, you don't have to pay, Casey. Come in." She pushed the two of them inside, saying, "I just loved your video from the other night. It was so funny. I'm glad you could take some time out of your busy schedule to hang out with us."

Casey shrugged as he stepped into the house. "I spend a lot of time online, so I guess I'm alone a lot," Casey said. "It's good to get out of the house. Thanks for your comment about the song… It was a comedy song, and it's really embellished, so I wasn't sure if it would resonate with people."

Marissa stared at him blankly, though she was still smiling. "Embellished?"

"Yeah, like, I use a lot of hyperbole in my songs. A lot of people on LitMille exaggerate their lives."

Marissa didn't know what the word 'hyperbole' meant either, but using her context clues, she figured that it meant 'funny.'

"Well, it was…comedic," she laughed, "If that's what you meant."

The point, although missed, still got a reaction that Casey could work with. He wasn't doing so badly, after all.

However, the night had just begun.

Anon stood in the doorway. "Come on, Casey. This is taking way too long to get to the good part. Stop building it up and just start partying." He tipped his hot sauce bottoms up, saw that there was none left, and threw the bottle out into the street. It shattered. No one noticed.

"Come on, Casey, let's get you a drink," Peter said, and he led the way through the living room. Dance music blared from the massive television. The bass thumped against Casey's ears and the dizzying chords bounced off the walls.

"GAH, this music is destroying my eardrums," Anon said. He clenched his jaw and pressed his palms against his ears in agony. Casey thought he was overreacting. "I'm going to go turn it down," Anon said. He proceeded towards the TV and the phone connected to the AUX cord. Peter and Casey continued to weave through the throngs of partying men and women.

Marissa's house was packed with people from their office, but Casey didn't see Charlie or Bill anywhere. There were other people everywhere, playing beer pong in the living room, crowding around a keg in the kitchen, and conversing in the hallways. There was a couple who were dancing on the countertop, and there were other couples walking up and down the stairs, to and from the bedrooms.

When Casey and Peter got to the kitchen, Casey saw a man's legs being held in the air by four strong arms while he himself held the top of the keg. The tap was yielding the frothy bounty into his mouth.

"FIFTEEN, SIXTEEN, SEVENTEEN, EIGHTEEN, NINETEEN, TWENTY!" The man's friends were counting very loudly before his knees buckled and he spit out the tap. When he was upright, he threw his fists into the air in triumph.

A woman was talking to someone else next to the keg. Casey couldn't help but listen to what she was saying. "The thing about parties is, they take place in a whole different universe, inhabited with its own species of symbiotic lifeform. After a couple of hours, when everyone is drunk, the conventions of normal society and pleasantry evaporate and anarchy forms from the absence of rules.

"It sounds scary, but this lawlessness is the main appeal of parties. Drunk people can do whatever they want to do: they can make out with someone who they've just met for the first time. They can sing their favorite song at the top of their lungs, even if their voice sounds like a garbage disposal. They can smash bottles and take their shirts off and basically 'act a fool,' because there is a double edge to alcohol. When taken in responsible doses, no one cares about what they do themselves, and no one minds what anyone else does, either."

Peter looked at Casey with a hint of schadenfreude. "You want to do a keg stand?" Peter asked.

Casey smiled sheepishly and shook his head no. Peter shrugged and led Casey to the kitchen sink.

Inside was a cooler halfway filled with a red liquid. Peter grabbed two red cups and dipped them into the concoction. Peter handed one cup to Casey and happily said, "Cheers!" The pair's plastic cups clicked together, and Casey cautiously took a sip. It tasted like fruit punch. When he lowered his drink, he saw that Peter was almost halfway done.

The woman at the keg continued, saying, "But this carefree utopia of parties comes from one substance: alcohol. Now, many people will say that 'Drunk words are sober thoughts,' and 'Drunk you is the real you,' but I vehemently disregard both options. When you're intoxicated, you aren't the real you. Heck, you cease to be yourself at all. You become part of the Drunken Hivemind, led by the Party God itself."

"What is this?" Casey asked.

"It's jungle juice," Peter said.

Casey looked at him blankly, then said, "Oh, Allie told me that before."

"It's vodka and, like, pineapple juice, lemon-lime, and sugary drink mix," Peter said. "It tastes really good, right?"

Casey nodded.

"It has a ton of alcohol in it." Peter pressed his cup with Casey's again. "Cheers," he said again, then added, "Finish it this time," with a wink.

The two men drained their cups and Peter moved to fill them up again.

The person at the keg was just finishing their train of thought. "The Party God is a singular personality that can inhabit many people's bodies. It is happy and stupid and carefree. It is quick to laugh, quick to fight, and quick to fuck. But when one is transformed into an avatar of the Party God, he or she will seek out and form close bonds with others who are manifestations of the God. Thus, when a party forms and many people metamorphose into the Drunken Hivemind, they all come together to bask in each other's drunken light, which appears much brighter in a drunken haze. In such an environment, cares are thrown into the wind and the Party God rides triumphantly (if not a little wobbly) into the sunset of bliss."

Casey felt awkward accepting alcohol and other substances so willingly. He wondered what his parents and grandparents would think. However, Casey's personal icon, Trevor, was very public with his love of drinking. Armed with that knowledge, Casey figured that alcohol couldn't be all bad.

He looked at Peter again, who reminded Casey a little of Trevor, even with his blond hair. Peter was so cute and charming, even if he was a little tipsy. Casey had always thought that drunk people were annoying, but he found that the feeling was negated when the drunk person in question is one's crush. Of course, Casey's judgment was clouded when he began to think that. The one cup of jungle juice had already given Casey a feeling that he had felt a few times before, but the drink tasted so good that he didn't even notice.

He chugged the next cup that Peter gave him to the halfway point, then stopped when a woman caught him arm.

"Casey? It's me, Abby. Russian Literature? In college? You usually sat in the back, but you know me, right?"

Casey nodded. Peter was looking at him dreamily. He turned to fill his cups back up, but a couple was leaning over the sink and making out behind them.

"Yeah, well, I just want to say that Jess and I love your videos, and you should come play beer pong with us." Jess stood behind Abby.

Although Casey possessed the allure of Zephiscestra, the room seemed to revolve around Jess.

"DAMN! She's a fox, Casey. How about you stop being 'Male Order' and go play with these women," Anon said, inputting the proper finger-air-quotes.

He drank deeply from a handle of Vladokov Vodka that he had pilfered from someone's hands. If the people in the room could see him, they all would have cringed: Vladokov Vodka tastes like nail polish remover. It was almost impossible to drink without a mixer or a chaser.

This stuff is better than that hot sauce, Anon thought. *I can still barely teste it, but it gives a stronger tingle to the taste buds.*

Casey whipped his head from Anon to the Jess and put his hands up defensively (almost spilling his drink). He was about to inform them that he wasn't interested in hooking up with them, when Jess spoke up.

"Yeah, come play some beer pong with us." Abby and Jess tilted their heads to the side and grinned. Casey flashed a burgeoning smile. In all of the commotion, he forgot that no one could here Anon's voice.

"Of *course* we'll play with you," Peter said.

Abby jumped for joy and Jess gave them a saucy smile. The girls started back to the living room. When Casey hesitated to follow them, Peter pinched his butt to spur him on. Casey yelped audibly, though not loud enough to be heard over the music.

Peter unnerved Casey with a coy smile. "Let's go, cutie," Peter said, and he flicked his tongue up and down between his teeth. Casey was startled, since he had never seen a man do something that femininely sexy before. He stood there like a deer in headlights until Anon grabbed Casey's nose.

"Honk, honk, Casey," Anon said. "Get your ass in the living room. Don't leave those girls waiting. Plus, if you play your cards right, this guy will definitely suck you off." Anon glanced at Peter, who was devouring Casey with his eyes. "Actually, play your cards whatever way you like, this one wants the D."

Casey got the hint and spun towards his new friends. The jungle juice had made him lightheaded. The three of them stumbled through the crowd into the living room. Abby and Jess were already waiting on the long side of the table. A game was already in progress.

"Nick, let us get a game," Jess said, leaning over the table to expose a healthy serving of cleavage to one of the players. At that moment, the player from the other side splashed a ball into one of Nick's cups. The resulting splash sent a squirt of beer foam onto the tops of her breasts.

Nick Werther, a man from the Casey's company, removed the ball, took a sip from the cup, and drank in Jess with his eyes. When he finished the beer, he regarded Jess with the warmth that only the drink could provide.

"We're in the middle of a game, Jess," he said. "Look, we've got five cups left, but they've only got three. Andrew and I can end this pretty quickly if you want us to."

Nick and his pong partner Andrew were both starting lacrosse players for their college a few years before. Nick was a midfielder and the leading scorer for the team. Andrew "Stonewall" was the impenetrable goalie. The two were incredible athletes. Nick, the quick and tireless midfielder, was a team player and liked to share the ball as well as shoot. He was so talented on the field that he often found himself getting assisted, but he always made a big deal of thanking his teammates for their support. Andrew, the goalie, was slow on his feet but had incredible reflexes that made him invaluable in the net.

"But we're going to play Peter and Casey," Abby complained. "They want to play right now." Nick and Andrew snapped their heads in Casey's direction so fast that he almost pissed his pants. For a moment, he thought that they were going to attack him. He had seen their prowess on the field and definitely didn't want to get on their bad sides. Casey was infinitely relieved when they smiled at him instead.

"Oh, I didn't know that Casey Benton was here," Nick said. "Hey, Stones, do you want to let Casey play? We can just end our game, now."

Andrew shrugged an 'okay,' his massive grin betraying his excitement to be even mentioned in the same sentence as Casey.

"It's fine, guys, really. We can wait," Casey blurted. "Right, Peter?"

Casey's escort was in a different world, at that point.

Anon smacked the back of Peter's head.

"Hey, yeah, let's play!" Peter said, raising both arms into the air. Peter's enthusiasm made the bottom of his shirt jump up, revealing his belly button.

Casey blushed. He took a sip from his drink absentmindedly.

Nick grinned. "Sure, anything for you, Casey."

Casey wondered why Nick would end a game prematurely just to let him play. Casey had never even spoken to Nick before.

"I liked your song, by the way," Nick told him. He smiled and waved at his opponents. "Hey guys, we're going to let Casey and Peter play against Jess and Abby, okay?"

The other players began to complain, but Andrew and Nick wouldn't be swayed. Nick gallantly moved aside for Jess and motioned for her to take his spot. "I told you we could end the game for you," he said, grinning. Jess rubbed her hand on his flank to show her appreciation. Jess wasn't a shallow girl, but if she could choose between the peaks of mental or physical capability, she would pick the athlete every time.

Peter and Casey took their places at the opposite end of the table. Peter began to set up six red cups into a triangle on the table while Abby did the same on the other side. As Peter began to fill the cups with beer, Casey quietly turned to him.

"Um," Casey whispered, "How do you play?"

Peter laughed. "How do you play pong?"

"Yeah," Casey said. "I've never played before, so I don't know the rules. What do you do?"

Peter put a hand on the small of Casey's back. Because of all the alcohol that he had drank, Casey didn't mind the invasion of personal space at all. He even leaned into his partner. "Okay, so we have two balls, okay?" Peter grinned and slurred his words. "And, we have to throw our balls into the other people's cups. Okay? When we do that, okay, then they have to drink out of them. And the first one to run out of cups loses. And they do the same for us. And then we have to drink. Okay? It's fun."

Casey understood the simple rules well enough. "Okay, but how do we decide who goes first?"

"You can just go first, Casey," Jess said. She rolled the two Ping-Pong balls across the table to Casey and Peter.

Peter shrugged. Somehow, she had heard him over the music.

"Thanks, girl," Peter said. He picked up the balls and swirled them around in his hand provocatively before giving one to Casey.

They both threw their balls at the opponents' cups. Both of them missed their marks.

"Boo, you guys suck," Anon said. He took a swig of vodka. Although he had already drank half of the bottle, the alcohol didn't affect him in the slightest.

Casey, on the other hand, was quite drunk, and Peter made him drink a full cup of beer when Jess drained a ball.

"Oh, shut up, you," Casey said. He swatted Anon's shoulder. "You don't even know me."

"I didn't say anything," the girl behind Anon said.

Casey's smile stretched across his face. "I was talking to my friend. My--The man... my friend."

"Your man-friend is behind you," the girl said. Casey turned around to face Peter, who looked more attractive than Casey had ever seen. He thought of leaning in for a kiss when Peter handed him a ball.

"How about you make it this time?" Peter said, playfully.

"You're one to talk, you didn't make it either," Casey said.

A large crowd had gathered around the table. Mostly everyone at the party had dropped what they were doing to watch Casey and Peter play. All of the drunks jostled one another for a better view of Casey and his date, who everyone seemed to be talking about. The partygoers were unabashed in their fascination and openly called Casey's name, wishing him good luck. Everyone's eyes were on the two players. A few camera phones were pointed their way, too.

"Hey, I love the fact that you're not embarrassed to talk to me in public," Anon said, trying to make himself heard over the swarm of people who were surrounding them, "But you're going to look crazy to all these people. I should leave you alone. Plus, this crowd is pissing me off. Everyone is bumping into me."

Casey ignored him, or maybe he didn't hear him over the music and the chatter of the audience.

He threw the second beer pong shot of his life. The ball circled the rim and then bounced away.

"AWWW," the crowd yelled.

Casey laughed. Usually, he was terrified of large groups of people looking at him, but his three alcoholic drinks made him more relaxed and comfortable. He drank the crowd's adoration.

Peter sank a cup on the other side and the crowd cheered again.

Peter gave Casey a high five. They looked into each other's eyes, beaming.

"Okay, I'm just going to step outside, then," Anon said.

Casey watched intently as Abby lobbed her Ping-Pong ball through the air.

Dejected, Anon turned away and made for the front door.

CHAPTER 11

ANON PUT HIS head down and shouldered his way through the crowd.

He didn't care if he pushed people out of the way. After all, he couldn't get reprimanded by people who wouldn't acknowledge his existence.

When he freed himself from the mass of bodies, Anon turned back towards the beer-pong table.

Casey threw a ball, which splashed into his opponent's cup. The people surrounding him clapped their hands and cheered. Camera phones flashed at Casey and Peter. Couples in the crowd hugged and kissed each other. Anon swallowed his jealousy with a gulp of Vladokov. He had seen enough of Casey and his new-found popularity. He opened the front door to get away from the others.

When Anon stepped outside onto the front porch, he saw that he was not alone. A man and woman were sitting on pieces of lawn furniture, smoking cigarettes. The man was making jokes and the woman was giggling.

Anon drank from his bottle.

"You know, at first I was happy to be invisible," Anon said. "It seems like the perfect power. I can do whatever I want. I can go wherever I want, whether it's a movie or the women's locker room at the gym. I can take whatever I want from anyone."

To prove his point, he took the cigarettes from the two smokers. They didn't notice. Anon put both of the cigarettes in between his ring and middle fingers and inhaled them. "You guys look better without cigs, anyway." Then, since they didn't have anything to suck on, the man and woman started to passionately kiss each other. Anon sighed.

"Well that's just great, leave me here alone," Anon said. "Gah, I hate this. I want to talk to someone other than Casey. Don't get me wrong, the guy is really nice, but right now I feel like I'm going crazy in solitary confinement. Sure,

I can do whatever I want, but now the only thing that I want is to be noticed… by anyone."

Anon shook his head. "I'm sick of being a ghost. Or a figment of Casey's imagination. Or whatever." He took a drag of his cigarettes. "And I can't tell you two how horny I've been lately. I've already jerked off in every room of Casey's apartment and pretty much all over town. It doesn't help that people keep hooking up with each other wherever I go."

Again, Anon put the two cigarettes in his mouth. He inhaled, then drank from his bottle before exhaling the smoke.

"And, no matter how many times I bust a nut, I keep getting hornier. And there is no one to quench this thirst… Not even you, Vlad." Anon gazed longingly at the bearded Russian man on the label. He finished the liquor and tossed the bottle away.

"I seriously cannot be sated. It's like I lust for something that simply cannot be fucked; something that doesn't exist. Nothing cures it, not eating or drinking or smoking. Shit, food doesn't even have a taste for me anymore, and apparently I can't get drunk."

Anon trailed off. He absentmindedly picked at his sharp teeth. He had drunk an entire handle of vodka in a very short time, yet he was still stone sober. Taking a bottle of vodka to the face could potentially kill a normal human. The poison did nothing to even dull his mind.

He could still hear conversations from inside the house. A lot of people were saying Casey's name. After seeing all of the attention that Casey was getting, Anon was starting to resent him, since he seemed to have the perfect life, a *real* life.

Casey was the light in everyone's eyes, while Anon stalked the darkness, away from perception. Casey's social media accounts all had tens of thousands of followers. Casey could send out a post and get thousands of interactions. Anon couldn't even communicate with the people sitting next to him. Casey's video from the night before had already amassed a view count of 250,000, with hundreds of comments from people that wanted to have sex with him. It didn't come as a surprise that no one mentioned how Anon was doing flips on the bed in the background.

"So, this is the afterlife, huh? Full of anxiety and insatiable horniness." Anon laughed aloud. "I used to think that being insatiable would be a good thing... How wrong was I?"

At the sound of a moan, Anon turned back towards his porch-companions, who were now engaged in porch-coitus. The man sat in his chair with his pants around his ankles, and the woman was bouncing up and down in his lap. The slaps and slurps rang in Anon's ears. He felt like he was getting punched in the gut.

"Ugh, were you two even listening to me?" Anon turned away and sat down on the steps that led up to the porch. He felt his eyes welling up with tears. He almost went back inside the house to see what Casey was doing. Probably already making out with that guy.

Anon shook the thought out of his head. Maybe the alcohol did make him drunk after all. Anon had gotten used to thinking about his next prank, not wondering what his tether to the world was up to. He sighed and said, "Ah, whatever. Good for you two. But, when am I gonna get some action?"

⋆⇒ ⇐⋆

"Over here, over here! Elliot!"

A silvery form sniffed the air, whining loudly. "Ohhh, I can smell him. I can smell him!"

Ravage spoke with a nasally voice, and he always seemed to snivel more noticeably when he got worked up.

"Calm down," Elliot said. "Don't get too excited. You're going to need to concentrate on this guy."

Ravage rubbed his paws together. "I can't wait any longer. Ohhhh," he whined. "He's so close. I can almost *feel* him in my grasp."

The two of them stalked down the street as quietly as they could towards Marissa's house. For Ravage, keeping quiet wasn't a problem. He could scream as loud as he wanted to, and no one else in town would hear him. Although he was big and bulging with muscle, Ravage was quick and light on his feet.

Elliot, on the other hand, was clumsy. The shopping cart that he pushed was jingling and clanking over every seam in the sidewalk. Shoes, flowerpots, and garden gnomes from the neighborhood piled on top of boxes of electronics with the security tags still attached. Elliot also had a backpack weighing him down, stuffed with watches and jewelry that his partner had pilfered for him.

Ravage had a unique knack for theft, one that a human master-thief could only dream of. He could walk right up to someone and take the clothes off of their back without his victim even noticing. Ironically, Ravage's appearance should have made him stick out like an anime cosplayer trouncing around a top investment bank. He was covered in a thick coat of silver hair and his eyes were dark and baggy. He towered over Elliot, who was about average height.

Although the cart and backpack slowed them down, both Ravage and Elliot regarded their haul as vitally important. Even more important to Elliot, though, was the small idol in his pocket, exquisitely carved from a single jewel.

"Our intel said that this guy is unpredictable. We don't know how strong he'll be," Elliot told his companion. He stopped next to a trashcan to dig through it.

Ravage sneered. "Our intel also said that the guy probably hasn't eaten a single sc'erva yet. He's a weakling. Ohhh, I'm going to eat him in one bite!"

"Don't get too ahead of yourself. Like I said, we have almost no intel on this guy. All we know for sure is that he's a Lust. Do you forget that he's going to be a tough matchup?" Elliot checked one of the three ornate watches on his arm. Ravage picked at his teeth with his razor sharp fingernails. "Hell, a Lust is a tough matchup for anyone. Remember that one back in Tucson?"

"He was easy for me. I wanted it more than he did." Ravage passed by a woman on the sidewalk who held exceptional contempt for Elliot's shopping cart. It was clear that she had never been in such close vicinity to someone who appeared homeless. In a single motion, Ravage reached up and cut loose the necklace of pearls from around her neck. The sudden lightness caused the woman to straighten her posture, but she paid no mind to her robbers. Ravage grinned, exposing his line off needlelike teeth. He squeezed the necklace as hard as he could. "Where is he? I want to have him."

"Don't forget the plan," Elliot commanded.

"Fuck the plan." Ravage was worked up into a frenzy. He was almost foaming at the mouth. "You know how I get before a fight. I've been itching to eat again, and now I'm finally going to have my chance." Ravage was heaving, his heavy back rising and falling at an alarming rate. They knew that the Lust was close. "Besides, I've beaten other sc'ermin who were tougher than him. Now, I'm not afraid of anyone." Ravage was almost writhing in anticipation. He sniffed at the air again, then turned his head to see Elliot fumbling with his shopping cart. Without another word, Ravage tossed the necklace into the cart and sprinted down the street.

"Rav!" Elliot called out, but his words were ignored. "Fuck," he murmured.

Ravage was out of control. He was always anxious for a fight, but Elliot had never seen him like this.

Zephiscestra forbid Ravage getting killed, Elliot thought.

But, this virgin Lust was probably a weakling. How could they lose? Especially when Elliot held an idol?

◆⭢═◑ ◐═⭠◆

Charlie and Bill remained on the outskirts of the mob that surrounded the beer pong table. Bill was dancing with his hands in the air, cheering on Casey. He was tall enough to see over the sea of bobbing heads. Charlie was much shorter, and he had to watch the game through a social media stream. His feed was saturated with pictures of Casey and Peter laughing and playing.

It seemed that the app was infatuated with Casey. People kept sending him mentions and spreading around the hashtag #CaseyPong, which was trending in the area. Casey didn't know any of this. He had drunk several cups of beer on top of his jungle juice, and he felt no pangs of anxiety. There was only one cup left on both sides of the table, and it was Casey's turn to shoot.

"I think he's going to make this one," Bill yelled down to Charlie.

Charlie shrugged. His phone displayed an action-shot of Casey with a determined look in his eye and his tongue poked out in concentration, throwing a Ping-Pong ball through the air. In the picture, Peter had his hands around Casey's waist. Charlie hadn't interacted with any post related to Casey. "Why do you care about this dumb game?"

Bill yelled over the music, "Casey is having a lot of fun, so you should be happy for him. Don't be the jealous type." Bill had accepted a cup of juice from a woman he knew, and he hadn't stopped dancing ever since.

Charlie felt his face go red. "He should be hanging out with us, though. We're his best friends."

"If he wants to be with his crush for a little while, then let him. We got here a little late, I'll take the blame for that," Bill said, adjusting the scarf that had taken him an hour to pick out. "We can talk to him afterwards."

Charlie shrugged again and locked his phone. He looked around and saw how much drunken fun everyone was having. He was hesitant to have a drink at first, but, now that he couldn't hang out with Casey...

Charlie tapped a woman on the shoulder. "Hey, where did you get that beer?"

The woman--along with the rest of the crowd--erupted in screams of delight as Casey's ball made a satisfying "plop" into the cup. Casey had just won his first game of beer pong. The crowd chattered in intoxicated, Indulgent bliss.

"Oh my god, I got the video!"

"I got the picture!"

"Reblog my post!"

"I'm putting this on my page!"

⇥⇒ ⇐⇤

Anon stood in the front yard with his back to the road. From street level, he could see into the large windows on the front of the house. Casey was obscured by the wall of people around the pong table. A thick bass beat pulsed from the confines of the home and could be heard on the street. Bursts of excitement periodically emanated from inside, as well.

Anon breathed slowly. He ran a thumb across his square jaw and absent-mindedly flexed his fingers. Parked cars lined the street in his periphery. Besides the vehicles, the street was empty. The couple on the porch were still wriggling in ecstasy. Apart from the sounds of the party, the world was quiet. Nothing would have alerted such a low level sc'ermin to the approach of a demonic assail-ant, other than the grace of the Goddess Herself.

In the stillness of the night air, the hair on Anon's arms stiffened. His ears perked up, and it felt as if a hood of sluggishness was pulled from off of his head. He felt the intensity of his body being filled with the energy of every blade of grass on the lawn, every piece of gravel on the street. Something was moving in opposition with the harmony of the world, and it was coming fast. Like a spiritual awakening assaulting the mind of one asleep, Anon's true purpose was about to be revealed in a most grueling fashion.

With blinding speed, Anon ducked down to all fours just as a clawed hand soared over his head from behind. Still squatting, Anon pivoted on his right foot and whipped out his left leg in a quick arc, sweeping his assailant off of his feet. Anon regained his stance as Ravage slammed against the pavement, scattering bits of gravel that *dinged* the nearby car doors.

Anon barely had time to catch his breath before Ravage exploded off of the ground and launched himself at his foe. Anon swung his fist, but Ravage evaded the blow and wrapped him up in a tackle. Ravage lifted Anon from the legs and stuck his shoulder into Anon's chest. Anon howled in pain when Ravage dug his razor-sharp nails into his calf muscles. Ravage bulldozed Anon's back into the dirt, his eyes gleaming with malice and glittering with gluttonous tears of relief.

Ravage loosed his hands from Anon's legs and straddled on top of him on the ground. Anon had no time to think. He looked up at his assailant and almost choked when he saw Ravage's face. The thing's dark eyes were wide with excitement, and a malicious smile exposed a row of teeth as thin as knitting needles. Anon snarled and bared his own teeth, large and broad like garden spades. Ravage was bigger than him, but Anon could feel that his opponent was lighter, somehow. Or, it was possible that Anon felt as if he would be able to bear the weight of this monster.

Ravage lunged his hands at Anon's chest, but Anon caught both of his wrists. The two wrestled for control, their biceps bulging from the effort. Ravage tried to snap at Anon with his jaws, but Anon held him at bay by manipulating his arms in front of him.

Ravage thrust his body to the side, and the fighters began to roll around the yard, snarling and bucking at each other. Ravage seethed—veins popping from his temples—and wriggled his fingers, trying to claw at Anon's hands, whose grip was too low for Ravage to reach.

Simultaneously, the combatants thought: *Fuck. This guy is tough.*

Allie stood with one hand on her hip. She traced the rim of a cup with the pointer finger of her other hand. Bob towered over her and rested his arm around her shoulders. Allie pouted, her lips barely touching. Bob had a drunken smile plastered across his face. He pounded his free hand on the folding table.

"Let's get this game on!"

The mob cheered.

Casey and Peter both had a ball in their hands. They looked at each other and grinned.

"Care to do me…" Peter trailed off, his lip curling into a sloppy smirk, before adding, "Th' yonor of brayking th' ishe?"

Casey nodded and tried to line up a shot. After a few seconds of concentration, he ended up tossing the ball into the air with abandon. In the early stages of the game, 'throw away and pray' was still a viable strategy, since all of the cups were on the table. The cup at the tip of the triangle wobbled as the ball splashed into it.

"Woooooo!" Casey jumped for joy with his hands high above his head. Peter caught him in midair, wrapping his arms around his waist. Someone put the picture online and garnered almost a hundred likes in less than a minute, much to his surprise.

"Got the bitch-cup," Bob mused. He drank it down in one gulp.

⋆⇒⇐⋆

"RAH!" Anon closed his eyes and clenched his jaw. Ravage was still on top of him, straddling him on the ground, but Anon was restraining his wrists with a vice grip. At breakneck speed, Anon flung Ravage's arms away to either side of him, allowing Ravage's straining head to fall forward. At the same time, Anon attacked with his own head. Ravage tried to open his mouth to bite, but he only made it worse. Anon's forehead crashed into Ravage's face, crunching his narrow features in on themselves.

Ravage recoiled in pain and emitted a high-pitched, nauseating scream. Dark black liquid squirted from his nose and filled his mouth where several of his front teeth used to be. Ravage sat back on Anon's legs and clutched at his own face with his hands. Ravage didn't stop screaming until Anon bucked his legs from under him like a catapult, sending Ravage headfirst into a parked car on the street. The vehicle's windows shattered instantly, and a large imprint was left on one of the doors.

Anon rolled onto his stomach and hopped upright. He shook himself off, panting heavily.

◆─═◗ ◖═─◆

"Ooh my gooiness, Casey! You've rEAAlly gotten that hang of shish game," Peter exclaimed after Casey sank his second cup.

Allie and Bob had three cups remaining on their side, while Casey and Peter boasted a full set of six.

"I guessh I'm just luckyyy is all," Casey said.

Bob's ball bounced off one of the cups, and a brief brawl broke out when bystanders fought to retrieve it for Casey.

"You jusht want to put on… a good shoow for the cameras," Peter said. He made Casey laugh when he posed with a 'peace' sign for the flashing lights. Casey suspected for a moment that Marissa had installed a strobe light, but in fact the flashes came from people's phones as they took more pictures.

Several people were posting live updates of the game:

bigPaPi82: Best party ever watching this epic game #CaseyPong

nos_WET_45: There are cops here and they're just drinking and watching #CaseyPong

mrs_LISS: This game with Casey and Peter is so exciting I don't even care about the car alarm going off outside of my house

◆─═◗ ◖═─◆

Ravage swiped wildly at Anon with his claws fully extended. Anon bobbed and weaved his way through Ravage's barrage. Anon was distantly amazed at his own reflexes, but was too focused on evading death to think about his skill.

The two were exerting incredible amounts of energy and moving at a lightening pace. But, as the fight wore on, Anon felt himself getting filled with even more power. In the beginning of the melee, Anon could hardly catch his breath.

Presently, he was brimming with a vitality that he had never experienced before. He could sense his opponent growing more sluggish as Anon evaded his attacks.

Anon ducked under a wild swing and moved in close to his opponent, delivering a powerful jab to Ravage's abdomen. Then, he brought up his other fist in a devastating uppercut to Ravage's chin, fully extending himself.

Ravage's head snapped back. Anon took the opportunity to plant a swift shin to Ravage's crotch. When Ravage doubled over, Anon brought his foot back like a professional punter and kicked Ravage with the ferocity afforded to him by the Goddess of his power.

Ravage assaulted gravity itself, not realizing that he had been sent flying in the air until he landed in the middle of the street.

Anon didn't break his pace. He vaulted over the mangled car with its alarm blaring and landed with sure footing on the pavement. He moved in to stabilize Ravage's head so that he could punch him squarely in the nose. Before he could grab him, Ravage flashed forward and slashed at Anon's face.

Anon howled in pain. Ravage's sharp claws split one of Anon's cheeks down the middle, a horizontal gash between his upper and lower jaw. A thick flap of Anon's skin hung down like a jowl. Anon squeezed his eyes shut and scrambled away, diving back over the car and into the yard. Ravage was close behind, scampering over the vehicle, revitalized by the sight of Anon's blood.

⊷⇒ ⇐⊷

This wasn't the first party that Elliot had crashed.

While in high school, Elliot was always "there." He didn't talk much, but instead he hung around the periphery of conversations and eavesdropped. Thus, he had always known about parties, but he was never invited. This lead him to "just be there" whenever he showed up unannounced at someone's house.

Elliot looked around at all the young, happy faces. He remembered how, long ago, the kids from his school used to have fun without him. He felt the Envy of years ago flood through him like water from a poorly patched dam. Elliot had never gotten over how he had wasted his childhood wanting things that his classmates possessed: He wanted to have Chris Hender's talent on the football field; he wanted to have Gavin Hardt's girlfriend, (and even now Elliot felt knots in him stomach when he pictured them having sex); he wanted to have the achievements of Greg Kite, his best friend, that caused Elliot's own mother to wish that he was her son. Elliot felt ashamed of the envy that gripped and squeezed his stomach, but he gave into its green temptation and let it feed off of his pain.

It will make Ravage stronger.

Ravage… who used to drive such nice cars, wear such nice clothes, who used to have relations with such a beautiful wife…

Elliot knew enough to only sneak into big parties where he wouldn't be too out of place. Marissa's party was just like that, except for the fact that he was now a 40-year-old man at a party for twenty-somethings. Elliot ignored the weird glances that the younger people gave him. He was used to being looked down upon, anyway. He didn't plan on staying long, either. That other sc'ermin was putting up too much of a fight, so he had to end this quickly.

How could that be possible when he hasn't even killed another sc'ermin yet?

Elliot wondered how he was going to find the Lust's human in such a huge gathering. Then, he saw the beer pong table, the crowd, and all of the flashing lights. He saw a young man with another man wrapped around him.

It all makes sense. That's how his Lust sc'ermin is so strong.

Elliot knew that he had to disrupt this game. Otherwise, Ravage might die.

And this time, I won't be the one that killed him.

Elliot pushed the thought out of his mind, and, going against his timid instincts, pushed himself to the center of the crowd. Partygoers spilled their drinks and couples dislodged their lips as Elliot shouldered through the drunken hoard. He narrowed his sights on the man with the ping pong ball in his hand.

The sc'ermin were wrestling in the yard again, although Ravage now appeared much more monstrous than before. Ravage's silver fur was speckled with black blood and it bristled against the air with each quick movement. His yellow teeth, stained mostly black, were already starting to grow back. His shadowy eyes rolled around and bulged out of his head.

Anon, although appearing mostly human, had taken on a more demonic aura as well. He fought with animalistic intensity. Thick veins, coursing with black blood, stood out on his taut skin.

They separated and sprung to their feet, the distance between them tethered with the gravity of battle and the urge to connect with deadly force. Anon lunged at Ravage, his fist drawn back in preparation to strike.

Ravage dodged the deadly punch, ducking under it. He once again launched his shoulder into Anon's stomach. Ravage churned his feet and blasted Anon into the sidewalk, rupturing the concrete. Anon found himself straddled by Ravage, a position he had struggled so hard to rid himself of before. Anon rasped for air, but Ravage's pressure was making it hard to breathe.

Ravage's tongue ran furiously over the teeth remaining in his dripping maw. He slapped Anon across the face, shocking the virgin Lust into a moment of compliance. Ravage seized the opportunity, deftly cutting an 'X' into Anon's chest. Anon screamed as thick black blood oozed through his button-down shirt. Ravage tore the garments as easily one might rip through paper, rendering Anon's chest bare.

The assailant began to squeal with perverted delight. He bore into Anon's chest with his honed nails, tossing away small chunks of flesh like a child in a toy box. Anon was blinded by the pain.

"Lust is resilient, isn't it?" Ravage complained. "Your muscles are tough to tear. I can't even break through your bones!" Ravage clutched one of Anon's exposed ribs and pulled, but the skeleton wouldn't crack.

Anon gnashed his teeth and glared at the butcher above him.

⊹≡◉⊜≡⊹

With Casey in his sights, Elliot retrieved the idol from his pocket. The jewel had been formed into the shape of a beast with the head of a lion and the body of a gazelle. The demonic idol was vaguely circular, with its teeth biting into its own flank.

Elliot's eyes glowed in triumph as he held the idol at arm's length, putting it between himself and his target in space. Such a treasure had been the source of his Envy ever since he had joined the commune, but his leader had always given from his horde of gifts to the other Zealots. Ravage was strong enough to win his fights on his own, and Elliot usually kept to the shadows during his deadly bouts. So, he had never needed to use a Zealot's weapon before. As if he had foreseen the turmoil they would face that night, Elliot's leader had finally bestowed him with an idol of his own.

With the revelation of acceptance, Elliot allowed himself to revel in his premature victory. Other Zealots had moved mountains with their idols. Surely, Elliot would lay waste to this human who stood in his path.

Elliot was the quiet type, never one to make a fuss outside of his own mind. But, with the power of Zephiscestra in his hands, he found himself emboldened.

Elliot held the idol in his hands and raised his arms, reaching them towards Casey. He pointed the idol at him and cried out, "My Goddess! Make me your champion! Subdue this human of virgin Lust so that my sc'ermin may drink the eternal blood of your Glory!"

Elliot's chest heaved in triumph, then stopped abruptly. Casey, unaware, laughed easily at Peter's touch. He remained standing, oblivious to the curse that was uttered towards him.

Most of the crowd continued to watch the game, but some others bore witness to a strange sight. Those chosen few saw the ecstatic glee in middle-aged man's face melt into abject horror as glittering sand poured from his outstretched hands.

Several onlookers screamed when they saw the deranged rage that overtook Elliot. Casey turned to face the Zealot, and, with him, the entire party looked his way.

Elliot had often had nightmares where he would show up to social gatherings after neglecting to get dressed. Now, weaponless, forsaken by his Goddess, Elliot's naked shame in the waking world shattered any disillusionment that he had ever harbored about true vulnerability.

Like a rat backed against the wall, Elliot went insane with desperation. He was on his own, thrust back to Earth from his seat of perceived glory. He had nothing left to lose, and nothing left to use but his bare hands.

"Come here, you little shit!" Elliot lurched forward with battered determination, knocking Peter aside and sending him sprawling across the table. Cups of beer flew at disorienting speeds into the crowd.

Casey was dumbfounded and paralyzed with fear. Elliot approached him with empty outstretched hands and quickly apprehended him. Women screamed, and some of the men ran away. Others shouted angrily at Elliot.

"One move and he dies!" Elliot bellowed, his voice cracking with the strain of pure terror. He wrapped his hands around Casey's neck and squeezed tightly. The music was still blaring. Casey clawed at Elliot's arm, but the man didn't let go.

Elliot had always dreaded getting into a fight, but this guy was easy to handle. If he wanted to, Elliot could snap his neck like a twig. Casey's face began to turn blue. However, Elliot didn't want to kill him. He just wanted Ravage to win his fight so that they could go home, stronger than before.

⟶◦⟵

"AIIIHAHAHA!" Ravage screeched wickedly when he finally got a good look at Anon's exposed heart. It was beating at an alarming rate in the crater that used to be Anon's chest. Scraps of bone and flesh littered the yard on either side of them.

"Finally! You little shit, you weren't supposed to be this hard to kill. But now I can finally eat your sc'erva! I've been waiting so long!" Ravage sniveled in ecstasy as he spread his mouth wide open. Several of his teeth were still missing, but the other needles in his gums would do the job fine.

He licked his lips and lowered his head into Anon's chest.

WHAM

Elliot saw stars as his head snapped to the side. Casey was released from his grasp and Elliot hit the floor. Bob stood over him, panting.

Someone turned off the music, and the house was silent. Bob looked around and noticed that he was the center of attention. Allie was still on the other side of the table. Her mouth was agape.

As Zephiscestra left him, Bob picked a neglected beer up from the ground, cracked it open, and took a gulp. He held the can above his head and yelled, "WOO!"

The rest of the crowd joined him.

A couple of people helped Casey back to his feet. Various others rubbed his arms and back to make him feel better. Casey just looked around, confused. He saw the man who attacked him on the floor at Bob's feet. Allie was already draped around Bob's shoulders, the two kissing passionately. Peter was still getting himself off of the table, wiping the beer off of his skin and clothes. Casey rushed over to him.

"Ohh my god, arne you oakay?" Casey helped Peter stand upright. When Peter was on his own two feet, he hugged Casey in a tight embrace.

"OH my gawd, Casey, I was soo scared. Who wash that guy?"

"I dunno?" Casey said.

They both looked back at the man on the floor, who was knocked out cold. Peter and Casey looked back into each other's eyes. It might have been the alcohol, or the fact that he was just in a dangerous situation, but Casey felt himself melting in Peter's arms. They were face to face, their noses almost touching. Peter smiled warmly and hugged Casey tighter. Casey closed his eyes and leaned in with his head. Peter did the same. Their lips brushed against each other's and Casey shuddered with pleasure. Peter's lips were softer than he could even imagine. Casey went back in for another kiss. Peter took Casey's lower lip lightly into his mouth. Casey sucked on Peter's upper lip. Then, he gently squeezed Peter's lower lip with his own. This continued while the people around them took tons of pictures. Casey and Peter were sent all over the internet in a matter of minutes. The picture that went most viral showcased Peter and Casey kissing in front of Bob, who presented an unconscious Elliot in one hand and a thumbs-up in the other.

⋆⇒◉⇐⋆

"EIIIYYYEEE!" Ravage shrieked as Anon's teeth sunk deep into his neck. Anon grabbed Ravage's arms so that he couldn't be scratched again. Ravage kicked with his legs, but Anon continued to manhandle him.

As Ravage's blood doused Anon's tongue, Anon felt a surge of energy kick in, and he no longer felt any of the pain that had come from his face and chest. His fatigue evaporated, and his fear fled his body. Ravage couldn't move his upper body at all, since Anon controlled the movement in his arms and neck.

Ravage snapped maniacally towards the concavity in Anon's chest, but the heart was out of reach. Anon rolled Ravage's body onto the lawn, still biting into his neck. Anon was now on top, straddling Ravage, hunched over and heaving into his enemy's lacerated skin. Since Anon's cheek was torn open and allowed for his mouth to open even wider, he was able to bite incredibly deep into Ravage's neck.

Anon clenched his teeth together with malevolent force. Ravage writhed on the ground until Anon's teeth connected, then went limp.

Anon spit the flesh aside. Ravage's head, with only half a neck to support it, drooped onto his shoulder; his eyes were open, but they saw nothing in the dark of the night.

With Ravage's defeat, the frantic fervor left Anon's mind, and opiate-like relief spread through his limbs. He gingerly touched the gorge that Ravage had burrowed into his chest. He could feel his heart pumping blood throughout his body, but he didn't touch the sc'erva with his hands. Inky black blood dripped from Anon's chest onto Ravage's twitching body.

Anon noticed for the first time that Ravage wore a torn business suit, black with thin white pinstripes. The seams had burst in several places and the sleeves had been split off. It looked as if the man had undergone a massive growth spurt while he was still wearing his clothes. Tufts of silver fur sprouted from the suit in various places.

Anon sat on Ravage's lifeless body for a moment, contemplating what he should do next. The party was still raging inside.

Should I see if Casey is okay?

Who the hell was this guy, and how could I have fought like that? Anon looked over at the wrecked car in the street.

I did that...

He wondered where the unparalleled strength and lightning fast reflexes came from.

Anon touched delicately at his chest again. A few drops of blood landed onto Ravage's right breast pocket.

Did he say he wanted to... eat my heart?

Carefully, he unbuttoned Ravage's suit from the neck to about halfway down his torso. Ravage's furry chest was now fully exposed.

Anon licked his lips. He suddenly felt very hungry. Anon bared his teeth and lowered his head. Ancient, supernatural instinct kicked in. Zephiscestra smiled as Anon began to feast.

CHAPTER 12

CASEY WAS SHOCKED to learn about Anon's fight when he emerged, bleary eyed, from a death-like sleep on Saturday.

At first, he didn't believe the story that Anon told him, even when he saw the thin scar on Anon's cheek. Casey's mind was irrefutably changed when Anon showed him the monstrosity of scar tissue that was now his chest. The proof was undeniable, although neither knew how it could be possible for such wounds to heal so quickly. Casey, though, was too hungover to truly process anything of worth. He slept for most of that day, ignorant of even his last bit of bliss.

They didn't know anything about the world that they had inadvertently stumbled into until Casey received a mysterious message on his phone that Sunday.

Casey woke up that morning in his bed. Sunlight flooded his room through the open window. He rubbed the sleep from his eyes and adjusted the loose t-shirt from around his neck. After a full day of sleep, he felt refreshed from the unprecedented night he had at Marissa's.

As he did every morning, Casey checked his phone. Whereas last week Casey would have woken up to one or two text messages, today Casey's phone boasted over a hundred texts. Casey opened the app to sift through the mail.

A few people sent multiple messages, despite the unspoken two-text rule. Casey scrolled down the screen and surveyed the texts. Bill's name was on the screen, as was his younger brother. Allie, Marissa, and other people who had put their number into his phone at the party had sent other messages.

Surprisingly, Charlie had not texted him.

At the bottom of the list, there were several texts from unsaved contacts. Most of them were benign, but the one in particular slapped the sleep out of Casey. He sat straight up in bed while he read it.

???-???-????: Casey, my name is Fix. That's all the information that I am willing to give to you about my identity. However, I will help you to navigate the peril that you have gotten yourself into.

Casey, spurred on by Zephiscestra, shakily typed out his response.

Caseybent44: What? Who is this?

Fix answered immediately.

???-???-????: Casey, I've already told you, my name is Fix. You may refer to me as that from now on, although I don't advise you to bring up my name to anyone other than your sc'ermin. Caseybent44: My sc'ermin?

???-???-????: Your demon, phantom, wraith, ghost. Whatever you have chosen to call the man that only you can see.

Casey felt his stomach constrict. His face turned pale.

Who the heck is this guy?

Casey flung his phone across the bed, then turned toward Anon. Casey said, "Are you pranking me or something? Are you texting my phone?"

Anon did not look away from the porn playing on the computer, but he dropped the bottle of HighCladd vodka from his lips and shrugged.

"I don't know what you're talking about. I don't even have a phone. I guess I could use the computer… but… I'm pretty busy here."

Casey's entire awareness was flooded with Fix's revelation, and facts that were on the periphery of his understanding violently integrated into his consciousness. He was not hallucinating: There was a real ghost following him, or a sc'ermin, that fought other sc'ermin. And the sc'ermin that wanted to attack them followed around other humans who might attack him.

And, the worst part of it all was that it was his own fault.

Casey's eyes watered as Zephiscestra allowed him to remember reciting the incantation. He experienced the memory from outside of his own body, and he heard himself speak the words in a voice that did not seem to be his own. And yet, he was the one who had bound Anon to this world as an abomination of his former self.

Casey was wracked with guilt, and he looked over to Anon again. He had to tell him the truth of his origins… but he needed more information. Casey considered the possibility that Anon would attack him for using his life as a bargaining chip for social media followers.

When you put it like that… maybe I deserve for him to kill me.

Zephiscestra wouldn't let Casey go that easily. In a twisted form of a blessing, She numbed his guilt so that he could fulfill his duty. Zephiscestra wouldn't do the work for him, nor would She allow him to know all that he needed. The search for the questions was a part of the answer, after all.

Casey, by his own will, didn't want the mysterious messenger to cause him any more trouble, and he especially feared for his family and friends. He wondered for a moment if this number could have been the man who attacked him on Friday.

The partygoers were so drunk that they forgot about him soon after he was unconscious. Even the police who were in attendance said that they were too intoxicated to drive him to the station. Casey himself, wrapped up in Indulgence, had found his hands full with Peter.

Consequently, after Bob had propped Elliot up for a picture, they all just left him lying in a pool of alcohol. When the people who stayed the night woke up the next day, Elliot was gone.

Casey reached across the bed and retrieved his phone. Another message was already waiting.

???-???-????: I'm not going to hurt you in any way, Casey. I want to help you. You have gotten wrapped up in something much bigger than yourself. Without me, your sc'ermin is sure to die, and you could possibly suffer the same fate. Now, let me help you.

Caseybent44: First of all I don't even know who you are. And I have a few questions before I talk to you anymore. I'll ask again. Who are you? How do you know who I am? And what do you mean by sc'ermin?

Casey paused for a moment, then sent another message: Are you an enemy or a friend?

The answer came quickly, as if the stranger already knew what Casey was going to say.

???-???-????: For the last time, my name is Fix. I cannot tell you any more about my identity. But I know about you and your situation. You and your sc'ermin were attacked last Friday night while you were at a social gathering. You were attacked by a human, while his sc'ermin attacked your own. Do you remember reading aloud a certain incantation recently? Does the name Zephiscestra mean anything to you?

Casey's heart skipped a beat. How does he know about that? Casey answered 'Yes.'

???-???-????: I will inform you of what you have gotten yourself into. The ritual that you manifested was an ancient and sacred pact between gods and men. By reciting its words, you have displayed a willingness to take part in a practice that has spanned millennia. I assume that you were unaware of all of this when you spoke them. Usually this would mean that you would die, but you chanced by an unwitting sacrifice, did you not?

The night on the bridge flooded back into Casey's memory. Fix was confirming what Casey had feared. If Anon had acted as a coincidental scapegoat for Casey...

Fix didn't wait for a response.

???-???-????: Think carefully, Casey. What did you desire when you read the ritual?

Casey scrunched his eyebrows in concentration. Before he read the words, he had been talking about his LitMille channel with Bill and Charlie. He was worried about his channel's popularity, and he wished that more people would view it. He also thought about how famous Trevor Greenbrook was, and how much Casey would love to work with him (or even just be with him).

Casey told all of this to Fix.

???-???-????: That's what I figured. I have been doing research on you, Casey. When I first saw your sc'ermin in one of your LitMille videos, I had a hunch that you yearned for fame. You see, the ritual doesn't exactly require you to make a literal wish. Your heart's deepest desire at the moment you say the words are enough. My postulate seemed correct when I tracked your channel's follower count. You have steadily increased this amount by more than 100,000 times. While this may appear to be good news to you, it does not come without cost.

Casey tried to swallow his anxiety and kept reading.

???-???-????: When humans incant the ritual and make a sacrifice, their wishes are granted. They get what they desire. In your case, this is fame. However, their sacrifices don't just disappear, like you know. Their spirits come back as sc'ermin, and they are bound to whatever Zealot summons them. No one can see these spirits except for the one who sacrificed them, as well as other Zealots that have made their own sacrifices. This is where your fame may become the death of you, Casey. Sc'ermin can increase their power by defeating other sc'ermin and consuming their bodies—the heart in particular. This leads the sc'ermin to seek food. Depending on what type of sc'ermin they are, the desire to feed may be greater or lesser. Unfortunately for you, your fame makes you a prime target for sc'ermin and their partners. You will be very high-profile in the coming months, and many other Zealots will learn of the origin of your fame. They will hunt you down so that they may become more powerful. The Envy that you encountered was just the first. There will be more.

Casey's mouth hung open in disbelief. How could any of this be possible? He never asked for this. All he wanted was for his content to be more popular, but Casey would never willingly go to such an extreme length for fame. He shot Anon a glare of contempt.

Caseybent44: Look, I didn't ask for any of this. I read the ritual, but I didn't make a sacrifice or anything. I tried to save him when he jumped.

Fix took a long time to respond. Casey looked at the back of Anon's head. Somehow, it looked more demonic than just a few days prior.

Casey almost jumped when Fix's message appeared on his screen.

???-???-????: I've heard tell of a Lust, taken against their will to appease our goddess, Zephiscestra. Whether you asked for it or not, you are now irrevocably involved.

"Look what you got me into!" Casey said, unable to contain his emotions.

Anon swiveled around in his chair. A busty woman's expression of ecstasy played on the screen behind him.

"You made me make a sacrifice, and now I'm getting hunted down! All because of you!" Casey's eyes were wide with fear and his stomach was doing somersaults. He felt a sheath of sweat leeching out of his body. He had never been so frightened in his life.

"What they hell are you talking about?" Anon asked.

Casey gulped when he realized what he had said.

Anon didn't know about the ritual, and he was in denial about his own suicide. Casey felt that, now that he knew the truth himself, it was time to let Anon know what was really going on.

"I didn't want to tell you earlier because I thought that you would freak out," Casey said, "But, remember when we first met? I said that you tried to kill yourself."

"Barely, but okay," Anon said.

"Well, you succeeded. You actually died. However, earlier that day, I... mistakenly recited an ancient ritual that brought you back to life and turned you into a demon." The adrenaline pumping through Casey's body wouldn't allow him to even think of smiling sheepishly.

Anon stared at him for a long time. Casey felt more beads of nervous sweat break out on his forehead. He expected Anon to get angry, to attack him with his teeth, to take revenge on the person who made him a monster.

"Before you kill me," Casey said, curling into himself on his bed, "Read this. Some guy texted me saying he knows what's going on." He tossed his phone to Anon, who started reading curiously.

"Actually, that makes a lot of sense," Anon said finally. He rubbed his chin and handed the device back. Casey threw his arms out in frustration.

"What part of that makes any sense? None of this makes any fricking sense at all!"

"No, hear me out. The guy that attacked me was seriously freaky. Like, his teeth were all pointy and thin like knives—"

"So are yours!" Casey said. "And, why aren't you freaking out right now?"

"Let me finish," Anon said angrily. "He also had a kind of snout, like a rodent. And his ears were pointy, too. Also, he was covered in fur. Not like your normal body hair, I'm talking real animal fur. It was grey and bristly. He definitely wasn't a human, and he could move way faster than one, too."

"So what are you saying?" Casey asked cautiously.

"I'm saying that it makes sense that the guy was like a sc'ermin, or whatever. It's like he was a demon, or something. What did he mean by 'type of sc'ermin?' Ask him."

Casey did as he was told.

???-???-????: It's perfectly natural that your sc'ermin isn't upset by this news. The undead were designed by Zephiscestra to accept their fate. Outside factors can complicate things, of course, but it's good that Anon is unperturbed for now. To answer your question, sc'ermin take several main forms. Seven, to be precise.

These descriptions of these archetypes survived the ancients and made their way into myth. You may know these types as the Seven Deadly Sins.

Caseybent44: Doesn't that seem a little cliché?

???-???-????: Make no mistake. The Sins evolved from the ritual, not the other way around. You wouldn't know about the Sins unless the sc'ermin came first to inspire them. But since I know this information, it is useful for me to classify the enemies that are out there. For instance, I have a feeling that your own sc'ermin is a Lust. I gathered this from the fact that most of your fans' comments have been aggressively sexual. Lust for fame makes sense, especially if there is a famous person that you desire sexually.

Casey thought of Trevor and how much he would love to be with him.

???-???-????: Are there any other signs of Lust around you? Do people start to act overtly sexual when your sc'ermin is around?

"Yeah," Anon said. "Wherever I go, people just start hooking up with each other. Like at your work, and even at shops and stores in public." Anon laughed aloud. "And that party was basically an orgy. Everyone just started hooking up all over the place. I saw two people fucking on the front porch when I was fighting that beast."

Casey relayed this information to Fix.

???-???-????: This is good news. Lust is not one of the most common sc'ermin types, but it is one of the most versatile and powerful. Lust is resilient, and your sc'ermin should be exceptionally durable. He will also be able to heal quickly from injury and will have incredible stamina. Also, in battle, a Lust will feel a unique passion and will gain more strength as the fight increases in length, like a lover in the heat of the moment.

Anon agreed that this sounded realistic. He reported feeling stronger the more that he fought, while his opponent lost his will when he had the upper hand.

???-???-????: I have reason to believe that your attacker was an Envy. Envies are strong during the beginning of a fight, but they lose their potency as time wears on. However, Envies are unique in that they can sense other sc'ermin over great distances. This is probably how that Envy found you in the first place. I know that he had encountered other sc'ermin before and was more powerful because of it. You are lucky that he attacked you when he did.

Caseybent44: Why was I lucky?

???-???-????: Like I said before, you and your sc'ermin are intertwined in ways that even I do not fully understand yet. But, as your sc'ermin will make you more famous, so can you reciprocate the effect. I saw the pictures of you that circulated popular media sites.

Casey found himself blushing at the memory of kissing Peter. It must have been the alcohol, otherwise Casey would never have done such a sexual thing in public.

???-???-????: Those pictures of you and your boyfriend were shared thousands of times, making you even more famous. The combination of widespread attention and sexual action gave strength to your sc'ermin. The goddess Zephiscestra gave us our sc'ermin so that they may serve us, and She enjoys it when we Indulge in the gifts that they offer. When we Indulge, when we partake in that which was our heart's desire at the time of the incantation, Zephiscestra grants strength and ability to our sc'ermin if we Indulge while they are fighting. Casey, if those pictures didn't make it online, your sc'ermin would surely be dead right now.

Casey couldn't help but feel pride that he had given power to Anon, but he was still embarrassed at the widely public displays of affection that Anon's strength had come from. He didn't even correct Fix about Peter's relationship status with him.

???-???-????: You see, you two are linked. Your sc'ermin will make you incredibly famous. It is no coincidence that your pictures, your LitMille channel, and your social media sites are receiving so much attention. The people of this planet will be supernaturally infatuated with you from now on. Whatever you do is sure to make headlines and dominate social media sites. While this will give you untold earthly wealth, it comes at a price. Like I said, other sc'ermin pairs will see you and know your secret. They will come after you in hopes of eating your sc'ermin's heart. They may also harm you in the process. I know that the human who attacked you was knocked unconscious, yes?

Caseybent44: Yeah, a guy at the party knocked him out when he tried to strangle me.

???-???-????: Humans and sc'ermin are bound together. I cannot stress that enough. But their relationship to each other is not symmetrical. If a sc'ermin is defeated in battle, its human will continue to live, although they will no longer receive its blessing. However, if a human is killed, the sc'ermin will instantly disappear. When the human lost consciousness, his sc'ermin was severely weakened, because sc'ermin share their human's strength. That was how your sc'ermin was able to win the fight.

"Hm, so we really lucked out, huh?" Anon said. He took another gulp of HighCladd.

Casey almost gagged, remembering the taste of a celebratory shot that he took with Peter and Bob two nights before.

"How can you be so flip about this?" Casey asked. "This is serious business. We are going to have people fighting us all the time, and you don't even seem like you care."

"Let them come," Anon said gravely. "I fought that fuckin' last guy and I killed him."

Although Anon pretended to be confident, his voice wavered when he said the word 'kill.'

Anon visualized himself digging into the silvery sc'ermin's chest with his teeth. Casey barely picked up on it, though. "If anything, this is good news. Before, we had no fucking idea what was going on. But now we actually know what I am, and who that other guy was. We know why everyone has been acting so fucking horny lately, and we know why you are suddenly blowing up online."

Anon tipped his bottle at Casey in a toast. "Fuckin'… This is a *good* thing."

???-???-????: I am sure that you still have many questions. I didn't think that you would believe all of the things that I am telling you now, but I wanted to share this information with you anyway. At least now you know that you aren't being haunted or punished, and at the very least it must be a relief that you haven't been hallucinating.

Casey had to agree with the fundamentals of what he was being told, but he would still consider himself to be both haunted *and* punished.

The totality of his situation still didn't make much sense to him; he had a hard time wrapping his head around all of it. But, in the end, Fix's texts were the only explanation they were going to get.

Casey had to be skeptical, but he chose to take Fix's word for it. The stranger knew enough details about Casey that his testimony seemed believable, although he was still creeped out by how much this guy knew.

Caseybent44: So wait, how do you know all this? Have you been spying on me?

???-???-????: Don't worry, I don't have your room bugged or wiretapped or anything of the sort. I have no need for such tools. As you probably have put together by now, I have made a similar sacrifice, although mine was wholly intentional. My sc'ermin gives me all of the information that I need. But I cannot see you, and you will not see me. At least for now. However, I would like to work with you. I think that we can be of use to one another. Of course, we will have to keep our distance. If we were to meet face to face, our sc'ermin wouldn't be able to resist devouring each other. That being said, I have given you a lot of information, but there is so much more: specifically, about your sc'ermin. Would you like me to share?

Caseybent44: What do you know about Anon?

Casey hit send before he realized that he had used his sc'ermin's nickname. Fix would presumably have no knowledge of such an intimate detail. However, Casey figured that Fix would have no problem putting the pieces together.

???-???-????: I'll get right to the point. Search Rowan Tarwick on your computer. The man who committed suicide last week has been found.

Casey almost choked. He looked up from his phone to Anon. The sc'ermin was back to watching porn on the computer, savoring 151 proof vodka.

???-???-????: I'm surprised the authorities haven't contacted you, since you were the last person to see him. The man's parents probably wouldn't want to bring any outsiders into such a private affair. The body was found a few days ago, and the funeral is tomorrow. The details should be online.

"Anon, you might want to check this out." Casey spoke in a measured voice. He didn't know how his sc'ermin would react to the news. Casey lifted the blanket off himself, stepped out of bed, and walked slowly to the computer. "Here, let me show you."

"Fuck you, I'm not done yet," Anon said, but he moved aside regardless. As Casey leaned over to use the computer, he noticed that Anon was larger than he had been before. His jaw was stronger, and his muscles pulled his clothes more tightly around him. (Somehow, his clothes had been repaired after the fight. Casey had found this unbelievable, but Anon found it inexplicable. Anon did not sleep at night but claimed that he didn't notice how his clothes were restored.)

There were also more subtle differences to him. Anon's ears had started to taper at the top, as did his fingernails. The stubble on his face appeared coarse and sharp. The hair on his neck, hands, and what Casey could see of his arms had grown thicker, as well.

"Here, you might be interested in this," Casey said. He stepped back from the computer and let Anon read from the screen. The only article that was available was just a short blurb on the local news site.

"Local man, 20, found dead in river. Police have identified the body as Rowan Tarwick of Greatwood County, who was a sophomore at Greatwood Community College. Authorities have ruled out foul play. Mr. Tarwick's family have requested us to respectfully withhold more information."

Anon stared at the screen. The exhaust fan inside of the laptop whirred loudly.

Anon exhaled. "So, what? That was me?"

"Yeah, that's what Fix just told me," Casey said.

"Oh." Anon clicked away from the article and back to his website.

"What are you doing?" Casey was incredulous. "We just found out where your body is, and you don't even care?"

Anon shrugged. "As far as I'm concerned, my body is right here. I don't know who that kid is that killed himself, but it's not me. I don't have any memory of that."

"But he was *you*. Don't you *get* that? This guy that died was you, and now you're here. I, for one, am really curious about this."

"Well, I'm *not*. Maybe it's because I'm a sc'ermin now, but I don't really care about this petty human stuff. From now on I'm just going to watch porn, drink vodka, and fight demons."

"How can you say that?" Casey was shocked.

Anon ignored him.

Casey sat back down on his bed. He sent a text to Fix, and only had to wait a couple of seconds for a response.

"The funeral is on Monday, at 9:00 AM. I think you should go," Casey said.

"Why would I do that?"

"Because you need to find out who you are. Who your *parents* are. Who your *friends* are," Casey said. "I don't know how you sc'ermin perceive the world, but this stuff is important to normal people. I would feel a lot better if you went."

Casey still felt guilty about Anon's death, but didn't vocalize his feelings to his family or friends. He recognized how important relationships were to one's mental wellbeing, especially because he was neglecting his own.

Anon finished his bottle of HighCladd, set it down, and cracked open a new one. He had stashed 30 bottles of it in Casey's closet, all of which he had stolen from various liquor stores.

"Okay, I'll go," he said. "If it will make you happy, I'll go. I live to serve you, don't I?"

Casey smiled apprehensively. He appreciate that. "Well, I wouldn't say that you're my slave or anything, but you could take my advice once and a while."

"Are you going to come, too?"

"I don't think I should. I didn't know you before… and anyway if your parents wanted me to come then they would have contacted me. You would be able to attend it unseen, though."

"And what if you get attacked while I'm gone?"

"I think I'll be fine for a couple of hours," Casey said. "Plus, now I have Fix who might be able to alert me about oncoming attacks."

Anon considered this and nodded his head.

"Okay, I'll check it out. But I'm not staying for long," he said.

"You can do whatever you want," Casey said. "It's your funeral." He tried to smile, but Casey realized that he found his own joke humorless.

He checked his phone again when he felt its vibration.

???-???-????: I need to go now, but you can text me whenever you have a question from now on. I will do my best to answer. By the way, I don't expect you to try to track this number but know that it is untraceable. I will keep in touch.

Casey was wary of the secrecy, but he felt better knowing that someone was looking out for him. Still, he was terrified of the information that he had learned that day. Secret informants, suicidal college students, and violent sc'ermin were all a part of Casey's life now. Was all of that a fair price to pay for untold fame and wealth?

Casey couldn't easily decide if it was all worth it. Having your life completely shattered will cause confusion in just about anyone, and Casey was not immune.

He looked over again at Anon.

My sc'ermin. My Lust.

Anon had made Casey nervous from the beginning, but now that the truth had been revealed, Anon seemed more concrete, and the threat that he represented was all too real. Casey was grateful for the information, but he wondered whether it would have been better to remain ignorant and just let Anon fight his battles.

Does that mean that I don't care if he dies?

Rowan was already dead. Would it be that much different if Anon died, too?

Casey shook the thought from his head. It would be easier for Casey to go on living without the danger that Anon would bring with him, but Casey thought that it would be inhumane for him to wish death upon his sc'ermin.

Even if he is no longer human.

Still, the thought of safety enticed Casey.

On Monday, Casey couldn't help but feel more at ease with Anon gone. At least, until 10:00 AM.

Casey felt a sense of privacy, increased by the lack of Anon's presence yet lessened by the social media engagement.

He had longed for time by himself ever since his sc'ermin first came into his life. Of course, even without Anon, Casey would never truly be alone. His hundreds of thousands of fans would assure that. But even his most fervent admirers—even those in his office—wouldn't fully share this particular experience with Casey.

A new film had to be edited for his company, and Casey was tasked with adjusting the lighting. He tried his best to pay attention to his work, but he could sense that some of his coworkers were craning their necks in his direction. He heard giggles when an email popped up on his screen and he jumped in his chair.

"Aw, how cute," someone whispered behind him.

Although no one else noticed it, the door to his desk's floor space swung open, and a horrifying woman stepped into the room. Her dull red high-heels clacked against the floor, although no one else could hear them. When she stepped in front of the window, dim light glittered off her sequin dress. She brushed long, platinum blonde hair out of her face and stood directly in front of

Casey, who gripped his desk's sides and sat as far back in his seat as possible with an expression of horror.

The woman spread open the blue, feathery wings from where her arms should have been and flapped them lightly. She fanned her extravagant eye-spotted tail feathers that completely obscured the rest of the room from Casey's view.

"Casey Bennnnnntoooonnnn!" Casey thought that he was going to pass out due to fear. He then wondered how this monster could trill her R's, since her mouth was a two-foot long beak. "I come bearrring a prrroposition for battle!"

CHAPTER 13

ANON SAT ON the stone steps in front of the church where, inside, his body waited.

Cars drove by in the street while humans walked past on the sidewalk. None of them paid any mind to the sc'ermin.

A dreary mat of clouds hung in the sky. It had rained lightly only a few hours before, while the sun still slept. The rain left the air clear and cool, and a light breeze caressed the sc'ermin's face. Anon could not feel the air. He hadn't felt much of anything for as long as he could remember. Not even the alcohol could deliver a sensation.

Although… Anon shuddered as he felt the phantom claws of the demon that had torn though his face, his clothes, his chest, and his ribs.

Anon sighed and he pushed himself to his feet. He had been fighting himself for the last forty-five minutes to walk through the doors.

If I stay here any longer, I'm going to miss my own funeral.

He had debated even entering the building. If he left now, he could simply lie to Casey and say that he went inside.

Or, I openly disobey him. I am his sc'ermin, not his slave. Who is he to tell me what to do?

Anon took a deep breath. He would only have to be there for a short time, since he had already missed most of the proceedings. Anon decided to swallow his unease and walk inside. As he grasped the iron handle on the door, Anon told himself that he wasn't scared.

He shook his head and pushed away his fear, replacing it with uncertain apathy.

Much better.

Anon entered the church. Overpowering, melancholy tones of an unseen organ boomed throughout the main hall. The air was much thicker than outside, past the massive oaken doors. Small candles burned inside the inner chamber, and a bowl of incense sent tendrils of smoke drifting towards the high, steeped ceiling. The interior of the church was impressive, its walls constructed from heavy grey stone. Ornamenting the rough walls were the fourteen stations of the cross. Seven were spaced on either side of the congregation. Anon noticed that the final station depicted Jesus Christ being laid in the tomb, but there was no sign of the Resurrection to be seen.

High on the walls, above the stations, were dozens of stained-glass windows of myriad colors and shapes. All of them depicted Catholic saints. Catherine of Alexandria, St. Stephen, St. David, and St. Paul gazed at the mass from their perches. Minimal light shone through the windows from outside, and the saints seemed somber in their motley of rainbow glass, especially with the harrowing tunes of the organ swirling about the room.

At the front of the church, flowers of red, purple, and yellow sprung from the foot of the white altar. A large picture of the deceased sat atop the altar, and a banner hung underneath. It read: "Our Dearly Departed, Rowan Tarwick," in ornate gold and white. In the picture, Rowan looked out over the crowd and seemed enchanted at their presence. Anon shared no similar sentiment.

Anon was surprised to see that the seats were filled with about a hundred people. Even though his face was displayed at the front of the church, Anon felt like an intruder; he didn't know a single person in the room. In the back of the church, where Anon entered, rows and rows of adults sat with small children. Everyone was dressed in suits or gowns of black, even the kids. Anon almost felt awkward that he was so grossly underdressed.

Whatever, it's my funeral anyway. I can wear whatever I want.

Anon feigned boredom and made his face implacable, but then he remembered that no one could see him. He scoffed bitterly at himself. Then, the sc'ermin paused for a moment to survey the rest of the crowd.

While the young ones didn't seem affected by the gloom around them, their parents held them tight. It felt as if the children's mere presence among the dead might make them meet the same fate. Anon turned from the uneasy mothers and somber fathers and made his way to the front of the church. The sorrowful sound of the organ seemed to be trying to crush him under its weight.

Near the front of the church, the casket stood in the middle of the center aisle. Soft light from the candles illuminated the darkly polished wood. Anon stood next to it. He ran his fingers over the thick golden railings on its side. For a moment, he debated opening the lid, to see what he once looked like. No one would notice. He could just take a peek, to see who he once was.

But I'm not that person any more, am I?

The woeful organ pressed into his chest, constricting his breath. Anon shuddered and wrenched his fingers from the casket's imposing surface. He moved on to the front pews, where the crowd was aged more homogenously.

Anon stood at the front of the church and faced the groups of people who he assumed were his classmates. They were all the same age as him and looked to be at least in college. Each of them was dressed in black, like the families in the back. Anon tugged uneasily at the white collar of his shirt. Most of the college students wore deep frowns, their faces downcast to their clasped hands. A woman in the third row sobbed silently into a man's shoulder. Anon felt his gut involuntarily clench at the sight of her. He quickly looked away.

It's not my problem anymore, is it?

"Why did he do it?" One man whispered to another. His friend didn't look up from the ground, but simply shrugged. "But he didn't show any signs, did he?" The other man gave no answer. Anon thought he saw the man's lip quivering. "I just wish that he would have said something, you know? We could have helped him."

"Yeah, just shut up, man," the other man said.

The first man's eyes went wide, but he calmed down once he registered the dolorous bitterness in his friend's voice and saw the white knuckles of his clenched fists. Anon felt anger rise in himself, but he didn't know where it was aimed.

It's not my fault, right

Elsewhere, red-eyed youths hugged each other or held hands in their seats. Few tried speaking through the organ's woeful cries. Suddenly, the music stopped. A man pointed to a section of the program paper on the second page. The hundreds of eyes in the church turned to the first row of pews on the right side of the room. Four people stood up, supporting each other, and made their way to the podium that stood at the right of the altar. Anon felt as if a punch hit him in the gut when he realized that those people were his family.

The Tarwicks' stoic walk to the podium was met with utter silence from the congregation, all the more conspicuous in the absence of the organ's throes. Anon stood completely still. Any breath that he would have used to make a sound had left him, but Anon didn't notice that he had stopped breathing. The male Tarwicks' footsteps echoed faintly against the stone walls, while the women's black heels pierced the silence repeatedly like a knife in a crime of indolence. When his former family took their places behind the microphone, Anon forgot that there were others gathered behind him.

They stood tall behind the podium. Rowan's mother and sister stood side by side in front of his father and brother, who rested their hands on the women's respective shoulders. Rowan's sister adjusted the microphone to her height. Her blonde hair tumbled around the black dress about her shoulders like sunlight breaking the dusk. Her deep blue eyes blinked back tears, matching those of her mother and brother. Rowan's father stood back, stolid and implacable, staring blankly before him. Anon noticed that Rowan's picture shared the same eyes as his father. While Rowan's eyes were bright, though, the light had gone out of Mr. Tarwick's.

"Rowan could light up a room in a way that no one else could, simply because he didn't try to," Rowan's sister began. She spoke slowly in a clear, unwavering voice. "His carefree attitude allowed him to laugh off his problems, yet he had a willfulness that made him help anyone in need. He was always quick with a smile or a lighthearted joke, even when no one else was in the mood for it." The woman stifled a cough, halfway between a sob and laugh. Her brother's lip quivered violently behind her.

"Rowan spent a lot of time alone, but I wouldn't call him lonely. When we would come home after a long day, he was always there to happily greet us like a puppy." This time, she managed a short-lived chuckle. Beside her, Rowan's mother let out a sob. Her husband squeezed her shoulder, his face still a mask.

"He was quiet, but that was because he was thoughtful. He was gentle, but he wasn't timid. He was always calm, but never passive. Although he kept to himself, Rowan always had a way of making others feel wanted. Just the atmosphere that he brought with him made others feel comfortable and content. Whenever Rowan was in the room with you, he made you feel as if everything was all right."

Rowan's sister sighed, then looked at Rowan's picture before turning her head to the ceiling. Moving her lips to the microphone again, and with a voice that was beginning to falter, she said, "But I guess now that you are in heaven, you will always be in the room with us, wherever we go. Whenever I feel anxious, or lonely, or scared, I will think of you, Rowan. I will ask for your smile, or a kind word, or even just to have you sit next to me, and I will know that everything will be okay."

No longer able to control herself, Rowan's sister turned to her mother and embraced her. "I love you, Rowan. I love you."

Rowan's mother seemed to be taking it the hardest. She buried her head into her daughter's shoulder, heaving between sobs. Through reddening eyes, the girl looked once again to the ceiling. Her brother wrapped his arms around the two of them.

Anon stood paralyzed.

It's okay, it's okay. It's not my fault. I don't even know these people, anyway.

Rowan tried his best to harden his heart, to quell the rush of any emotion before he lost his cool. He had no connection to these people... And yet there was his face, gazing out onto the crowd. There was his mother and his sister. There was his brother, who looked so much like him, and the father that he would have surely grown to resemble. Anon couldn't remember the love that he had for all of them, but he felt it rising inside of him, heating up his chest like a furnace and making his heart beat faster. Anon turned his head away. He wanted to push away the feelings that were gushing into him. He couldn't bear to face the people that were hurting so much in front of him, until he heard Rowan's father make a sound.

Mr. Tarwick, a solid, rugged man, began to weep. The tears broke through his implacable features and ran down his cheeks. For some reason, the sight of this man's agony especially filled Anon with incredible sadness. Maybe it was because it's rare to see a grown man cry, but Rowan's father's bared emotions expressed the reality of the situation. It was no time for patriarchal expectations or cultural gender roles. Rowan's father, who loved his son with fathomless propensity, broke down before his entire community, stricken with the grief of a collapsed home and a shattered heart.

Anon felt unbidden tears run down his face. He blinked them away angrily.

No, this wasn't—NO! This wasn't me! I didn't do any of this.

He wanted to scream, he wanted to run up and hug his family. But they aren't my family, are they?

"Are they?" Anon asked aloud.

Even if he were to run up to the podium, yell out for his brother and sister and parents, ask for their forgiveness, tell them that, yes, he was here, it was going to be okay... it wouldn't make a difference. They couldn't see his tears, they couldn't feel his embrace, they couldn't hear the reassuring words that he could offer.

Anon felt sadness weigh him down from the pit of his stomach, yet aimless anger bubbled up from beneath it. The Tarwicks' sorrow flowed through the microphone, resonating throughout the chamber, even more harrowing than the organ's dreadful song. Anon yearned for that depressing organ to flood the church again, to drown out the awful cries of Rowan's—no—*his* own family, who stood all alone behind the podium.

Anon turned back towards the congregation. "How can you just sit there?" He screamed at them, but they simply hung their heads. No one made a move to rise and console the family. "You call yourself my friends? Go help my family!"

Anon heard his screams turn into shrieks, yet he felt no shame. If his own father could bare naked emotion, Anon could do the same. When no one in the mass acknowledged him, Anon felt his anger turn inwards. He clawed at the tears that stained his face with the pads of his fingers.

"How could you do this to them?" Anon whipped his head towards the poster board that displayed his smiling face. Where before Anon interpreted innocent cheer, he now saw only snide ungratefulness. "How can you be happy like this? How can you smile?" Anon ran to the front of the church, poised to rip the smirking poster in half. He caught himself right before his sharp claws could rend the icon.

That would make me no better than you. I won't take anything else away from my family.

Instead of the poster, Anon turned again and stomped towards the casket, hot tears blurring his vision. Anon clenched his jaw in frustration as he fumbled with the clasps. "How could you do this?" As he flung open the lid, the organ began to play again.

Anon was suddenly bombarded with an assault of sensations. His family's sobs still sounded through the church speakers. The invisible organ once again resumed its ubiquitous, melancholy cry. Anon experienced an intense bout of vertigo and dizziness. His eyes wrapped into tunnel vision, and he felt like he was looking into a mirror with another behind him, gazing into an infinite and terrifying recursion.

And then there was the stench.

Anon reeled as the noxious odor erupted from the open casket. The rotten stench of death curled into his nostrils and clawed its way straight to his brain. Anon could feel the putrid smell coursing through his veins, working its way into every cavity of his body, feeding off his insides like a disgusting parasite. Anon tore away from the open casket and stumbled down the aisle until he doubled over, his hands on his knees, and retched. Thick black phlegm spattered the marble of the floor. Anon convulsed violently until his stomach was empty.

That face. That face… That's not my face!

The encompassing, omnipresent organ made him want to curl up into a ball, and the Tarwicks' cries made him want to scream. The overload of sounds made Anon feel as if the walls were caving in around him, constricting his chest and denying him breath.

That face…

Anon regarded the dark slime on the ground with disgust. He then straightened up and turned back to the casket. Anon covered his nose with both hands and gazed down at the one who had caused all of this pain.

The water-logged cadaver had been found in the river after a few days. Rowan's bloated face stared back at him through one sallow eye. The other eye was missing; a brown mass of goop was nestled in the otherwise vacant socket above bulbous cheeks, a clogged nose, and swollen dripping lips. Its pallid skin looked slick and waxy. Thin strands of hair clung to its head like scattered bits of seaweed. Black scabs littered his face, neck, and hands like barnacles. Someone had stuffed his body into a suit that had become soiled and rank as it slowly wrung moisture out of the dead man. The noxious fumes that seeped out of the body were almost too much for Anon to bear. He was about to close the lid when he noticed a defined protuberance beneath Rowan's left lapel. With one hand still secure over his nose, Anon reached under the jacket to remove the item. He gagged when his fingers brushed against the squishy polyps through Rowan's shirt, and he quickly removed the object of his curiosity.

Anon shut the lid on the nightmarish corpse and examined the treasure that he had procured: It was a small notebook. Worn, nondescript black leather covered the pages that stacked about an inch thick. The edges of the pages were damp and yellowed. The book itself reeked of dank carrion. Anon flipped through the moist, crinkled pages that were covered with scrawling of black, blue, and red ink.

He turned to the first page, which, in faded letters, read: "I Earnestly Request that You Not Read the Contents of this Book, Unless, of Course, You are Its Owner."

Under that was a different message written in blue ink, which appeared to have been added more recently:

"If this is found before I am buried, which I presume that it will in its current place, please leave it with my body. It is not an overly long suicide note. It is simply my journal. I promise that its contents are not at all interesting, yet I retain the request above. Please, as my last wish, do not read past this page out of respect for me. Mom, Dad, Kim, Rob, you may find my note where I left it in the kitchen."

With no small guilt, Anon slid the book into the back of his waistband. As he closed the lid of his casket, his family passed by him and made their way back to their seats. His father led Kim and Rob, presumably, into the first row of pews. His mother, however, deviated toward the coffin. Anon backed away to give her space, but she came to rest mere inches away from him. Those in the congregation whom she faced lowered their gazes; those behind her watched with fearful expressions.

Anon's mother ran her fingers over the smooth surface of the casket, shuddering with grief. Her head downcast, with bitter tears burning holes in the floor, his mother whispered to herself so faintly that only Anon could hear.

"Who did this to you," she breathed, not for the last time. "Who took away my son?"

CHAPTER 14

*JANUARY 8*ᵀᴴ*: I can't help but believe that we are in hell. Falling though a bottomless pit of darkness; stuck on a crusty blob of magma; and surrounded by debris, balls of fire, and chaos. We are all unhappy for one reason or another, and eventually we disappear forever, burned into dust. We've forgotten where we are, though, and we've grown accustomed to the evil that we live within ever since we've gained control of our corner of hell. But, when we realize that we can unlearn all of the habits and shortcuts that we use to navigate our existence, and perceive reality through a strictly objective lens, we realize how strange of a place the world is. Ferocious beasts room the land, seas, and skies, but now we keep some of them as pets. Creeping tendrils and ragged twists of sharp wood cover the earth, but they no longer hinder us, and we use their reproductive organs as food. Even humans, the most unimpressive looking creatures on this earth, are grotesquely biological on the inside. If not for our smooth skin, we would look as terrifying as the rest of hell's inhabitants.*

It was 6:00 PM when Casey burst into his room after work. He wore a pallid complexion that had plagued him for the entire day. At first, the look came with the social anxiety of the bombardment from his coworkers. From 10:00 AM to the end of the day, however, Casey's fears had become more malignant.

"Fuck—get up—this is awful," Casey said hurriedly, shutting his door. Anon, still lying on Casey's bed, broke from his uneasy reverie. Six empty bottles of HighCladd and a half a bottle of mouthwash were scattered around him. Instead of sitting up, Anon simply turned his head towards Casey, who had begun pacing the room in a panic. When he spoke, his words came out in a fevered rush.

"I was at work, okay? And this, this... *thing*! It—or she—I don't know. She walked right up to my desk and started screaming at me." Casey threw his hands above his head, still pacing the room. "It was the most terrifying experience of my life. She was tall, and she was covered in feathers. Fucking feathers, man.

And she had these big wings and this frickin' tail! And that was made of feathers, too. But this is the worst part, she had this beak. Oh my God I swear it was longer than my arm! And she pointed it right at my face! I thought that she was gonna kill me!"

At that thought, Casey put his hands to his face and started to quiver. After a moment, he exhaled to regain his composure. "I mean, you should have seen this thing," Casey said. "It was the single most terrifying experience of my life," he repeated. "And no one tried to help me. Well, how could they? I mean they couldn't see it... But then all through the day people just kept coming up to me to try to talk. And I didn't want to talk to anyone after that. How could I? All I could think about was the frickin monster! And those eyes... I can't even tell you..."

"Are you done?" Anon asked. His eyes were closed again. Casey blinked in disbelief. "Am I done? What are you talking about? I just had the single—"

"The single most terrifying experience of your life, I know," Anon cut him off. "You don't think I had a rough day, too? You don't think that my experience wasn't the most terrifying fucking thing that I have ever seen?"

Casey was about to ask how anything Anon had seen that day could be scarier than coming face to face with a demon, but he held his tongue when he thought: *I forgot about the funeral.*

He quickly exhaled a few more times, leveling his hands to bring his emotion down.

"Okay, I'm sorry," Casey said, "But, what I'm saying affects the both of us. I really think that you'll want to hear what she said."

"You know what? I don't really care what she said. I don't really give a fuck anymore, okay? How's that?" Anon's eyes were still closed, so he didn't see the look of revulsion morph onto Casey's face.

"First of all, why are you being such a dick," Casey said, stifling his attempt at compassion. How can you be so inconsiderate, even after I told you what I've gone through today? Casey thought that he was going to explode; the heat between the two of them created mounting pressure in the room like gas. Suddenly, Casey scrunched his nose. "Fuck! What reeks in here?"

Anon's eyes snapped open, although he remained rigid in the bed. He pictured the rancid journal in its hiding place under the bed. "You can smell that?"

Casey covered his nose. "Yeah, it stinks."

Anon was quiet for a few moments. "Sorry, I just ripped a fart."

Now it was Casey's turn to hesitate. "Well, it smells like death."

Anon turned his head towards Casey. Their eyes met, and for a moment they shared an awkward silence. Then, they both started to laugh hysterically.

"On my bed, too?" Casey asked, through bouts of giggles that hardened his face and scraped viscous stress from his forehead.

"Sorry, man, I drank a lot, as you can see." Anon chuckled as he motioned to the bottles on the floor. He acknowledged internally that Casey had simply been broken by the violent absurdity, yet he was grateful that he could keep his journal a secret.

"At least your breath doesn't stink," Casey said, pointing to the half empty bottle of mouthwash.

"True," Anon said. He sat up and moved to the edge of the bed, putting his feet on the floor. He reached back and grabbed the mouthwash, unscrewed the cap, and took a gulp. He swallowed it without swishing it in his mouth. "Ahhh."

Casey made a face. "You're gross." He moved to open his windows. A cool breeze drifted into the room, and Anon's stink was more easily tolerated.

Anon smiled. "Well, you're stuck with me. So, tell me more about this big bird."

Casey laughed again. Surviving such a life-threatening encounter left him more susceptible to intense emotion on both sides of the spectrum. While he was first smoldering mad in fight or flight mode, he found himself strangely joyous in safety once the danger has passed.

"No, no. Tell me about your day. I was the one who suggested that you go to the... to the funeral. I want to hear about it."

Anon sighed and scratched the back of his neck. "It was okay," he said. "No, I mean, it wasn't okay, but you know what I mean."

Casey folded his hands and looked at Anon expectantly.

Anon looked up at the ceiling. "There were a lot of people there. They all seemed really sad. Especially the family. There were four of them. A brother, a sister, a mom, and a dad. Other people were crying, but the family hit me the hardest." Anon looked back into Casey's eyes. He found them comforting.

Casey, however, averted his gaze after a moment. He hadn't ever had an experience talking about death before. While he usually pictured these conversations as profoundly sad, he found himself, in the moment, feeling strangely awkward.

"Well, yeah, that's normal, right? I mean, it's your family."

"That's the thing. I didn't feel like they were my family. I didn't have any connection to them, really, since I don't have any personal memories from when I was alive. Or, I mean, when I was Rowan. But either way, I felt. . . I dunno. Guilty. I had this profound sense of guilt. Like, what's the guiltiest you've ever felt before?"

Casey thought back to when he had taken a Chemistry final in college. He failed the test and ended up having to retake the class. Confronting his parents with his failing grade had made him miserable. His stomach turned into a pit that seemed like it was expanding and contracting at the same time. An unseen weight crushed his arms and shoulders. The worst part of it was that he felt naked when his shame was bared, like Adam when he sinfully stood before God's judgment.

"Well, it was worse than that, I think," Anon replied. "I knew that I had done something that hurt a lot of people in ways that I will never fully understand. And even worse, I knew that I could never take it back. That guy in the casket... it was permanent. He's always going to be there, and his friends and family are always going to feel this hurt, this emptiness. I don't even feel bad for doing it to myself. I feel bad for how it made everyone else feel. And it's all my fault." He stared Casey right in the eyes and said earnestly, "I swear I will never do anything like that again."

"Well, do you want to go to the Tarwick's house? It could be good to be with them for a while. If, I mean... If you think it would help."

"No, I don't want to be around them. They are just torn apart, and I don't need to see any more of the consequences of Rowan's actions. Plus, when I went up to them after the funeral, they became a disturbing mixture of depressed and horny. Not a pretty sight." Casey nodded his head, unsure of what to say next. "Enough about me. I don't really want to talk about it anymore. What happened with this other sc'ermin?"

"Come on, we aren't done talking about you yet."

"I said I don't want to talk about the funeral anymore. And besides, what happened to you effects both of us. I'm the one who's going to have to fight her."

"You have a point," Casey said. "Okay, here goes." He took a deep breath and replayed the day's events.

The woman had burst through the door, waving her wings in a grand entrance. She strutted up to Casey's desk and flaunted her tail. Then, when she was sure that Casey was thoroughly impressed by her majesty (although horrified was more appropriate) she began to deliver her decree. The woman tilted back her head and raised her two-foot beak in the air like a trumpet. With the aplomb of a royal announcer, the sc'ermin declared her demands.

"She said that you two are to fight at high noon this Friday," Casey said nervously. He was shaken after telling Anon about the sc'ermin's entrance.

"She said 'high noon?' Does she think she's a fuckin' cowboy or something?"

"From the way she presented herself you would think she was more like the sheriff's royal benefactor. But, yeah, that's what she said. She set the time and date like it was some kind of Roman sporting event."

"Well, fuck that," Anon said. "Why should *she* get to pick the time?"

"Hey, at least she was up front about it," Casey said. "It's better than getting ambushed, right?"

"I guess so," Anon said. He remembered the surprise attack of his first foe. "Did she specify a place for this fight?"

Casey thought back to what the woman had said. "She wants to fight in the parking lot of a movie theatre. Says that it will be wide open and empty."

Anon snorted. "The parking lot? Fuck cowboys, now she sounds like a high school bully."

"How can you be so cavalier about this? This–monster—wants to fight to the death, and you're making jokes about it."

Anon shrugged. "I dunno. I'm just not scared. And if you haven't noticed, I'm a monster, too." Anon bared his sharp teeth in a broad smile. "I can take her."

"No, you don't understand," Casey said, wiping sweat from his ever paling forehead. "You still look human. She was like a literal monster. I told you about her beak and the feathers and the wings… and… oh…" Casey trailed off, too frightened to continue.

"Don't worry about it, Casey. I can take her. I beat that last guy, right?"

"But we just got lucky last time," Casey blustered. "You said that your whole chest was ripped out. If Bob didn't knock out his human, I bet you would have died."

Anon scowled. "I wouldn't have died. I had that guy right where I wanted him." He cast his gaze aside. "But you're right. We need to have a plan. What are we going to do?"

"I don't know," Casey said. He fanned himself with his hands. "I'll talk to Fix and see what he thinks."

The pair's informant attempted to shed some light on the situation.

???-???-????: I believe that this sc'ermin is a Pride based on your description. Pride is a unique type. Based on my research, Prides' strength is highly influenced by the tide of battle. If she finds herself losing, she will ultimately give up fairly quickly. However, if she perceives herself to be winning, she will gain power.

Caseybent44: So what do you suggest we do?

???-???-????: This sc'ermin sounds very advanced and developed, and she has probably already defeated several others. Since Rowan has only absorbed one other sc'ermin, this fight should be tough. However, I have located a weak sc'ermin that he can consume in the meantime to prepare.

Casey excitedly showed Anon the phone. "See this? Fix said that this one is gonna be hard to fight, but you can get stronger beforehand."

"I know how to read," Anon said.

Casey was dismayed to see that Anon's mirth had been short lived and his hostility was creeping back.

"And my name isn't Rowan. I'm not him, and he's dead."

"Okay, okay," Casey said, putting his hands up in defense.

Caseybent44: So where is this sc'ermin?

???-???-????: I can send you the address and the instructions about how to get there.

Caseybent44: Thanks. Is there anything that Anon should know about this guy?

Fix took a little longer to answer than usual.

???-???-????: I believe that this sc'ermin is a Sloth. Since he and his human never leave their house, they have never had to fight before. This means that Rowan should have an advantage. He will go at night when the human is sleeping.

Caseybent44: But you said that the human's behaviors affected their sc'ermin's strength so if a Sloth's human was sleeping wouldn't that make it more powerful?

???-???-????: Very perceptive, Casey. You pick this up fast. But don't worry. My intel leads me to believe that this fight should not be an issue.

Caseybent44: Ok I believe you but if you don't mind me asking where you get this information?

???-???-????: I'm sorry, but I do mind. I cannot disclose that at this time, but perhaps if we keep working together you may find out my methods in the future. I will send you the address, entrance route, and blueprint of the apartment. Send a message when the sc'ermin is defeated.

CHAPTER 15

JANUARY 27ᵀᴴ: Is it any small wonder the self-contempt that I feel, as I sit in this closet lined with perverted, distorted mirrors? Alone, within this confine, there is nothing to examine but the wretched creatures that surround me. To my left, the twisted, ugly shapelessness of the hunchback, who constantly thirsts for men that cringe at the mere thought of holding his hand and would rather vomit than press their lips unto his. To my right, the despicable wonton who lusts for ecstasy, allowing his grotesque shame to spill forth whilst wearing a greasy smile meant to disarm but that only manages to simultaneously terrify and invoke pity. Behind me, the contorted blue face and protruding eyeballs of a panting figure wracked with pain, who tries to bear an unseen weight in a panicked struggle like a rat caught under an unyielding boot. And in front of me, a pallid visage that somehow expresses immense and ghastly horror, though the milky portals to his soul have rolled back and he has no mouth with which to twist into a terrible frown or visceral scream.

Late that Tuesday night, Casey smiled as he turned off the notifications on his phone. His microblog mentions made his cell phone vibrate so hard that the device seemed apt to break.

That should be enough questions for the Q and A.

He looked over at Anon, who was leaning against Casey's bedroom door.

"What are you so happy about?" Anon asked. He scowled, and a dark cloud seemed to hang over his head.

Casey's smile dissipated. "Why are you mad at me? I purposely set up this Q and A so that my fans would be paying extra attention to me tonight. This way, you'll have that much more strength while you fight the Sloth."

Anon make an exaggerated frown, waved his hands on either side of his face, and mocked him, saying, "Oh, you're so smart Casey. How ever will I thank you?"

"You know what Fix said. You and I are linked. When *I* get attention, *you* get stronger." Anon ceased his mockery, replacing his fake frown with a sneer. "Just don't act so smug about it. Don't you forget: without me, you wouldn't even be famous in the first place."

Casey furrowed his brow. "You know what? Why don't you just leave, if you're going to be such an asshole to me."

"Fine! That's all I'm good for anyway, right? Fighting your battles for you, putting my life on the line. And you don't even care, do you?"

Casey's face reddened as he tried to push back the tears he felt welling up behind his eyes. "I just thought that I would help," he said.

"Whatever," Anon said. "Make your little video. Just remember what it could cost me." With that, Anon left the room, slamming the door behind him.

Left alone, Casey sniffed back his tears.

Why does he have to be so mean?

Casey stared at his wall. Anon had turned downright cruel. Before, he was aggressively lewd, but it was a less biting type of rudeness.

Casey tried his best to repress the thoughts of Anon, tried to wrinkle over the parts of his brain that thought of him. There was no time to think of anything else other than the important livestream that had to be recorded. The camera was set, the lighting was perfect, and the questions were in. Casey flipped the switch on his camera and saw himself in a little box on his computer screen.

"Oh no," Casey said to himself. Red, puffy eyes would not be appropriate for this video. His audience would see through his phony joviality after Anon's harassment. If he shot a video when he felt this depressed, his audience would get depressed while watching it. No, he would have to wait a bit until he calmed down.

Casey decided to do what he always did when he was feeling down. He clicked on his browser to visit Trevor Greenbrook's social media page. He scoffed, though, when he found what Anon had left on their browser.

"Slut Gets Split In Half By Massive-"

Casey clicked away from the porn that put him in an even fouler mood. Sure, Anon was a Lust, but his usage of pornography was disgusting. The other day, Casey accidently saw a frame of fetish porn that Anon had found somewhere in the darkest, most depraved hole of the web.

Casey, again, tried to physically mold his brain over the thought. He proceeded to his favorite corner of the Internet.

Trevor stared back at Casey from behind his black frames. The green haired man smiled in his familiar half smirk that Casey was so fond of. It made him seem mysterious, yet inviting, like he was harboring a code to a private game. Casey would only have to play along to find out what it was. He longed to hear what Trevor would say to him if they met in real life. Casey often fantasized about the moment.

They would meet in a coffee shop. Trevor would be standing in line in front of Casey. Casey would want to say something, but he would be at a loss for words. Then, when Trevor ordered his coffee, he would casually glance back and ask Casey what he would like. Casey would tremble and be left speechless. Trevor would simply chuckle and order Casey the same thing that he ordered for himself, then ask Casey to sit with him.

They would talk for hours, complimenting each other and teasing each other's mouths by leaning in for kisses that never met...

Casey blinked suddenly. His eyes felt as if they were burning after inadvertently staring at the screen for so long.

I told myself that it was no use thinking about celebrities in that way. I'll never be with them, so there is no point in giving myself so much false hope. I'll just get hurt when it finally sinks in that I will never get to date him.

Yet, the newly perceived inevitability of their marriage was rooting deep within him. What had before been an impossible probability, might now be within his reach. Anon held the key to make it all possible, yet he acted as an emotional gatekeeper that had Casey doubt himself.

To Casey, Trevor wasn't like other personalities who only appeared on TV and in movies, never really communicating with their fans. Trevor's brand of social media celebrity offered much more intimacy. It seemed as if Trevor created his videos specifically for Casey. They sat down with each other every week and held conversations about pertinent issues that Casey would coincidentally be dealing with, such as problems with straight men, the newest fashion trends, or what happened on their favorite reality show. Trevor sent Casey pictures of his face, his hair, what he was eating or what he was watching, as well as messages about his mood and his opinions, even interesting pictures or videos that he found online.

As far as Casey was concerned, he and Trevor shared a close friendship. Tragically, this was one friend that he may never meet in person, a friend that he could only listen to, never interact with. Casey's heart ached at the thought that he could never be with someone whom he felt he knew so well.

Remember, you don't know the real him. Only the persona that he created for the public. But I could get to know the real him. If only we met…

Casey covered Trevor's page with his instant messaging app after several minutes of deliberation. The visits always gave Casey mixed feelings. Sure, seeing his crush's face again filled Casey with joy. But, at the same time, he felt the pain of an outsider who watches someone from afar but can never reach them. Casey went through periods where he shunned this shining star, whom he admired from so far away, but he always relapsed into his addiction. The only cure from the tears was talking to his real friends to distract him from the one he only wished that he had.

Luckily, Bill and Charlie were both online. As soon as Casey signed into his messaging app, he was invited to their group chat. The window popped up where Bill and Charlie's usernames were waiting.

Trevor's face peeked at him from behind the text box.

Bb_cakes720: Casey good thing you're on I was about to text you

Bill answered the chat a mere moment after Casey logged in, meaning that he had already been eager to share some news.

Caseybent44: Hey Bill hey Charlie whats going on

Bb_cakes720: Casey Charlie has something that he wants to tell you

Charlie368: Bill do you have to be so up front about it? D:

Charlie368: D:

Casey could imagine the look on Charlie's face signified by the emoticon.

Bb_cakes720: Why the sad face? This is good news!!!

Caseybent44: What is it?

Charlie368: I know but I'm nervous.

Bb_cakes720: Don't be nervous we are all your friends

Caseybent44: What is it?

Charlie368: I know but this is nerve wracking and you know how I get

Bb_cakes720: Okay but you know that Casey is gonna be here for you and I am already here.

Caseybent44: lksajdfhlkjdhf GUYS

Caseybent44: What is it?

Bb_cakes720: JEEZ Charlie tell him.

Charlie368: Ok

Charlie368: Casey, I've been keeping this a secret for a long time. But I finally need to tell you

Casey misunderstood people, in general, while he was in the closet. When someone harbors a secret that consumes their thoughts day in and day out, they might begin to believe that others are holding secrets, too. If someone is in the closet for a long enough time, they may begin to think that other people that they meet is also in the closet.

Like a raw nerve, the topic of homosexuality is in the forefront of a closeted person's mind, especially during conversation. So, whenever someone told a secret to a closeted Casey, he would always hope that they would come out to him. That way, the two could share their secret together.

A secret kept by one person gnaws away at their insides, starting at the corner of their mind and working its way in, but a secret shared by two acts as a glue to strengthen the bonds between them. Thus, Casey would always want his secret to transform from a corrosive to a cohesive whenever the topic of secret subjects emerged.

Now that Casey was out of the closet, however, he did not think about his sexuality as much. He was no longer required to "maintain" it, so to speak. Someone in the closet tends to keep thinking about his sexuality, lest it escape their lips, as if it were a balloon tied to a string liable to float away forever at the slightest neglect.

Another reason sexuality is so salient in a closeted person's mind is that they frequently project opinions of it onto everyone that they meet, an exhausting and alienating practice that only serves in exacerbating the person's own worries about themselves.

So, now that Casey was out of the closet, he no longer jumped to the conclusion that every secret would involve coming out. Thus, Charlie's message thoroughly surprised him.

Charlie368: Casey, I've already told Bill this. I am gay.

When Bill had come out to him, he sat Casey down after school and confessed the secret that he had been keeping his entire life. Casey felt relief when he heard that he wasn't alone. He also felt fear; that someone might hear, or that he had misheard, and that one of his best friends was experiencing the same tribulations as he was. Casey and Bill's hearts connected as equals that day.

Charlie's confession had a completely different effect on Casey. Instead of a mutual confidant, Casey felt like an authority on the subject receiving a request for advice from a novice. Casey had experiences of coming out of the closet, and he knew that it felt good. Coming out was one of the best things that he had ever done, even though sometimes it came with pain. Charlie, unfamiliar with the process, was still afraid. But, Casey felt that he could be a good guide to assist him.

Casey was speechless for a moment, but quickly typed in a response so that Charlie wouldn't feel awkward in the silence.

Caseybent44: OMG Charlie! That is so awesome! I had no idea!

Charlie368: Thanks I don't know why I kept it secret for so long

Bb_cakes720: Really? You didn't know?

Caseybent44: Of course I would understand Charlie I'm also gay in case you forgot

Charlie368: I don't know its just that I was really nervous to come out and I didn't know what was going to happen after I did I should have known that there was no problem coming out to you

Caseybent44: we are your best friends you know that and we will always be there for you

Bb_cakes720: you mean u really didn't know?

As a newly appointed liaison for Charlie between the closet and the rest of the world, Casey proposed that he should ask some questions to find out how he was feeling. He was online, after all, and emotions could not be perceived through facial expressions or body language. When Casey had come out to his family, there was a lot of hugging and crying, signifying acceptance, relief, and happiness. Online, there were only words, so Casey had to get as many words as he could out of his friend.

Caseybent44: how long have you known that you were gay?

Charlie368: I don't know as long as I can remember it might have been since I was like 10 maybe

Caseybent44: Yeah I was the same way

Bb_cakes720: me too

Charlie368: I feel like Ive been holding on to this secret forever its been eating me up inside

Caseybent44: I felt the same way I had to come out to my family because I just couldn't lie anymore

Caseybent44: is that why you decided to come out? You couldn't hold on to the lie anymore?

Charlie took a while to answer. Three dots bounced in harmony to denote that Charlie was writing a long message.

Charlie368: I just hated having to look over my shoulder all of the time to make sure I didn't do anything that could be perceived as gay, to accidentally out myself. I hated having to act as masculine as I possibly could in order to hide the fact that I am gay and I couldn't admit that I thought certain male celebrities were attractive to me. I hated leading girls on as a cover. Remember Alexa a while back? She was really sad when I broke up with her for no reason. I couldn't bring myself to tell her that I was gay so I just broke off communication from her. I know that she blames herself. I really hate being a liar and feeling disgusted with myself all of the time never knowing if what I feel is right. I just hated being in the closet.

Caseybent44: wow that's a lot. Im sure that it feels the same way to a lot of guys who don't come out.

Bb_cakes720: yeah, it must be really tough to hold on to a secret for that long to always be scared of being found out

Caseybent44: its really a bad secret to hold especially when it turns out to be no big deal when you come out

Charlie368: thanks for cheering me up guys good thing I came out in time

Charlie368: but then anyway that all piled up in my mind all day every day 24/7 and all I could think about was how much I hated being in the closet and how much I wanted to come out but I never could do it but it was always on the tip of my tongue but I could never get the chance to say it

Caseybent44: sometimes it feels easier to say nothing but it is so much better to be active and just say it

Charlie368: but then when I was driving to the supermarket for my parents this afternoon I got stuck behind this car on Freidman Road you know the one with all the trees? So I was on this road behind all of the cars, and their back window was really reflective in the darkness of the trees and there was this shape in the window but I couldn't tell what it was. And then we got out of the trees and the light shone through the back window and I saw all of these balloons in the back seat and they were all jostling around each other pressing up onto the roof of the car and the back window and I just stared at them for so long because they reminded me of people jostling each other in the back seat trying to get a better look out the window, and then I had a sense that they were like dogs in a cage trying to get closer to someone who might set them free. And I stared at it for so long as we drove down the road, I almost forgot that I was driving. The associations I was making kept changing, but the *vibe* was that it was a group or collective trying to go beyond themselves. When we got to a red light I wasn't paying attention and almost crashed into it. And all that I could think of then was that if I had crashed into the car then all of the balloons would have exploded, and even though that wouldn't have been the biggest issue there I just started crying.

There was a pause in the conversation until Bill answered:

Bb_cakes720: that's really cool and all but wtf does that mean ahah

Caseybent44: come on Bill that is a beautiful moment its really symbolic

Charlie368: I know it sounds cheesy but it literally happened to me like I am not even lying at all it happened for real today and it totally affected my decision

Caseybent44: well I'm glad that you finally get to live truthfully. Trust me it feels really good

Charlie368: thanks Casey

Caseybent44: You're welcome charlie

Bb_cakes720: guys guys I'm sooooo happy. Now we have a big gay trio!

Caseybent44: now all we have to do is wait for Shiest to come out

Charlie368: oh god no pleeeease I don't want him to ruin this great community that I have just entered

Bb_cakes720: noooooooooo

Caseybent44: its fine guys I was just jokin arounddd

Suddenly, Bill sent a private message to Casey. When a group chat was going on, an unaffiliated private chat was the equivalent of a whisper or a passed note, completely invisible to the other conversationalists.

Bb_cakes720: Casey

Caseybent44: whats up Bill?

Bb_cakes720: how excited are you that Charlie came out?

Charlie368: guys seriously just thanks for making me feel good about this.

Caseybent44: im really excited about it. I mean that's awesome.

Bb_cakes720: and you really didn't know about it before?

Caseybent44: I really didn't know why

Bb_cakes720: I mean he was really hushed up about it but sometimes it showed through the cracks if you know what I mean

Charlie368: I mean it just feels so good to finally get rid of that secret

Bb_cakes720: yeah he told me not to tell you but I think you should know. The reason that he was so nervous to come out to you was that he has massive feelings for you.

Casey involuntarily gasped, and his heart skipped a beat. He saw his face go red in the recording window that was still open on his desktop. Trevor Greenbrook's face still stared longingly from behind the chat box.

Casey didn't know how to answer Bill.

Bb_cakes720: Isn't this good news? Don't you like him?

Casey's feelings were complicated by Charlie's previously incompatible sexual orientation. When he had first met Charlie, Casey experienced intense infatuation for him. However, he tried his hardest to suppress those feelings since he would never have a chance to date a straight person. Years of suppression stomped flat the fields of Casey's attraction to Charlie, although a few sprouts still clung to life amid the trampled debris.

Long ago, Casey would have jumped at the chance to be with Charlie, romantically. Now, though, his attraction had gone stale. And, with Casey's growing popularity online and the possibility of Anon bringing him into the arms of Trevor Greenbrook, Casey did not know whether he even could connect in such an intimate way to one of his best friends.

Casey had evidently been taking a long time to answer, so Bill sent a message to lessen any possible tension.

Bb_cakes720: its fine if you don't like him I wont tell him that I told you anything you know its really fine

Caseybent44: I just need some time to think about it Charlie is one of my best friends and I don't know if I can break a friendship to be with him like that

Bb_cakes720: well you wont be breaking a friendship wouldn't you be strengthening it by taking it to the next step

Caseybent44: but like what if it doesn't work out then what it would ruin our friendship

Bb_cakes720: that's the worst-case scenario why are you being so pessimistic

Caseybent44: Bill why are you pushing this so much just give me some time to think about it

Bb_cakes720: well you don't want to break his heart

Caseybent44: what about my heart? This is just so complicated

Bb_cakes720: idk whats wrong with you the other day you said that you wish that Charlie were gay

Caseybent44: that was hypothetical it doesn't mean anything when you say stuff while shooting the breeze

Bb_cakes720: well you shouldn't say stuff like that when the guy came out for you

Caseybent44: he came out for me?

Bb_cakes720: yeah he really likes you and he came out to be with you

Caseybent44: that's putting a lot of pressure on me you know you cant just do stuff like that like choosing what you want other people to do

Bb_cakes720: hey it wasn't me who did it

Caseybent44: but you didn't have to tell me about it

Charlie368: hey are you guys haven't answered in a while

Bb_cakes720: but isn't it better to know?

Caseybent44: no because now I am no longer innocent in the situation.

Charlie368: hey are you guys in another chat?

Bb_cakes720: but now you have all of the information to act in the best way

Caseybent44: but I don't know the best way to act

Charlie368: omg you guys are in a side chat

Caseybent44: sorry Charlie I was editing

Charlie368: oh ok are you sure

Caseybent44: yeah and I should probably get back to it

Caseybent44: but thanks for coming out it really means a lot to me and Bill and you know that we will be there for you

Charlie368: thanks Casey I know

Caseybent44: okay I g2g but ill see you tomorrow babe

Charlie368: yupp ill see you tomorrow ;)

Casey gazed back Trevor's full face once he closed his chat tabs. His idol seemed so calm, so secure. Casey put his face into his hands.

Babe... why did I have to call him babe... I never call him babe.

CHAPTER 16

February 4th: I used to think that God came to Earth in human form so that He would know what it was like to be human. He would probably be confused as to why humans are so evil and disobedient, since God is so perfect and unlike us. However, I have come to a different understanding. God must have grown to hate humans, who He previously thought was His greatest creation. He made us in His image, and we showed Him that that image was evil. When He realized that a "perfect" creator who creates an imperfect self-portrait is therefore Himself imperfect, He judged that He couldn't live anymore. Since He is immortal, the only way to do this was to first become human. Then, He tried to give us a parting gift of knowledge and we crucified him for it. The worst part is that even though He resolved to die, we didn't have to kill Him. What an ironic end, that the beings that He gave life took life from Him. If His own creation brought about His end, does that mean that He killed Himself?

Anon arrived under the cover of darkness. Breaking into the Sloth's apartment wasn't difficult the second time around. The first time, though, Anon fell as he attempted to scale the building to the third floor. A spiked fence broke his fall, and Anon was left to climb the wall again with only slight impalement damage to his left glute.

When he reached his target's window, Anon used a tool that Fix had prescribed. He had taken it from a hardware store earlier that day. The tool hooked under the top of the frame, and Anon undid the lock with a twist. He could have easily smashed the window, but Fix had warned against waking a sleeping Sloth.

What kind of beast will this thing be? An actual sloth? No, that is too obvious. A sleeping bear? I would not want to wake that thing up.

The apartment was pitch black, but Anon was able to see well in the dark ever since he had eaten the heart of his first sc'ermin. Anon shivered at the thought. He suddenly regretted his duty as a sc'ermin.

In the heat of the moment, Anon had no qualms about devouring the heart of his enemy. Now, though, the mere thought of the action made him nauseous. Of course, he would do anything for Casey. Anon could never say no—ultimately—to that pretty face. Any words that came from those soft lips were his commands. Anon felt bad for yelling at Casey earlier, but he had just felt so neglected. It's as if Casey only cared about Trevor Greenbrook, and not the person who was standing in front of him.

Not that Casey even counts me as a person anyway...

Either way, this enemy had to be defeated. Anon wished that he could simply do his duty instead of contemplating what it all might mean. Unfortunately, he brooded over his life—if you could call it that—after his funeral.

No. After Rowan's funeral.

Before that, Anon had felt invincible. Afterward, though, he could sense his mortality like a raw nerve. His obsession with his humanity stemmed from seeing his own decrepit, bloated carcass. That, and reading the book that it had left behind. Anon had only read a few pages of Rowan's journal before having to put it down.

That kid must have had a seriously fucked up mind if that is the kind of journal he kept. No wonder he killed himself.

Even if the *words* on the pages weren't unsavory, the putrid *smell* of the pages themselves would have made Anon close the covers. The rancid smell of death and decomposition had become infused in the book from its time in the noxious coffin. Each foul page stung Anon's nostrils when he tried to read them. There was no way to wash out the stink, either, as treating it with any sort of cleaning supplies would ruin the paper and ink.

As much as Anon detested the tainted tome, he had resolved to read it. Even though he didn't fully admit it to himself, Anon wanted to know more about the person whose death had created him. He wanted to keep the book a secret, though. One reason for this was to honor Rowan's request for secrecy on the first page. The page asked that no one read the rest of the journal. After much consideration, Anon decided that it was fine for him to read since it belonged to his former body.

Keeping it from Casey was hard, though, because of the stench. Anon was able to blame it on flatulence the first time, but it would be impossible to hide the book in the house for long. Anon opted to bury the book in the back yard like a dog with a bone. He stole a small chest from Casey to keep the book from incurring any damage underground. There, the stink couldn't be detected and the chances of anyone stumbling onto it were slim.

Anon didn't know if sc'ermin could become depressed or not, but he was in a bad mood ever since finding that book. He ha transitioned to drinking mouthwash, and he had snapped at Casey earlier. While Anon was regretful about being so harsh, his austerity wasn't totally unwarranted. After all, Anon was breaking into a third story apartment to fight a demon while Casey was at home microblogging.

I guess I really got the shit end of the stick in this deal, huh.

As Anon crawled through the window, he pushed all thoughts from his mind to focus on the task at hand. Distraction might cost him his life.

Anon found himself in the kitchen. The room was enveloped in darkness, but a dim strip of light shone from under a doorway across from the window. The kitchen was small, crammed with boxes of microwavable food that should have been kept cold. A refrigerator with bare white doors stood next to a cluttered sink. Dishes, silverware, and glasses were piled into the sink, all of them covered with stains to match the counters. On the other wall was a microwave with a forgotten cup of instant soup inside; empty cupboards surrounded it.

Anon crept to the door and put his ear to the wood. On top of Anon's improved eyesight, his hearing had been dramatically enhanced as well. The sc'ermin could clearly hear voices from the other side of the door. He silently cursed Fix for giving him a bad time to sneak in. Then, he heard a tune that he recognized. Anon slowly pushed the door open and stepped into the living room.

The first thing that Anon noticed was the massive television that stood at the front of the room facing the kitchen. The large screen was displaying what a reality program that Casey and he sometimes watched. Anon hated reality TV, but this time he was glad to see that the room was otherwise unoccupied.

A bewildered looking man was being interviewed on the show.

"You know these 'reality' programs are poison, right? All of this bickering, gossiping, and bi*ching makes people think that they want drama in their lives. My wife starts petty quarrels with me all of the time because she sees it on your show."

In the center of the room, facing away from the kitchen, sat a recliner that matched the TV in size. Anon snooped behind it and peered over the headrest. The cushy chair was filled by an equally cushy woman, snoring softly. Her greasy tank top, stained with cheese dust and various sauces, heaved as each ragged breath squeezed between her jowls. Anon felt his chest tighten with anxiety. He didn't want to wake this leviathan from her apparent food coma.

Ugh. If that behemoth is the human, I hate to think what her sc'ermin looks like.

Anon carefully eyed the woman's mouth for a set of tusks, just to make sure. All he found was a sparse set of yellowed—albeit otherwise normal—teeth.

That would be too easy, huh. Well, let's find this hibernating beast, then.

"The fact that you're letting me say this on your show either tells me that you guys are really ballsy or really fu*king stupid."

The bleep that the show used was brief enough that the entirety of the swear could basically be heard.

Anon prowled back around the chair and surveyed the room. A small side table stood to the left of the recliner, holding a laptop. Its charger ran from the table to the wall about 6 feet away. Discarded pizza boxes and Chinese food cartons took up a lot of the space in between. The area to the other side of the recliner was much more interesting.

A heap of papers and envelopes were piled by the door on the right side. Anon noticed that the door was the main entrance to the apartment, judging by the mail slot. Out of curiosity, he investigated some of the papers. Many of the unopened envelopes contained spam mail, but dozens more were checks and prizes. Several different sweepstakes companies' logos were stamped onto checks that ranged in worth from $1,000 to $15,000. A large cardboard check worth $13,000 was propped up against the wall next to the door. Estimating only from the opened checks, Anon guessed that there was around $500,000 in prize money.

Maybe that's what her sc'ermin does for her. Keeps winning her money so that she can sit on her ass and order pizza.

Aside from the kitchen, the only other way to go was through a dark hallway to the right of the TV.

Anon skulked through the corridor. Three doors were in the hall. Anon opened the first one, closest to the living room.

Drip. Drip. Drip.

Anon found himself in a small bathroom with a sink, a toilet, and a tub. The shower curtain was drawn, and small splashes sounded from behind it. Anon bared his teeth, then slowly peeked behind the curtain. He was expecting to discover some kind of whale or snapping turtle resting in the water. All he found, though, was an empty tub with a pink ring around it. The rusty faucet dripped droplets of water into the dirty puddle around the clogged drain. Anon snuck back into the hall and closed the door.

The next room appeared to be the master bedroom. Although this room was almost pitch black, Anon could see relatively well. Baggy clothes covered the floor like hay in a stable. The bed was disheveled, although it didn't look like anyone had slept there for a while: clothes and delivery boxes were piled on top of the mattress. A yellow smiley face, printed on a bib, suffocated under a heap of dark clothing.

Anon made his way to the dresser, which stood at about waist height. Leaning on the wall was a slightly concave mirror that gave Anon a slimmer appearance. A framed picture sat atop the dresser, too. In it, the beastly woman wore a wedding gown. Her arm was draped around an equally obese man who wore a suit. They both smiled weakly. Anon only glimpsed at the picture for a moment. He turned around to resume his search for the sc'ermin. There was a closed closet in the room, and Anon slunk over it.

Looks like a good spot for a lazy lion to make its den, no?

Anon grabbed the door with his left hand. He crouched, bared his teeth, and readied his right claw to swipe at whatever might pounce from inside. When he opened the closet, though, he only found more women's clothes hanging from the railing. Anon sighed his relief and shut the door.

That left only one room to check. His prey must be inside.

Anon crept towards the final room. When he was back in the hallway, edging toward the door that must have contained his enemy, he heard a snort from the living room.

He froze and prayed that he didn't disturb the Sloth. It was the one thing that Fix had warned him against.

He stalked back through the hall and peeked his head into the living room. The blob on the chair shifted a little, let loose a fart, and nestled its head back within its bosom like a gelatinous turtle. Anon narrowed his eyes and turned back towards the final room.

Anon placed his ear against the door, listening for any snoring that might come from a slumbering giant. Instead, he heard the muffled sound of white noise.

Well, it's now or never. Anon gritted his teeth. His last assailant had caught him off guard, but this time he was the one with the element of surprise. It felt good to be on the opposite end of the veil of ignorance. He mustn't let his advantage go to waste, though. He needed to pounce with all of his force and end the fight before his enemy even knew what was happening.

He's probably asleep. That's probably why Fix said this fight would be easy. Either way, I need to keep my guard all the way up.

Anon turned the knob, opened the door just wide enough, and slipped silently into the room.

His eyes quickly adjusted to the black. The room's soft white walls were painted with light blue trim. Yellow ducks with smiley faces formed a ring around the ceiling. The room was bare, apart from one piece of furniture. In the middle of the room stood an empty, stark white crib with a light blue skirt dusting the floor.

Still poised to attack, Anon crouched and surveyed the room again. He saw no other places for an enemy to hide. There was no closet, no window, and no hatch doors anywhere. Only the crib took presence in the room.

Anon checked the inside of the crib. The only thing resting inside was a blue and white striped pillow. Anon scratched his chin with a long nail. He considered whether he should leave the room, but then decided to peek underneath the crib.

There wasn't much space beneath it, so he doubted that anything worth fighting would be hiding within the confines of the skirt. He backed away from it and lay prone (after checking his surroundings again for any danger) and strained his eye towards the space between the skirt and the floor.

I swear if I get attacked while I'm face down ass up peeking under this thing... While there didn't appear to be any life underneath the crib, there was a dark shape that Anon couldn't fully identify. The shape was perfectly still, though, so he didn't think that it was alive. It looked more like a box than a sleeping sc'ermin.

Anon crawled towards the crib on his hands and knees. Tentatively, with more fear than curiosity, he lifted the skirt, half expecting something to jump out at him. Instead, he discovered a hidden container.

Anon reached under the crib, gripped the object, and extracted a metal safe that was cool to the touch. On its back, with the door on top, the safe was about two feet tall, three feet wide, and three feet long. "Arthur's 'Unbreakable' Firearm Storage" was printed in typical Wild Western script on the door. A thick black dial protruded from the left side of the door and an 'L' shaped handle stuck out underneath it.

Anon lifted the safe with ease and slowly inspected its sides. The bottom of the safe read, "Impenetrable. Steel Alloy. Empty Weight: 150 pounds."

Anon laughed to himself. In his hands, the safe felt like 5 pounds. He considered trying to spin it on his finger like a basketball but thought better of it.

Also on the underside were directions to open the unit:

1: Spin dial to the right five (5) times
2: Turn dial to the right to the first number
3: Turn the dial to the left, passing the first number once, until you reach the second number.
4: Turn dial to the right directly to the third number.

I wonder what's inside anyway...

Anon idly spun the dial around, following the directions but landing on random numbers. When he was done, he gripped the handle.

How funny would it be if I actually got the code right?

Anon wrenched the handle with all of his strength. It splintered away from the safe, leaving a gaping hole in the door.

"Holy fuck," Anon hissed. He looked around in fear hoping that he didn't wake the giant in the other room. He sat, petrified, for a full minute. When no one else came into the room and he was sure that the human was still in her chair, he sighed his relief.

Anon looked down at what he had done. The door sat lamely on its hinges with a jagged hole where the handle used to be. Anon suddenly noticed that his whitened hand was still tightly wrapped around the mechanism. His fingers creaked when he straightened them out and dropped the now useless piece of metal on the floor. Soft bubbling sounds started to drift from within the hole. Anon didn't have a clue where the noises came from, but he guessed it came from the hot steel being torn apart.

Anon dipped two of his fingers into the hole and gently pulled open the door. When he saw what was inside, he whispered, "Holy fuck," this time with awe instead of fear.

Gingerly, he produced from the safe the most magnificent object that he had ever seen. Anon held a florescent pink conch shell, the size of a watermelon, that seemed to glow in the darkness. It twisted into a point like a unicorn's horn. Brilliant spindles jutted from the shell in rings like the points of a crown. The shell was as smooth as the surface of a rainbow. At the bottom, the brilliant shell flared out, leaving an opening underneath. Anon turned over the beautiful shell to examine the bottom. He couldn't see inside, because the opening was blocked by the smooth gray foot of the creature within.

Anon didn't realize what he was holding, so he poked at the foot. He was startled to see that the hard surface retracted when he prodded it. Curiously, he kept poking the foot until it suddenly regressed into the shell with a slurp. With the inside exposed, the fleshy pink body of the inhabitant was visible. With more bubbling sounds, the body twisted inside of its shell, until a face turned toward the outside.

Anon stared, aghast, at the slimy face of the infant that was housed in the shell. The baby had its eyes closed, and it yawned softly, sticking out a slug-like tongue. The baby smacked its lips and opened its eyes. For a tense moment, Anon and the infant stared at each other.

Then, the tiny sc'ermin screamed.

CHAPTER 17

SOMETIMES I WONDER if the world religions are correct, and the meaning to life is love. I suppose that any meaning would be better than a nihilistic wasteland, and what better meaning than love, something that everyone wants to have? I've felt love, or at least I think I have. If love is one sided, is it even really love? Does it need its other half to be complete, elsewise withering under its own weight? This must be the case, because the only love I have known has hurt. Maybe that's what love really is. Just a nightmare disguised as a daydream, lulling us into its grip with sweet nothings whispered in our ears. Love is suffering if you ask me. And if the meaning of life is to suffer, then nihilism seems all the more attractive.

Casey scrambled out of his bed when he saw Anon's bright eyes staring at him in the inky dark of night. He had awoken at the dreamlike sensation of someone watching him. He quickly came to realize that his nightmare was a reality.

"I'm back," Anon said as Casey flicked on the light. Casey could see his sc'ermin's pupils contract when the lamps were on. Other than the look of snide frustration that he wore plainly on his face, Anon looked exactly the same. "How did your little livestream go?"

"Uh, well… it was amazing. I was keeping steady six hundred thousand viewers for about two hours." Casey hugged himself at the thought of his stream, where the questions exploded onto the screen in real time, much faster than he could read them.

"Good," Anon said. He took a seat on the floor and scratched his ear. Casey looked for a sign of mutation that may have occurred. Fix had told him that eating sc'erva would make someone more demon-like. Stronger. More terrifying. More likely to kill.

Anon didn't appear to be any of those things. He was presently downing a bottle of mouthwash that he found on the hardwood beside him.

Anon continued, saying, "I didn't really need the help, either way. The fight was easy." He thought back to when the infant started its cry that almost burst his eardrums. He knew he had to find a way to make it quiet, one way or the other.

"Just like Fix said."

"Right. You see, the thing was just a baby." Anon could hear the pounding of the giant human's footsteps down the hall. "It was just an infant, and that bitch had to go and ruin it."

"What are you talking about? Do you mean that—" Casey's voice trailed off when he put two and two together. The other sc'ermin's own mother killed it to reap the rewards.

Well, she had nothing left now.

"Yeah, killed her own child. For what? A bunch of scratch off tickets and some pizza." Anon saw the door open and the mother squeezing through the frame.

"That's terrible," Casey said. "I'm really sorry that you had to go through that."

"Me, too." He felt the heft of the safe in his hands, which was easily lifted over his head.

"Do you want to talk about it?"

A metallic crack as the safe decimated the murderer's skull. A shimmer of light as the infant sc'ermin drifted away into golden dust.

"Nah, not really."

"But, did you…"

"Did I eat it?" Anon eyes were wild with a malice that made Casey withdraw. When the human died, her sc'ermin disappeared before Anon could consume it. Not that he had wanted to eat it.

They said nothing more for several minutes.

"Well, I need to tell Fix this," Casey said, finally.

"Whatever," Anon said, and took a swig of mouthwash.

"Hey, this is a good thing," Casey said. "Even though it seems really fucked up, this is what is supposed to happen."

"None of this would have happened if you never read that ritual," Anon shouted.

"Keep your voice down," Casey said, only catching himself at the end.

"Or what?" Anon was yelling louder now. "No one can fucking hear me anyway. All I'm good for is fighting your battles and doing some fucked up shit." Anon stood up and walked to the door. "I just came here to tell you it was over. I'll meet you at the parking lot tomorrow for the fight."

"Wait, you're just going to leave?" But Anon was already gone. Casey looked down, dejected, and found his phone. Within minutes, Fix was going over a plan for the next day.

In the outer hall of the apartment complex, Anon bumped into some people who fell to the floor after he jostled past them. He took the stairwell two at a time down to the lobby. A custodian had her cart next to the elevator, waiting to go up. Anon snatched a bottle of glass cleaner and unscrewed the spray nozzle. He drank from it as he exited the lobby.

Anon walked around to the back of the building and got on his hands and knees in a patch of dirt in the parking lot. He started digging, his long nails rending the soil and tossing it aside. He reached the box with the journal inside—a new hiding place—and pocketed his secret treasure. Anon replaced the dirt and wiped his hands on his pants. He continued away from Casey's apartment building and hopped a chain link fence into another parking lot.

Anon had been thinking about the journal since he killed the Sloth and its mother. He wanted to write down what he felt, after ending the life of his first human. It felt different than killing another sc'ermin, almost as if it were unfair for him to attack her like that. Anon was much stronger than she was. She didn't have a fighting chance.

He could also read some more things that Rowan wrote. Anon's past-self had recorded a fair sum of pensive passages, and Anon couldn't help but to keep digging up the book and pouring over it. Although he didn't identify as Rowan, Anon felt an overwhelming sense of curiosity to peer into the man's life and try to see the world how he saw it. Rowan had never seen death in person, though. That was why Anon had to add to the notebook's narrative.

He approached a corner store with some teenagers loitering by the shop front. They were vaping and drinking bottles with paper bags around them. It was only Tuesday.

But that's what people do. That's what they do until they die.

Anon went inside and found some pens by the cash register. He took one and debated sticking around for some more free stuff. There was a homeless person stuffing candy bars into his own hoodie.

Anon couldn't judge him, since he was shoplifting, as well. Candy didn't taste like anything to him, though.

Anon took another gulp of the glass-cleaner and exited the establishment. He wandered down the streets, drinking his chemicals and looking on as drunk people stumbled past, laughing and jeering. He yearned to be with them, to forget the troubles of the world and simply have a good time. Not that he could get drunk, anyway. At least, he couldn't achieve the state with countless bottles of vodka.

Either way, chemicals tasted better.

Anon eventually reached an empty park, save for a couple in the bushes making love. They were hidden from other humans; only Anon's enhanced senses allowed him to notice them. He created some distance between him and the four-legged beast, sat down on a bench, and opened the notebook.

If we are all One in body and spirit, then how can one person contemplate suicide on a daily basis while another thinks only of candy canes and rainbows. I've been both types, and neither time did I feel the influence of the other while I was immersed in the feeling. We do not share minds, that much is sure. We are each individuals in a world split into atomic fragments. Nothing is One, everything is Separate. Complete chaos with the illusion of order. College teaches me the limits of physics, but I know what lies past them. A swirling void of emptiness, meaningless, the basis of our reality. Out of it springs endless pain. Observe the void for too long, and you unlock its secrets. Secrets no one should ever know.

Anon wrinkled his nose as a breeze wafted the noxious scent of the book into his face. It was truly no wonder that Rowan killed himself. He lived in a universe of suffering, built from his own perceptions. All he saw was devastation around him and he let it creep into his very being. The devious thoughts turned into dark ideations once their grasp on his mind took firm hold.

Was Anon much different? He lived in a true hell, one filled with demons. Only, he was a demon himself. Were they, too, tortured in the lake of fire along with the sinners? In fact, the opposite seemed true. The sinners, the murderers, lived comfortably while the demons slaved in the heat. There was a hierarchy to hell, and Anon was on the bottom.

And what was to happen the next day? Anon knew well that he did not consume the Sloth's sc'erva like he was supposed to. Blinded by rage and confusion, he attacked the human first. Anon ended up killing both human and sc'ermin in the process, with nothing to show for it but a mountain of guilt. He had snuck into their home and murdered them both, and he felt weaker because of it.

How was he expected to fight the Pride now? She was described as incredibly mutated, which meant that she was strong. Anon could still pass for human if people could see him, which meant that he was outmatched.

Fix and Casey had better come up with a plan.

Casey would have to livestream again, or maybe have sexual contact. Either way, Anon might become strong enough to beat his adversary. He didn't see much of a choice in the matter, anyway. Whether or not he showed up to the fight, the sc'ermin would find him eventually. It was now or never.

Never wasn't an option. The sc'ermin could kill Casey, and then he would die as well. Although, fading into light didn't seem like such a bad way to go. It sounded much less painful than getting his heart plucked out by a giant condor.

Anon flipped through the pages until he was about three quarters of the way through. That was when he finally found a blank page to write on. He considered what Rowan would write, since he would be continuing his legacy. Rowan would probably write about whatever he was thinking at the moment. He wouldn't try to come up with something out of the blue. It would have been on his mind for a long time.

Anon held the pen in the air, poised for action, and began to write.

Back at the apartment, Casey was still on his phone, talking to Fix.

???-???-????: Why don't you bring Charlie with you?

Caseybent44: I just don't feel for him the same way that I do for Peter.

???-???-????: For this plan you work, you need someone with a strong connection to you, sexually. From what you've told me, it seems as if Charlie has had intense feelings for you for a long time. Those feelings must be building up inside him, especially with your Lust running around. We saw a leak in the hull today. Charlie came out to you. And, now, what would throw him into a frenzy more than you presenting yourself to him?

Caseybent44: first of all that's my best friend you cant just say presenting like its no big deal

???-???-????: If you only knew the stakes, you would do what it takes. You would let nothing stand in your way. You need some type of physical contact to increase your sc'ermin's powers, and the more they feel lust for you, the stronger the augmentation will be. Charlie is perfect.

Caseybent44: I think Peter is even more 'in lust' with me. We never even spoke before that night, and then he was all over me.

From what Casey could remember of the later hours of the party, Peter was definitely lusting for him.

???-???-????: That was because your sc'ermin had just defeated another and his strength was reverberating through you. Peter didn't have a chance.

Caseybent44: You do seem to know a lot about this...

???-???-????: So will you listen to me?

Casey thought about whether or not to go with his gut, or to trust a stranger from the internet. Fix displayed exemplary knowledge of Casey's situation, and he was dying to learn more. Maybe he should go with Charlie. The thought of kissing Charlie was...

Casey realized that he had never pictured himself doing anything romantic with Charlie. In fact, he had never allowed himself to. Perhaps it was the jading years of falling for emotionally unavailable men that turned Casey away from him. But, since that he was out...

Caseybent44: ok, I'll do it

CHAPTER 18

I FEEL LIKE *there is something in my story that is missing, like a name or a face. It's right in front of me, but I cannot see it. A man, a college, and something left behind. These are the clues that Rowan left me. No, these are the notes that I left myself. The more I read about Rowan' deepest thoughts, the more I connect with him. I think I am becoming myself. Through reading my past life, I merge with Rowan until it's like I never died at all. I must face Pride, a sin that Rowan couldn't claim to have committed. Will it give me an edge? Or, will it prove to be a weakness? Must I give in to the temptation or should I fight it. What about myself, and my own powers? Indulging in Lust would make me stronger, but does that mean that sin is rewarded? What kind of goddess would bless those who do the world harm, like unleashing their Wrath? Should we worship this deity or curse its name? What does Zephiscestra do to blasphemers?*

"Casey, thanks for bringing me," Charlie said, blushing.

Casey smiled as best he could and turned his car into the parking lot of The Hallgrove Theatre. He checked the clock on the dashboard. It read 11:45 AM. There were only fifteen minutes left until the Pride's deadline.

Where the heck is Anon?

Charlie was staring at him dreamily.

Maybe it was a good idea to use him. Take him. Along.

Casey hit the brakes a bit too hard. Charlie didn't seem to notice.

"Of course, Charlie. I mean, what better way to spend our first date than by going to a movie?"

That was it. A date. Casey laid all his chips on the table. Fix had convinced him that keeping Charlie on as a boyfriend would increase Anon's powers for a longer period of time. Casey couldn't help but feel as if he were only manipulating his friend into doing his bidding. He tried to focus on the date, for Charlie's sake, but his mind kept fighting back to the Pride sc'ermin that would be arriving shortly.

"I know. It's so classic, isn't it?" Charlie reached over and touched Casey's hand, who flinched until he remembered where he was.

"Yeah, it is. I can't wait for dinner later, too," Casey said.

"Me, too," Charlie said. He kept staring into Casey's eyes whenever they faced each other. Casey broke their contact when he reached for the door. They exited the car, and Casey looked around for Anon.

He hadn't come home since the night he walked out, and Casey hadn't seen him at all in the meantime. Casey hoped that Anon would arrive, otherwise he could be left defenseless against their opponents. And, with Charlie there, an innocent would be thrown into the mix.

Casey clenched his jaw. He had debated even coming, since there was no guarantee that his sc'ermin would show up. What a fool he would look like then, Indulging in his desire just to get torn to shreds by a conceited canary. Casey winced at the thought of his opponent and realized that he truly couldn't do anything without his partner.

They walked in a zigzag through the spaces in the vast parking lot to the theater doors. Scattered cars occupied spaces all around but left enough room to walk between them. Nobody else could be seen in the vicinity.

Casey became all the more worried, since Anon was nowhere in sight.

Maybe he's inside.

Charlie held open the door for Casey when they reached the entrance.

"Thank you so much," Casey said. Charlie tried to hide his glee. Casey did the same when he saw who he was looking for, drinking from a gallon of industrial toilet cleaner by the concessions stand. Casey was about to head right up to him until Charlie grabbed his hand and dragged him to the box-office.

Charlie stepped up to the booth and asked the cashier for two tickets to Broken Faucet, a foreign film about a man who finds love on a job search. "Uh, sorry, but we're not letting anyone into that theatre anymore. The movie started at eleven o'clock.

Charlie looked at Casey, eager with worry. "That's fine. What do you have showing now?"

"Uh." The cashier looked behind him at the schedule, even though he already knew the answer. "Looks like they all started at eleven."

"You've got to be kidding me," Charlie said. Casey's heart sank. He hated to see Charlie shot down, and, even more worrisome, his sc'ermin might lose because of it. Casey took a deep breath and nudged his way to the counter.

"Is there any way you could let us in? For me?" Casey battered his eyelashes. The cashier looked around nervously.

"If you download my mixtape, I'll sell you some tickets," he said.

Casey smiled, surprised, and said, "Sure, send me the link."

Rowan noticed them as the cashier was linksharing with Casey. He looked at the clock on the wall. It was eleven fifty-three. He put his bottle of chemicals on the counter and glided toward his human.

"You seeing a movie, Casey boy?" He did not seem happy.

Casey looked in his direction and nodded subtly, careful not to let Charlie see him.

"Enjoy yourself. I'm about to go get penetrated by a flying demon." He brushed him aside and was out the door, just like the night he left.

Casey, startled, said, "Charlie, I'll be right back. I forgot something in the car."

"Oh, I can come with you," Charlie said, apparently not too keen to let Casey stray too far from him.

"But, then, who's gonna listen to my music?" The cashier put his hands up defensively when Charlie shot him a beam of distaste. He whipped his head back around at Casey, who expressed his apology through a cocked head.

"You stay here. I'll be right back." He left the building before Charlie could say another word, and just as the first piano notes started dropping from the box-office.

Casey ran until he caught up with Rowan.

"Fix said to taunt her," Casey said, out of breath.

"What?"

"It's a Pride. If you hurt their feelings, they get weaker."

"Good to know," Rowan said.

"That's it? You're not going to say anything else to me? You were missing for days."

"I knew exactly where I was," Rowan said. "Casey, I need to focus. Go make out with your new boyfriend so I don't get my face impaled."

Casey scoffed, then felt the relief run through him when he realized that his sc'ermin was really going to fight for him. "Got it," Casey said, and for a moment he was more focused on the thought of Charlie's lips than the death battle that was about to happen.

Then, he saw her.

The sc'ermin stood on the tips of her toes in the center of the lane. Her slender neck was craned upward, and her massive beak shone in the sunlight. She had a thin tail of feathers that doubled her height. Casey could tell from even that distance that she was definitely taller than his sc'ermin.

The Pride held her majestic pose as Rowan drew nearer.

Casey issued a 'good luck' in a hushed whisper and ran back to the door. When he got inside, he hugged Charlie tightly.

"I got the tickets," Charlie said in a daze. He melted into Casey's body and gripped him closer.

Casey, in a move of desperation, lightly squeezed Charlie's butt. Casey felt his partner stiffen.

Charlie looked up at Casey and said, "We should probably go into the movie now, right?" He turned to look back at the cashier, who quickly averted his gaze.

"Yeah, that's probably a good idea."

They walked to Theater 10 where their seats were waiting for them. Casey put his arm around Charlie's shoulders. Charlie leaned into him. They entered into the darkness together, and they sat down in a seat with as much privacy as they could find.

Outside, Anon stood fifteen feet away from the Pride. She unlaced her exquisite pose and fluttered her wings.

"Casey Benton's sc'ermin. My name is Sc'ermicia De Lailla. You have been challenged to battle at high noon today. Heralded by your arrival in this world, the fracas shall presently begin. Plead amends with Zephiscestra so you may not disgrace yourself with your early arrival unto Her heavenly domain."

Rowan took his hands out of his pockets and crossed his arms. Throughout the days he was gone, he had written down his thoughts and examined them concretely. He came to the realization that he was absolutely going to die. However, he had to fight. He couldn't let this other sc'ermin take him down too easily. He decided he would try to disfigure her at least, to injure her vanity.

He said, "Whatever, bitch. Can we just get this over with? I've got shit to do."

De Lailla twitched her head to the side. "Things to do?! Darling, you won't have anything to do in a few moments. Don't you worry." She tittered at her own joke.

Rowan flipped her a middle finger, and her amusement abruptly faded. The simple gesture broke any semblance of decorum that the Pride could feel between them.

"You insolent plebeian. I will defeat you handily."

The Pride took a step back and bent her knees. She leveled her beak like a lance and held her wings horizontally for balance and speed. Then, she charged like a jouster in full tilt.

Rowan gasped and readied his stance. De Lailla approached at lightning speed and stabbed at Rowan's face, pulling back in a feint at the last moment.

Rowan dodged to the left and saw that De Lailla was ready for another blow. Instead, she opened her beak wide and screeched with an equally powerful flap of her wings.

Rowan fell back and hit the ground. De Lailla was already poised to attack and brought her beak down towards Rowan's torso. Rowan rolled to the side and the beak buried itself deep into the concrete.

Rowan jumped to his feet and raised his claws.

De Lailla ripped her beak from the lot, sending debris scattering. A large chunk of asphalt encased the lower half of her beak. Rowan saw his chance to strike now that his opponent was disabled. He lunged at her with his nails, ready to rend her flesh to ribbons.

De Lailla snapped open her beak, exploding the rock with a loud crack. One of the chunks hit Rowan in the face and he lost his momentum. With one swift motion, De Lailla closed her beak and jabbed it at Rowan again. He only had time to lift his hand in defense.

Blood spattered Rowan's face as the beak punctured a hole through the center of his right palm. He screamed and gripped the beak as best he could to keep her from snapping it open again.

It took only a moment before De Lailla screeched her beak wide open. "Gaaahhh—"

A shower of black blood erupted from Rowan's hand as his middle finger flew through the air and landed helplessly on the pavement.

◆═◎═◆

Casey and Charlie held hands in their seats. Charlie constantly cast glances in Casey's direction, perhaps to try to get his attention. Casey was too nervous to look anywhere but the screen.

He wondered how his sc'ermin was doing when his phone vibrated continuously in his pocket, signaling a call.

Casey debated whether or not to pick it up. He *was* in a movie theater. However, it could be something important.

Great another thing that I have to worry about.

He pulled the phone out of his pocket. ???-???-???? showed on the screen.

"Fuck, I have to take this," Casey said. Without thinking, he put the phone up to his ear.

"Casey, what are you—"

Someone shushed Charlie before he could finish.

"Give Charlie a passionate kiss, and then excuse yourself to the bathroom without him."

The voice was heavily distorted with what sounded like a modulator. It sounded ominous and 'in charge.'

Casey hesitated, then did as he was told. He pulled Charlie's head in towards his own with his free hand. Their lips embraced and danced on each other in a thrilling tango. Then, as soon as it happened, Casey was gone.

"The human is augmenting the Pride's powers. He's nearby, locked in the bathroom. You're going to need to embarrass him."

Casey was in the hallway, right in front of the bathroom. He put his ear to the door and heard snapping sounds.

"He's on the Wi-Fi. Now, listen carefully, I need you to go on social media and start a smear campaign against him, something that he will see right away."

"Is he big on social media?"

"You guessed it. Seems that you two aren't so different after all."

Casey paused when he heard a scream from outside.

"Give me the username, now."

⊹⊷⊜⊶⊹

Rowan almost bit his tongue as he rolled around the Pride. His hand was a ragged mess, and he tried to hold the two halves of it together by clenching its own musculature.

But, things were suddenly clearer, and Rowan distinctly heard the whistle of an imminently approaching beak. He whirled around with a speed he didn't know he possessed and deflected the attack with the back of his good hand, sending De Lailla reeling in a circle. With a smooth motion, he leaped at the sc'ermin's exposed neck from behind. Rowan clawed into her back and opened his jaws for the killing blow.

Before he could deliver the execution, De Lailla swiveled her thin neck and the beak swung towards his face. Rowan ducked and dug his nails deeper into his enemy's shoulder. De Lailla screeched, spread her wings, and took flight.

⊹⊷⊜⊶⊹

Fuck, fuck, fuck.

The human's online handle was @theicecreambro. When Casey got to his page, he saw that he was a man in his thirties who owned an ice cream truck geared towards adult entertainment. He was also incredibly handsome, and Casey saw pictures of the man with beautiful women licking their cones sensuously. Casey cringed and copied the name into his message board.

He wondered what he would say. He had never bashed anyone on social media before, especially someone who he knew nothing about. He figured that, with Zephiscestra's help, a simple online mob would overwhelm his foe.

On his own microblog, Casey linked the Pride human's username and typed "Tell this man he's a bitch."

He looked at his screen. Then, he heard another scream. Rowan was in trouble. Just a few more seconds, but Casey always had a glut of fans that re-freshed their social media pages neurotically in the hopes of seeing a new post from him...

Casey counted to ten and refreshed the page.

⋆⊱═◎═⊰⋆

De Lailla circled the lot from above in an inward-leaning pattern. Rowan clutched her shoulder with his hand and hung beneath her, swinging wildly in the wind. He tried to bat at her wings when she flapped them too close, but he could never get a good swipe.

⋆⊱═◎═⊰⋆

Inside the bathroom, Paul Russell's mind was spiraling. The inflated high his ego was riding on—warm, amorphous, and strong—had turned cold and terrify-ing as his awareness took on a sharpness that seemed to stab into his brain. He scrolled through his precious social media feed, a place where beautiful women commented on his body and sent pictures of their own, a place where men told him how great his muscles were looking. His feed was his haven, and it was pres-ently under breach.

⋆⊱═◎═⊰⋆

De Lailla suddenly did a nosedive and plummeted towards the ground. Rowan knew instantly that she meant to scrape him off on the pavement. Rowan started heaving back and forth, regaining his balance. He put out his feet and bent his knees to brace for impact. The earth was rapidly approaching, but Rowan was ready.

⋆⊱═◎═⊰⋆

More and more people were commenting terrible things on his pages. His most popular posts took serious hits to their ratings, too. His vision constricted as waves of insults battered his ego in a relentless onslaught of terror and shame. His throat began to tighten as slurs were jammed down his throat.

⊷⟾ ⟾⊶

With a shriek, the Pride pulled her trajectory back and up into the air so that she wouldn't crash. Rowan kept his feet poised until the last moment, then slammed his heels into the cracked asphalt and swung his arm down with all his might. De Lailla spiraled, free of her foe's grasp, and skidded into a car.

⊷⟾ ⟾⊶

Paul strode over the Polaroid photos scattered on the tiles and put his shirt back on, suddenly shameful of his torso. Then, he heard loud knocking at the door.

⊷⟾ ⟾⊶

"My—my—" De Lailla's voice sat paralyzed in her throat. She stood weakly to her feet, majorly off balance to her right side.

"My… my…" Gushing blood along the way, she took step after step through the distance to reach Rowan. The Lust licked his lips as the crippled sc'ermin edged closer.

"My, my, my. Looks like I found myself some dinner." Rowan laughed and ripped into the piece of De Lailla's arm that he was holding, its feathers on the ground at his feet.

CHAPTER 19

PAUL BURST THROUGH the bathroom door and into the face of a man with a phone's camera trained on him.

"Hey, Paul. What do you have to say to the rumors that you scratch dandruff into your vanilla bean ice cream?"

It's him.

Casey Benton: The target that that woman had given him.

Was he the one who started all of this slander against me?

The woman from the commune didn't give him much information, which Paul had found strange. She usually gave him everything he needed for a kill.

But this Casey...

She said he was an Envy.

Envies are easier to kill, but they can get the drop on you by sensing your location.

Paul had wondered why Casey's sc'ermin didn't pick up on their approach and had left Casey alone at his office when De Lailla first arrived with the proposal. He figured that his enemy was so weak that they couldn't even fulfill the most basic functions that a sc'ermin can provide. He wasn't worried about the fight at all.

That's because De Lailla is strong, and stronger than ever. She won't lose, especially not to a sc'ermin who could still pass as human.

But now its human was here, taunting him. A smart move.

"Trying to hurt my pride, are you?" Paul yelled, fully aware that the camera was listening to his every word. "Them's fightin' words. You know that, right? A scrawny punk like you?"

"No thanks, *I* don't want to fight you," Casey said into the phone's microphone.

Paul advanced on him slowly. "Why not, Casey?" He could corner him, right here.

"If I punch you in the face, I don't want to see what falls out of your hair."

Then, they heard an inhuman scream from outside. It was unmistakably a cry from De Lailla.

Paul almost puked. He advanced towards Casey and attacked him.

Casey was knocked to the floor, but he held on to his phone. The livestream continued to play, and Casey's fans continued to post obscenities about Paul.

⟢⟣

De Lailla struggled to keep her balance as she sent a volley of weak jabs at Rowan. He dodged and parried them easily. The Pride screeched and whirled her wing at Rowan, who caught it and gripped it as hard as he could. He ripped free a handful of feathers when he yanked on her arm.

De Lailla fell to the pavement.

She looked up at him, wounded beyond imagination, and hurled a desperate peck of her beak at his chin. Anon caught her beak in midair and quickly stooped down beside her before she could take off any more of his fingers.

Flecks of blood splattered from Rowan's mouth as he tore into De Lailla's tender neck. He ripped open her chest from her neckline down. The black blood mingled with saliva as Anon laid eyes on her beating heart. Rowan couldn't control himself when he saw it. He grabbed it with prying fingers and pulled with all of his might, which turned out to be overkill.

⟢⟣

For no apparent reason, Paul stopped kicking Casey.

Casey held his stomach and moaned. Paul had kicked him all over the torso, arms, and legs. He was competent enough to block his head from the blows.

Paul bent over and shuddered. He looked at Casey through the sides of his eyes, his pupils contracting with shame. "Who did this to you?"

"What? You...?" Casey didn't know what to say. Paul had experienced a sudden change of heart and was acting like a completely different person. Paul stooped low to the floor and continued to quiver, his sobs wracking his body.

Casey got to his feet and looked down at Paul.

What happened? Is this because...

Casey picked up his phone and turned off the livestream, ceasing the flow of angry emoticons that were flooding his screen.

Then, Rowan walked through the door looking much more at ease. The front of his shirt had soaked up a horrifying amount of inky blood and Rowan left dark stains on the glass door when he pushed it open.

He let the door shut behind him with a *click*.

Paul looked up and said, "Ah!"

Rowan froze. Casey flinched.

"There's the door, let me out of here." Paul ran for the door and shouted, "Don't look at me!" He exited from the building, looked around, and then took off again.

Rowan and Casey looked at each other. Casey's chest expanded when he understood, without a doubt, that Rowan had won. The relief in his posture sent pains shooting through his body, and he put his hands on his knees.

"Took a beating there, did you?" Rowan walked up to Casey and examined his bruises.

"He got me pretty good," Casey said through gritted teeth. "You?"

Rowan laughed and held out his right hand. It was caked in dried blood and his middle finger was missing. Rowan wiped away some of the residue and revealed that the area was completed healed over.

"That one hurt. Not anymore, though. Actually, I feel pretty incredible right now. Plus, I have this."

Rowan presented the yellow bone that he was holding and started nibbling at it. "This thing tastes incredible."

Casey was surprised by the next new thing that Rowan had.

"Is that... a tail?" Rowan contorted himself so that he could see behind him and laughed again.

"So it is. When did that get there?" He started wagging his new appendage, its black fur tossing side to side.

"You ate her heart, didn't you? You're mutating." Casey's awe matched the intensity of the pain he still felt from Paul's assault.

"Yeah, I probably am. I've eaten two hearts already." Rowan scratched behind his ear with a blackened nail.

"I thought this was the third," Casey said.

Rowan looked away and said, "Right. Three. Who can keep track of all of this?"

Casey nodded his head and winced in pain. Paul had kicked him squarely in the neck. Rowan smiled and closed the short distance between them. Surprising them both, he gave Casey a hug.

"You took a beating for me. Thanks. You may have saved me out there." Rowan grinned with his pointed teeth and held Casey closer. "I was so pissed at you since my first fight. I don't know, I was just mad that you were getting all of the attention and I had to get my ass kicked. But when you put yourself out there on the front lines. . . I have nothing but respect for you." Rowan let Casey go, but they still stood closely under the theater's chandelier.

"I respect you, too," Casey said. "I know that you are kind of foul mouthed... and foul in general—"

Rowan cut Casey off with a cough.

"But, because of you, so many amazing things are happening to me. I owe you, big time, and I'm going to keep repaying you. I know you try hard, but I'm trying, too. I'm trying my best. And I'm having fun along the way, sure. That doesn't mean we can't have fun together."

Rowan scratched his chin. "That was pretty deep, Casey. Thanks, it means a lot to hear that."

"You got deep first, Anon." Casey furled his eyebrow when his sc'ermin looked away. "What is it? You can tell me."

Rowan mumbled something and looked away.

"What was that?" Casey tilted his ear to hear more clearly.

"I said, call me Rowan."

Casey brought Rowan back into a hug again. "Aw, Rowan. Okay, I'll call you that from now on."

"Thanks," Rowan said. "Hey, shouldn't you be getting back to your date?"

Casey jumped and said, "Oh, my god. I totally forgot. I gotta go. Get yourself something to drink, if you want."

Rowan laughed and said, "I think I'm good with my chicken wing, for now."

Casey agreed and they parted ways, Rowan gnawing on his new treat and Casey nibbling on his fingernails.

When Casey walked down the dark aisle to take his seat, he couldn't help but feel that all eyes were trained on him. He sat down and instinctively put his arm around Charlie, wincing with pain as he stretched his abdomen.

"What took you so long?" Charlie looked worried, but he was ultimately relieved that Casey was back.

"I was on a call with my mom. She just talks forever." Casey absently observed that he could lie with ease.

Charlie nuzzled his head into Casey's shoulder, and they both stared up at the silver screen.

With all of the craziness going on, Casey realized that he didn't spend time enjoying the good things that were coming to him. The battle was over, and Casey thought that it was the opportune moment to sit back and revel in the blessings that he had received.

There he was, curled up with Charlie, who he could finally consider having a relationship with. He had hundreds of thousands of followers online, and his name was spreading around the world at lightening pace. It was everything that he had ever dreamed of.

Except, for now, it was his reality.

If he kept gaining followers, pretty soon he would be able to get a leg up in auditions for movies. He had never taken acting classes before, but he acted like a straight person for years, so he had some practice.

He also wanted to sing on an album. He had released some covers on his channel, so it was possible that record producers were already scouting him. Even though he knew that their interest was supernatural, he still felt proud that he could say he was in the running for greatness.

Casey felt Charlie nestle into the crook of his neck. He sighed his satisfaction. Although he didn't know what was going on in the movie, everything else in his life seemed to be lining up perfectly. Rowan was getting stronger, and he finally accepted his true identity. They had made their amends to each other after the fight, and it was possible that they would become closer together in the future. Casey would much rather have a friend in Rowan than a clingy demon-man skulking around.

Maybe they *could* become friends.

And, there was always Fix who could help with any issues that arose.

Ah, crap.

Casey had forgotten to alert Fix of their victory. He shrugged and settled back into his seat. Fix could wait until after the movie. He probably already knew that they won. Fix had solutions to situations that Casey didn't even have questions for, so it wouldn't be too hard to believe that he was plotting their next move at that moment. They weren't in any immediate danger, anyway, so there was no need to rush.

Just sit back and relax.

Rowan lounged on the roof of an SUV and tapped his foot on the windshield. He picked off bits of feather from his wing and tore into the flesh whenever there was a spot that was clear of its avian trappings.

Rowan was glad that he and Casey apologized to each other. They needed each other, in more ways than one. Sure, Casey could augment Rowan's strength, which had saved him on that very day. But he could also be there for emotional support.

Rowan experienced a prolonged influx of negative emotion in the recent nights, compliments of his past life. He was going to keep it bottled up, but he realized that he could truly share it with Casey. His human seemed to be empathetic enough with his other friends.

Friends.

Could Rowan say that he and Casey were friends? Maybe not yet. But, with some work, they could get there. Rowan thought of his other friends, the ones from the funeral. They were confused and saddened by his death. And it *was* his death. He did it to himself. He dragged Casey into it by sacrificing himself. Could he ever forgive himself?

No, Rowan never would have come back to life unless Casey had said the incantation. But, was his resurrection a blessing or a curse? Rowan had power that he could innately feel but couldn't grasp the full extent of. Because of that power, his presence put himself and Casey in danger. His fight with the Pride was a close call. Rowan thought that he was finished after De Lailla drew first blood.

He looked down at the spot where his middle finger used to be. It looked as if it were never there, the space between his index and ring fingers was smooth.

Thinking back to the funeral, Rowan remembered his family, his mother in particular. She seemed the most broken out of anyone in attendance, even more than their father. The way she cried... the way they all looked at her. Rowan vowed that, someday, he would make it up to them. He had so much power. He could get them almost anything.

Would material things fill the void left behind by a brother, son, and friend?

Rowan didn't know the answer, but he had plenty of time to think about it. Their enemy was defeated, and they could unwind for a while. This must be like what an athlete feels like after winning the Olympics.

Of course, in the Olympics, there is the Village, and they don't give out hundreds of condoms there for nothing.

Rowan didn't have a significant other, or anyone other than Casey for that matter. There had to be someone out there for him. If not, then what did he die for?

CHAPTER 20

MARCH 15ᵀᴴ: IT was 2:00 in the morning. Somehow, I had stayed up that late, even though I had a terrible night. The bars were the same as always: too loud to talk, too crowded to move. The alcohol kept me going, kept up my social life. Steve appreciated me going out with him. He always bought me drinks when I came out, since he said it was reason for celebration. He was always saying things like that about me, and it made me feel amazing. Last night, he bought me a few shots and then asked me to leave the bar early. I had never known him not to close a bar, and I agreed eagerly. We went back to his place, he offered me a bottle and I took it. I'm always drinking more when I'm around him, maybe in the hopes that I will finally have the courage to confess my love for him. At that BAC, the confession would turn to word vomit, and probably regular vomit as well. But when we laid on his bed, I looked into his hazy eyes and leaned forward and kissed him. He grabbed onto the back of my head and pulled me closer.

Nothing eventful happened for a couple of weeks after the fight.

Rowan sucked on his bones, having cleaned the meat off of them soon after their acquisition.

Casey, feeling inspired, created a few more videos to upload to his channel. They became the most popular posts on his account with supernatural speed.

Casey wanted to research Paul some more, but he found that his account was gone. Everything was deleted from each of Paul's social media pages. There wasn't a trace of him left.

Casey wondered what had happened to him and decided to ask Fix.

Fix said that, if a sc'ermin dies before their human, the human will live to fear their deepest desire from when they made their sacrifice. Paul had been proud of his achievements online, and now they scared him. He would withdraw from such a life into obscurity, most likely.

This information did not sit well with Casey. If Rowan died, then he would have a similar fate to that of Paul's

Faded away into obscurity.

Casey shuddered at the thought. What Fix told him brought rise to more questions, but, of course, Fix also had answers.

He said that, if a human dies before their sc'ermin, they are brought to the afterlife to present their sacrifice to Zephiscestra. If their offering is accepted, they will be placed in Zephiscestra's court to serve Her in one way or another. Depending on their strengths, they could be anything from cooks, to handmaidens, to warriors, and more. Her vast kingdom spread around the universe, and much was to be done in Her name.

Casey almost didn't want to ask what would happen if the ritual was rejected. Fix said that Zephiscestra could be so offended that she would inflict True Death upon them: their souls would be obliterated, and they would be wiped from the past, present, and future.

Casey was brought nose to nose with the thought of his own mortality. He suddenly felt the gravity of his predicament, felt it weighing on his shoulders. His stomach tied in a knot and he felt like he was going to puke.

When the sensation subsided, it allowed another question to flow into its place, a question that had been asked before: How did Fix know so much about sc'ermin and Zephiscestra and the ritual?

Where did he gain the knowledge?

Casey was relieved that Fix was on his side, since having him as an enemy would have been devastating, and not having him at all might have cost them their lives.

???-???-????: If you must know, it is because I performed the ritual myself, many years ago. My sc'ermin is a Lust as well, but instead of fame I lust for knowledge. Because of this, I gain relevant information at the most opportune time. It has aided me in support as you have seen.

That was all of the information that Casey could get out of him. That was fine, because Casey had to check his business email every few hours for opportunities.

Agents of all kinds had started contacting Casey with offers for auditions. A disturbing amount of them were pornography agents, but Casey figured that that was to be expected as a result of the ritual.

He ignored them. No amount of lust would direct him to shoot porn. Casey was too protective of his body to exhibit himself in such a provocative way.

There were a few mentions in his emails about something called the Starlight Convention, a large gathering for fans of fantasy and science fiction. Particularly, he was contacted by people related to a series of novels called the Prime Eternity Tetralogy. There was a private room at the convention where auditions would be held for the long awaited first installment of the movie series. Casey was invited specially to attend by several representatives online. The books were loved by millions, and the series could run for years if handled correctly.

It seemed like an excellent venture, and Casey was suddenly even more excited than usual. The unease—and injuries—of the fight had healed and he was ready to move on to the next step, reaping the rewards of the victory.

Casey discussed the audition with Rowan, who shared his enthusiasm. "Yeah, that sounds great. I think it will be awesome for you to get out there and show everyone what you can do. You already have a lot of practice in front of the camera, so just give it your best."

Rowan' friendly disposition still surprised Casey, but it had been that way ever since the theater. They both complimented each other, but Rowan showed loyalty towards Casey that he really appreciated.

When Casey uploaded onto his channel, Rowan was on the edge of his seat, watching the view count climb higher and higher. Each time they broke their record, Rowan celebrated by crunching into a bone.

"With you by my side, I'm sure that I'll do a good job. I might even get a part."

"With me by your side, you'll get the lead."

"Yeah, maybe I will," Casey said. In the past, he dared not dream so loftily. What Rowan said was true, though. He possessed a supernatural advantage when it came to fame. As long as Rowan stayed alive, Casey could accomplish anything he wanted.

Fix agreed and immediately clung to the idea of Casey in a lead role.

???-???-????: Think about it. Your face on the silver screen in theatres all over the world, twenty-four hours a day. Your name would constantly be in the daily news cycle, on social media, and in everyone's conversations. You would be more powerful than you could even imagine.

"Looks like it's settled, then. We're going to L.A."

The agent that had reached out to him about the Prime Eternity Tetralogy, Nancy Parkin, paid for the ticket. The event was the next weekend, and Casey decided to ask for time off of work on that Friday to travel. He rarely used his vacation days, so the HR Department had no qualms granting his request.

When the day came to leave, Casey was packed and ready. He brought a few outfits and his laptop and camera for his plans to shoot a video in California. Rowan lugged a backpack filled with the few remaining sc'ermin bones and some industrial solvents to wash them down.

When they got to the airport, Casey gained insight into how people could not see Rowan but could feel his presence. Strangers flocked around them as if enticed by instinctual pheromones. The younger people asked to take pictures with Casey, and some of the senior citizens asked for his autograph.

It was sobering connecting this feeling of joy with the pain of blood on the pavement. Casey felt himself getting sick.

"Drink some water," Rowan said. "You look dehydrated." He handed Casey a bottle of clear liquid which they both sniffed after opening.

"Thanks," Casey said after a few refreshing gulps. "I really needed that."

"I could tell," Rowan said. Casey kept his head down until they got into their seats. He made a mental note to bring a disguise for the next time they were in such a public place. Casey fell asleep immediately after they captain announced cruising altitude. Rowan waited in the back of the plane, helping himself to "complimentary" bottles of liquor and checking out what he called "the talent."

When the airplane bottles lost their appeal, Rowan found an empty seat in first class next to a businesswoman who was focused on her laptop.

He decided to match her energy and work on his own journal. His diary felt like opening a portal to another life, in another world. Rowan's old problems seemed so different than his present ones, now that he had passed away. He could get glimpses into what it was like to be alive, although most of it was painted as a depressing affair.

There were glimmers of happiness here and there, wedged between tides of gloom like coins dropped into shallow depths. A man's name was mentioned every so often, her essence a soothing juxtaposition to the feelings of despair that Rowan used to experience. They hung around in the same circles of people whenever Rowan could get out of bed to meet them. Steve, his name was. He was a good friend who would always lend an ear.

Rowan marveled at his own delight while he read an entry about them cooking dinner together, even if it was only a can of refried beans and some garlic bread.

He tried to imagine how Steve looked but could not conjure an image of his face. Rowan's memories of his past life were gone for good. The only ties he had were the journal, but Rowan could sense that there were some fantastical elements to the stories contained therein.

Rowan had written down an experience that he had with Steve on a drunken night where they shared a kiss.

Rowan found himself wholly engaged with this passage in the text until it was revealed that it was only a fantasy.

Rowan concluded, in the journal, that acting on his love for his best friend was mere folly. Even thinking about it could be harmful, lest he lead himself on.

Rowan felt a pang of regret for dreams he could not remember, which prompted a trip to the cargo bay in search of hazardous chemicals to ease his mind.

Meanwhile, Casey reclined in his seat, deep in slumber. Visions of faces floated around him.

Trevor, Charlie, and Peter's visages were arranged like a totem pole climbing towards the sky. Rowan was at the bottom of it and waved to him before turning towards the first face on the ground. Peter stuck his tongue out and Rowan gracefully jumped up onto it. Peter smiled and launched Rowan upwards to Charlie's face, who had his eyes closed. Rowan clambered up Charlie's cheeks, smooth as a sheer cliff. His sharp nails dug into Charlie, and rivulets of blood streamed from the fresh wounds. The blood seeped out and collected on Peter's head before it fell to the ground, each drop hitting the surface with a different musical note. Finally, Rowan leapt from the crown of Charlie's head and flew to Trevor's forehead. A bright light erupted from Rowan the moment he touched the top of the totem pole, and suddenly everything was gone.

In their stead was a void, a place so empty of matter that it could only exist outside of the infinite dimensions of the multiverse. From the void sprang forth a word, each of its syllables uttered instantaneously and curving back on itself in cyclical space. The word sounded like a bird's chirp, a lightening bug's glow, and the scraping of rhinoceros horns.

Casey awoke a moment later to a flight attendant coaxing him out of his seat like a sire from a stable. The plane had landed, and it was time to go.

CHAPTER 21

MARCH 21ST: I woke up the next day and didn't remember much, but I remembered the kiss. I couldn't tell if I was dreaming or if it actually happened, but I was too nervous to text Steve about it. So, I didn't. And I didn't text him when the next weekend came, and he didn't text me, either. I realized that he never really reached out to me unless I initiated the conversation, but I had never put two and two together that he was just a nice person who didn't have deeper feelings for me. Weekends slipped by and I was still too nervous to send him a message. He was apparently neglectful and did the same. That was the last time that I saw him, on that night. And I'm not sure if we were ever even together in his room or if I had imagined the whole thing in a drunken stupor. Without Steve to buy me drinks, I had to go to the liquor store on my own. Without the social convention to drink on Friday and Saturday nights, I found that I could drink every night of the week by myself and no one would say anything. Not even the liquor store cashier, who I saw frequently, gave me a hard time about wasting money on pints of whisky when there was work to do.

Casey peeked through the window of the shuttle when they arrived at their hotel, which was just a few blocks from the convention center. Nobody was supposed to know where they were staying, but Casey did not want to get mobbed by strangers who wanted to take pictures with him.

Rowan opened the door to step out and Casey yelped.

"What? There's no one here, really," Rowan said. "You didn't post your itinerary online, so we should be good."

Casey hesitantly slinked out of the van with his head down. Rowan held the hotel door open for him and they escaped from the California heat. Casey kept his sunglasses on in the lobby, just in case anyone might recognize him. Nobody did, but Rowan saw someone that they knew quite well.

"Hey, isn't that your boyfriend?" Rowan pointed to a lounge area lined with cushy chairs. Charlie was sitting in one of them, looking down at his phone.

"Holy shit," Casey said, approaching his friend. "What are you doing here, Charlie?"

Charlie looked up with an expression of sheepish excitement. "Casey! I've been waiting for you. I wanted to tell you earlier, but I also wanted to surprise you." Charlie embraced Casey in a tender hug. The tactile contact helped to dissipate Casey's shock. Charlie held up a ticket for the convention, and Casey could clearly see the word "FREE" embossed on it with deep black ink.

"Where did you get that?" Casey was now ecstatic that Charlie was there. He could not remember his dream on the plane, but he had been thinking about his feelings for his new boyfriend. Their relationship started off as a tool to keep Rowan alive and further Casey's career, but the manipulative origins of their status fermented into an intoxicating elixir.

Casey began to allow himself to once again experience the romantic feelings that drew him to Charlie when they first met. The amorous thoughts towards Charlie were suppressed when Charlie announced that he was only interested in women. Now that they began their relationship, Casey could not help but to reignite the flame that had been built in his heart for his friend.

"I got an email offering me a free ticket," Charlie said. "Usually, I just disregard those types of things as a trick to steal my money. They didn't ask for my credit card number, though, and sent me this along with a plane ticket. I called the airline and the convention center and it all checked out. I wanted to surprise you."

"A plane ticket and a ticket for the convention," Rowan said. "Did he get a free night in this hotel? No offense, but I don't think he could afford this place."

Casey shared this sentiment and asked, "Where are you staying tonight?"

Charlie's face turned pink. "That's why I was waiting for you. I was wondering if I could sleep with you tonight."

Casey's heart skipped a beat while Rowan slapped his knees. "Doesn't get any clearer than that," Rowan said. "Only question I have now is what am I going to do while you two are plow—getting to know each other intimately."

Casey subtly elbowed Rowan and said, "Sure, I have a queen-sized bed in my room, so we can share."

Charlie's face lit up and he hugged Casey again, this time with deliberate tightness. "Thanks so much. I knew that you would say yes."

"I wonder if he sleeps naked," Rowan mused.

Casey ignored him and motioned for Charlie to follow him to the check-in desk. The three of them stood there while the attendant reminded Casey that his room was only paid for one person.

Charlie smiled sweetly and said, "Oh, I already have a room booked."

Rowan laughed and said, "I'm actually two people, so looks like we're four times over the limit."

Casey said, "Just for the one, please."

The attendant addressed Charlie and said, "I'll just have to check for your room. What number was it?"

When Charlie faltered, the attendant said, "That's what I thought. Now, I can let you go on one condition."

Casey rolled his eyes imperceptibly when he figured out where they were going with this.

"Casey, could we get a picture together?"

"Actually, I don't want people to know where I'm staying," Casey said. "If you post it online, the word will spread because your friends know where you work. But tomorrow I'll be out of here, and then we can take a picture."

"I'll switch shifts with someone in the morning, so I'll get to be here," the attendant said. "And I'll be the one checking you out, so we won't forget."

"Sounds like a plan," Casey said with a wink. The attendant felt a sense of warmth as Casey's room key was conceded to him. Charlie waved goodbye to the attendant as they moved towards the elevator.

"Quick thinking," Rowan said.

"Thanks," Casey said, holding up a hand to the attendant in case Charlie heard him speaking to his ethereal partner.

They entered the elevator and Casey pressed the button for the top floor. The agent set him up with a penthouse suite, undoubtedly to entice him to audition for the role at the convention.

Rowan noted, out loud, that Charlie could not take his eyes off of Casey the entire time their compartment ascended the shaft into the sky. Casey snuck glances and saw that there were no secrets between them: Charlie grinned every time they made eye contact.

When the elevator opened and the trio unlocked the door to the suite with a slide of Casey's key card, they each noticed only specific parts of the penthouse's accommodations. Rowan saw a countertop lined with bottles of expensive liquor and the open cabinets below it filled with cleaning supplies. Charlie fixed his eyes on a hot tub planted in front of a tinted window. Casey somehow noticed the doorknob to a side room turning slowly.

A burly man, dressed in a black collared shirt and black cargo pants, appeared in the common area. Casey and Charlie jumped, with Charlie making a move for the exit. Rowan bared his teeth and shouted. He and Casey realized that the man winced at Rowan's outburst and put up his hands.

"Don't be afraid," the man said, looking directly at Rowan. "I was sent by your... *contact* to escort you to the convention tomorrow. Although, I was only expecting... one of you."

Casey asked, "Our contact? Do you mean the talent agent?"

The man looked overtly apologetically at Charlie and said, "Sorry, I'm speaking about the person who *fixed* this place up for you."

Rowan spoke up and said, "He knows I'm here, and he knows Charlie doesn't. I think he's talking about Fix."

The man pointed at Rowan showily; for Charlie's sake, it would appear as an innocent gesture. "My name is Alex Vernon. You can think of me as a bodyguard. You have a lot of... *ravenous* fans, Casey. I'm just here to make sure you get to your audition without getting mobbed."

"How do I know that you—" Casey's line of questioning was disrupted by a vibration in his pocket. He unlocked his phone, already knowing who had sent him the text.

???-???-????: You can believe him, Casey. Alex is one of my most trusted and capable acquaintances. He is only there for your protection. I wanted it to be a surprise as a show of my devotion to your wellbeing.

"Okay, if you say so," Casey said, waving a hand at Rowan. The sc'ermin took the hint, relaxed, and then bolted over to the liquor cabinet. "Why were you waiting in that room?"

"Those are my quarters for the night," Alex said. "I would please ask that you refrain from entering that room, as I have my personal effects in there. I will leave you alone until tomorrow if you wish, but I will remain in there in case you run into any issues. Now, if you will excuse me, I want to give *your* bedroom a final sweep to make sure that everything is up to code."

Charlie, back at Casey's side, huffed as Alex went into the master bedroom. "This should have been a night with just me and you," Charlie said. "This is all wrong."

"Don't worry, Alex doesn't seem to care about what we do," Casey said, closing the distance between himself and the hot tub to examine it more closely. He had seen such things in movies, but had never dreamed he would actually be in the same room as an indoor hot tub.

"Yeah, but I wanted to tell you something special," Charlie said. He sat down on one of the couches and motioned for Casey to sit next to him. "I wanted to tell you that… There are so many ways to say this, so I'll just make it plain. I love you, Casey. I've loved you for a long time. I wanted to tell you earlier, but I had been pretending to be straight for my entire life and didn't know how to go about it. I don't know, I guess I just had this idea of how you all perceived me, and I didn't want to change it. I mean, we were already close as it was, and I was scared to take a step forward. Lately, though… I don't know. My feelings for you have been ready to burst out of me. I love you so much I can hardly stand it, and I couldn't live with myself unless you knew about that."

Between the surprise appearance of both Charlie and Alex, as well as the fact that Charlie thought that he was making a private admission when there was an invisible sc'ermin listening in on the whole thing, Casey did not know what to say. He had not expected any of this to happen right before his audition, and his nerves were starting to affect him. Charlie's revelation should have eased the butterflies in his stomach, but it added another layer of confusion to the whole situation. Charlie may have been right in his assumption that a change in perception could be jolting. However, it only took a moment for Casey to make his decision.

"Charlie… I've been in love with you for a long time, too," Casey said. He could feel the relief emanating from his new boyfriend. "I had to stifle my feelings for you, but now that I know how you really feel I have to tell you that—"

Their conversation was interrupted by a cough from Alex, who was standing in the doorway to the bedroom. "All clear in there," he said.

Charlie shot a look of annoyance at the bodyguard and said, "Do you want to continue the conversation in there?"

"Sure," Casey said, and he took Charlie's hand. Alex seemed troubled as he let them pass through the doorway but went back to his room when Casey closed the door.

Charlie laid on the bed as Casey went to close the drapes. He looked down below to the building adjacent to their hotel and saw that its roof had a collection of red spots on it. When the spots blew around in the breeze, he realized that they were rose petals.

"Come join me," Charlie said. "We have a lot to talk about."

CHAPTER 22

THE NEXT DAY, when they had arrived at the convention center, Alex led them around the building to a side door which he opened with a key card.

Through the door was a small room with a private security scanner attended by people dressed all in black. While Casey and Charlie placed their phones and wallets in a bin to be scanned, Alex put two pistols into his own bin along with a slew of extra magazines. The security team did not bat an eye as they let them pass.

When Casey asked about Alex's belongings, the bodyguard said only that their mutual contact had ordered him to be present at the convention. Where Alex was present, so were his guns and munitions. Asking him why he was carrying them would be like asking why he had brought his hands along.

Rowan skipped the security scanner and opened the door to the main hall. Immediately, the group could hear the cacophony that came from within the building.

Casey had almost no time to gawk at the cosplayers dressed in their elaborate garb. Thousands of people were dressed as powerful wizards, grizzled space marines, and deadly monsters. The more impressive outfits obviously cost a small fortune, but there were still others who seemed to have been created by their wearers in their homes. The theme of the day was play, and all were merry who took part.

Alex rushed Casey along the wall that they had come out of, past fans who began to recognize them. Fairies and soldiers alike were thrown into a frenzy at the sight of them, unsheathing their phones to get a picture. Demons and divine beings called out for Casey, while martial arts masters were repelled by Alex's strong arms.

"Keep moving, Casey," Alex said. Casey was instantly grateful of Fix for sending him this savior. He would never have been able to make it to the audition if he had to deal with the fans who were presently trying to get a piece of him.

Eventually, the group found their way to an unassuming door with a small queue of people lined up before it. There was a woman blocking the entrance. When Alex flashed his key card, they were granted entry. Casey walked inside this other room, but the woman held up a hand to halt Charlie in his tracks.

"Your escort's authorization only allows one other charge," she said, clearly unwavering in her orders.

"So, Charlie can't come in with me?" Casey was forlorn for a moment, wishing that his lover could watch him during the audition. It would give Casey the motivation he needed to perform at his top level if he could have someone special there to impress.

"That's okay," Charlie said. "There are a lot of cool booths here. I can go check them out instead."

"That's a good idea," Rowan said. "I'll follow him around and make sure that nothing happens to him."

"Off you go, then," Alex said, and followed Casey into the room. The woman closed the door.

Charlie, an ordinary human amongst magical beings, was lost from sight.

Casey turned back around to face the others in the room. There were three of them: two women and a man. Small stacks of papers filled the folding table in front of them, and each of the agents had their own laptop. A camera was set up on a tripod to the left of the table and there were two unoccupied chairs by the wall.

"Hello, Casey," one of the women said. "My name is Margaret Burnside, and I'm in charge of the auditions today. With me are Tom and Tina Longwood."

The other two examiners waved to him silently. Margaret picked up a packet of paper and flipped it open to somewhere in the middle.

"Tom will read you in. The character that you will be trying out for is named Harmony, and he is being asked by his lover to step through a transformational portal that will make them the rulers of the earth. We need to keep the contents of the script a secret, which is why you'll be doing a cold read today. Let us know when you're ready."

She passed off the script to Casey, who received it tenderly. He could tell that this moment could change his life forever. Something that he had fantasized about for so long was within his grasp, and the only thing he had to do was read some lines from a page.

In the back of his mind, he hoped that Charlie's presence at the convention would give him the power of magnetism that he needed. He was beginning to understand the utility in using Charlie's effects for his own supernatural benefit, now that he knew their mutual feelings.

"I'm ready," Casey said. Margaret nodded and Tina pressed a button on the video camera.

Tom said, "Harmony, I've been subtly preparing you for this moment. All we have to do is walk through this portal. No time will pass, but the eons will shift in our favor and the space around us will be transformed forever. Take my hand and follow me."

Casey looked down at the script to guide him. He could feel the artificial emotions gathering like solid objects in his mind. Feelings of absolute trust and unconditional love enveloped him.

"Take me where you will," Casey said. "You have proven your worth to me. Without you, I could know nothing, yet you have all of the answers. You see all, surely you know I will go with you wherever you wish. Together, we will rule the next world that is already ours." Casey's lips curved into a faint smile and his eyes had assumed a dreamlike focus. "You will give me anything I ask, for I know that you love me as much as the oxytocin in your brain itself. We are one, you and I, yet I wish to be closer. Let us overcome all obstacles so that we may be smelted in the furnace of forever, to live everlasting in each other's arms, to breathe each other's breath and never tire. Answer me this, mine own heart: You wish to live in a world of 'us.' I wish to live in a world of 'you.' What I ask of you is to tell me truly: What do you see in me?"

Casey looked up from the page and back at the assembly of examiners seated before him.

Margaret had remained standing, apparently frozen in place once Casey started speaking. Tina looked uncomfortably at her brother, then stood up in applause. Tom looked as if he wished to rise from his seat but adjusted his belt tenderly and wiped his forehead.

"That was excellent, Casey," Margaret said. "We will give you a call when we make our decision. Please, enjoy the rest of the convention."

The trio appeared as if they did not want him to leave, as if they desired for him to remain with them during the auditions so that they could snark at the others who were not to move on. But, as Alex opened the door and appraised him with a new understanding, Casey turned and followed him out of it back into the reality of a fantasy world.

⊷⊨◉⊨⊶

Elsewhere in the vast convention hall, away from the eyes of Casey or Alex, Scorn sold her last plushy. Charlie had handed her twenty-five dollars for it and taken it away.

She had recognized him as Casey's lover and almost laughed hideously when they made the transaction, but kept her rage contained so that she would not be given away. She had sold dozens of the toys, but she made sure to keep one for Charlie, just in case she ran into him.

Zephiscestra smiles upon me this day, she thought.

With her supply of plushies finally exhausted, Scorn dropped the empty container she was using on the floor and made her way to the stockpile that was concealed in a men's bathroom not far from her. One of her partners had gotten a job setting up the convention and was able to hide what she needed in the ceiling tiles of the last stall.

Since her face was covered, she knew that no one would stop her from entering the bathroom, and she giggled maniacally at the queers who dressed up in women's clothing to make this possible for her.

Her excitement rising rapidly, she pushed and shoved her way through the crowd, elbowing the adults and kneeing some of the children in their tiny faces. Shouts chased after her, but the convention-goers were too wary to actually pursue her. If they had tried to confront here there, they would have had to meet their deaths before her plan called for it.

She picked up her pace before a premature act of incredible violence could alert the security team of her presence. With each step, she thought of the sc'ermin pairs that Casey and Rowan had killed.

Ravage was a good man, always game for crushing the spirits of his enemies. De Lailla was ruthless and so sure of herself that it infected my own mind with pride. How beautiful it was to feel their energies pouring into me. Truly I saw Zephiscestra in their faces! That Lust... he is the devil incarnate. What our Greed sees in them I will never know. But if he is the devil, then I will usurp the king and take his throne.

Finally, Scorn pushed her way into the bathroom, ignoring the line of people waiting to get in. They issued stifled gasps of protest, but Scorn could feel their fear peaking in their guts.

They would let her do whatever she wanted without putting up too much of a fight. Her power was too great, and the killing would only make her and her sc'ermin stronger. Such was the benefit of Wrath. Murder would quickly snowball into massacre.

Scorn kicked open the last stall and barked at the man sitting on the toilet to get the fuck out. He pulled up his pants and scurried away from her.

Smart man.

Scorn closed the door and lit a cigarette. The smoke drifted towards the ceiling, then filled the hollow space where her weapons were cached. She procured an assault rifle and enough loaded magazines to snuff out the lives of hundreds of innocents. She felt around the far reaches of the hollow space until, at last, she found the detonator.

She caressed the handle with her fingers, relishing the power she held in that moment. The dozens of plushies packed with micro-explosives were following the random paths of the people who bought them and were now spread throughout the convention hall to cause maximum damage. Scorn fantasized about the ecstasy that squeezing the trigger would bring when someone banged on the door and yelled, "Hey! You can't smoke in—"

Scorn kicked the door with force enough to send the man reeling into the sinks. She walked to the center of the bathroom, gun raised, and shouted at the men inside to "scram." Those that hadn't already immediately fled the bathroom when she had entered took her present advice.

Scorn performed a quick sweep of the bathroom to make sure that none of her customers were inside. The bathroom was completely empty except for one final person who remained hiding in a stall. When Scorn kicked open the door, she didn't recognize him as someone who had bought a plushy. Meeting his gaze, she smirked devilishly and balled a fist around the detonator.

First, there was a quick series of ear-splitting bangs. Then, a moment later, the sprinkler system extinguished her cigarette.

CHAPTER 23

CASEY WATCHED THE world fall away as rough hands forcibly removed him from the ground. He couldn't see anything except for flashing lights, and he heard a mix of high-pitched alarms and devastating pops that gave him a cold feeling. His entire body felt cold, and he suddenly realized that he was soaking wet. He rubbed the paste of grime from his eyes in order to recognize the gruff voice shouting at him over all of the other noise.

"Keep your fucking head down and follow me," Alex commanded. Casey instinctively crouched low as a fearful sweat mingled with the water from the sprinkler system. Alex turned and waved him towards a pillar about ten yards away from where they were standing.

Pop pop pop pop pop pop pop pop.

Screams blasted Casey's ears and he heard a faint sound of dead weight collapsing heavily to the floor. Alex forcefully pushed flailing arms and legs to the ground as they rushed past. Casey wanted to help them, to reach out and bring them with him, but each successive *pop pop pop* instilled terror into his heart. He could not even distinguish one person from the next as they covered their heads, shrank their forms, and huddled against one another in the endless artificial rain.

Pop pop pop pop pop pop pop pop pop pop pop pop.

Casey looked for the source of the shots and found it. A woman in a white dress with bright red hair was firing into the convulsing mass of people running for their lives. Blood spurted into the air from the frantic forms racing around the convention hall. More pops and more screams filled the cavernous room, and Casey put his hands over his ears to try to make it all stop until Alex grabbed him again and threw him behind a pillar. A moment later—

⋆⟫═◉ ◉═⟪⋆

"Casey! Where the fuck are you!?" Rowan scanned the tumultuous crowd but could not see his partner anywhere. There was also Charlie to worry about, but Rowan would try to find him later. He had left Charlie alone for a minute, then all of this happened. His top priority, though, was his tether to this world, and the only person who he could call a friend.

Rowan looked toward the main exit and saw a funnel of people jostling each other to get outside. The gunshots continued, the alarm was still sounding, and the screaming persisted.

Rowan heard booms from far away, a different percussive than the gunshots. The unsteady, rhythmic booms were coming from outside of the building. He listened as they got louder and louder until there was a *CRASH* and the wall by the main entrance exploded in a shower of reinforced concrete.

Rowan watched as a massive form burst from the dust at startling speed, then felt his own stomach wrap around itself when he recognized what the shape was. A giant sc'ermin barreled towards him, trampling people under its hooves. It had two swirling horns that tapered into sharp points, and it was covered in thick brown hair. Rowan looked into eyes of pure black and could feel the Wrath directed at him. He turned to run, but the creature closed the distance with flying bodies and splintered concrete.

At the instant that Rowan was to be impaled, he grabbed the horns with all of his might. He instantly discovered that the tremendous amount of force couldn't be redirected. He pushed off of the danger and shot to the ground underneath them, trading one peril for another. The sc'ermin stomped on his chest in its stride. Rowan's eyes bulged and his breath left him.

⋅⟩═◉ ◉═⟨⋅

There!

Scorn cackled as Zephiscestra's Light shone down from non-dimensional space and revealed her targets. Her Source of Wrath illuminated a pillar fifty yards away from her where Casey must have been hiding. Another light appeared elsewhere, but her sc'ermin was already handling *that* problem.

Scorn flashed a wry smile. Everything was coming together. The Great

Goddess had shown Her favor. The Lust and its human were betrayed by Her light, and Scorn felt her imminent victory course through her veins.

With a determination that only vengeance could provide, Scorn locked the pillar in her sights and pulled the trigger.

Pop pop pop pop pop pop pop pop pop pop

⋅⊶⊜⊰⋅

Bullets exploded into the pillar and Casey screamed. "Fuck!"

Alex shouted at him, "Stay right here, I'm going after her." Alex wielded his pistol as he crept away from Casey in order to get a better shot at Scorn. He snuck quickly behind booths and bodies to get a better vantage point.

⋅⊶⊜⊰⋅

Elsewhere, the Wrath skidded to a stop and turned his sights back on Rowan. The other sc'ermin charged, and Rowan could barely stand fast enough to put his hands up in defense. It did not matter. The Wrath pummeled Rowan in the face with a giant fist and sent him sprawling back into the dust. In another instant, the Wrath was on him again. This time, it picked Rowan up by the leg. Intense pain shot through Rowan's body when the vice grip of the Wrath enclosed on his calf, and Rowan thought that his bones were going to break.

The Wrath lifted Rowan high into the air and then slammed him into the ground, again and again. Rowan lost count of how many times his face hit the concrete. With all of the bludgeoning, it was hard to keep track of anything other than the pain.

Finally, the Wrath let Rowan go. In fact, he sent him flying through the air, high over the piles of bodies and tumultuous chaos, until he pulverized a thick plate glass window above the main entrance.

Rowan flailed his arms and legs in his descent, eventually coming to an inertia-halting rest in the front seat of a newly totaled minivan.

⋅⊶⊜⊰⋅

Alex slithered behind overturned booths and stepped over lifeless corpses to get closer to the source of the convention's despair. He put on his earpiece and pressed the button, connecting himself to the only channel available for the device.

"Hostile confirmed, it's Scorn," Alex said. He turned back to the pillar, which was temporarily free from the hellfire of bullets. Scorn had focused her attention on other people, probably to build her rage for more power.

"Just as I feared," Fix said over the line. "Are there any others with her?"

"Negative," Alex said. "She's here alone. Probably thought that she could take out Casey and Rowan on her own. Enough have died in their path, why bring anyone else along with her?"

"Her rage builds in isolation," Fix said. "Losing her friends has only made her power grow. The death toll will be immense. Surely this will be the largest mass shooting in the history of the country."

"By my estimate, it already is," Alex said. "I'm moving in for a closer shot. I don't think Zephiscestra has given away my position. She hasn't fired on me yet."

"Good. The Goddess smiles upon you this day," Fix said.

Or does she ignore me? Alex thought.

"You have your orders. Eliminate Scorn and dispose of the body. We can't have her traced back to us. You should have no problem incinerating her with all of the chaos around you as a distraction." "Roger," Alex said. He fingered a small idol in one of the pockets of his cargo pants. The statue was made of a black jewel and was shaped like a cat with four wings instead of legs.

"Make haste," Fix said. "Rowan is on the verge of death. I will not lose him. Understood?"

"Understood." Alex heard the fear in Fix's voice, something that did not manifest often. Alex felt a pang of envy for the people that he had to protect, but quickly pushed it away with a deep exhalation. He knew the love that his leader had for him, a love born of usefulness and need. What Fix needed from Casey and Rowan was something else entirely, something that Alex would never be able to provide.

He exhaled again, clearing his mind. Getting distracted and failing the mission would make him lose what he had worked so hard to gain. Alex gripped his pistol tighter and edged closer to Scorn, his orders laid out before him.

⋆⟶◯⟵⋆

At that instant, the Wrath dropped an expensive car on Rowan's head, then grabbed him by the arm and wrenched him out from underneath it before he even understood what had happened. The Wrath held Rowan up to its face and screamed at him, sending globs of blood and spittle into his eyes. Rowan tried to avert his eyes but could not help to look at the rows and rows of jagged teeth that lined the sc'ermin's gaping maw.

Rowan felt the fear in the pit of his stomach. He jerked his arms in an attempt to rip away the fingers of rage that tormented him.

It was no use. The Wrath was too powerful, and the senseless slaughter inside the convention hall only added to its might.

Deranged from his failure, Rowan howled in desperation.

The Wrath roared right back, and Rowan was once again overcome with fear. He saw inside the jaws of death itself and wished desperately that he could save Casey.

Since Rowan himself was still alive, that meant that Casey was, too. But for how much longer? Without a sc'ermin to protect him, Casey was a sitting duck on the killing floor. If Rowan died, Casey would have no memory of why he was even there or how the massacre had come to pass. Casey would become like Rowan: a person inhabiting a body with a missing past. Rowan could have wept for him in that moment, and maybe even wept for his own demise, but there was no time—no time left at all.

Scorn cursed at Casey, cursed at Zephiscestra, and cursed at her own weapon. The pillar was still standing, and the light was still bright behind it. No matter how many rounds she sent into its metal surface, the structure would not fall. Scorn gnashed her teeth and advanced on Casey's position.

Frustration coursed through her veins, and she expelled her rage by pulling the trigger at anything that was still moving in her way. She got closer, and closer, and closer, until—

⋆⟶◯⟵⋆

Casey heard the gunshots getting louder as Scorn approached him. He wailed and looked around in desperation, searching for an escape. Beyond the haven of the pillar was only carnage. There was no escape, no escape.

"No escape!" Scorn shrieked her victory when she was fifteen yards away from Casey's position.

"You got that right," Alex said to himself. He aimed at Scorn's head and fired two quick rounds into her.

Zephiscestra's Light disappeared from the arena as Scorn and her Wrath were sent to the afterlife.

CHAPTER 24

"WITH TWO HUNDRED and seventy-seven dead at the time of this report, this has been most deadly mass shooting in American history—"

Casey did not notice the dryness in his eyes, but blinked unconsciously.

"So far, we have no known motive for the attack, and no manifesto or list of demands has been received from the shooter, whose whereabouts are unknown."

Rowan sat cross legged on the couch, listening to the news while staring at Casey. He tried to figure out how to reach him. They were only a few feet apart, but Casey seemed miles away.

"The shooter appeared to escape from the convention center, as no trace of them was found after the destruction stopped."

Casey whimpered and Rowan turned off the television to stop the pain that was coming out of it. He examined his human partner and tried to imagine what, exactly, was going through his mind. He knew that Casey was grieving the loss of Charlie and the massive sacrifice of human life that perished along with him. But, since Casey hardly spoke, Rowan didn't know how his human was going to proceed. Casey had shut off from communication with Bill, his roommate, and his family. Rowan did not know how to approach Casey in conversation when he was like this. The only thing to do was to ask him what was on his mind.

"I don't want to do this anymore," Casey said evenly. He looked at Rowan with eyes that cast a certain dullness that could only reflect deep introspection. There was a taste of revulsion in his voice as well.

"You don't want to do what?" Rowan already knew that Casey was talking about him.

"This whole sc'ermin thing. The ritual. The fighting. The killing. I don't want to do it. There was a moment in time during all of this when I thought that we were doing something good, taking the evil out of the world one sc'ermin at a time." Rowan flinched at the words. "But I realize that other people can get hurt in this never-ending battle, people close to me and others that I don't even know. And we are not better than the other people who did the ritual, either. We still feed off of the power of Zephiscestra, a goddess of death and sin. It's not right, what we're doing. We're stomping over others so that I can, what? Get famous enough to date Trevor Greenbrook? It's not worth it. Would I even be happy if I achieved my goal? After all of the destruction left behind in our wake?"

Rowan put a finger in the air and said, "Just wait here a minute, will you? I have to dig something up from behind the building."

Casey curled his upper lip in a snarl. "I'm not going to eat a sc'ermin bone or drink any toilet cleaner if that's what you're thinking."

Rowan put his hands up defensively and said, "No, it's nothing like that. I haven't told you this, but I found my old journal at my funeral. It's the one I kept when I was alive. I didn't tell you about it because I knew you would want to read it, and I just wanted to process it by myself first. I want to read you something from it now, though."

Casey's own harsh words slapped him in the face, and he felt tears coming on again. "Rowan, I'm so sorry. I didn't mean to insult you. I'm just feeling depressed. It's really not your fault."

Rowan tried his best to smile and said, "I can just give you the gist of the journal entry if you want. The journal got a bit rotten before I could retrieve it."

Casey nodded, and Rowan took that as a sign that it was okay to share. He exhaled and began his story.

"When I was alive, I was madly in love with a man named Steve. We went to the same college, you know, the one around here. We were friends, even though I wasn't as outgoing as he was. I admired the fact that he was kind to everyone, especially to me, because I was so shy that I couldn't really connect with people. But, with Steve, it came easily. He was just so put together while I was a fucking mess. I couldn't burden him with a romantic relationship. I loved him too much to subject him to my patented brand of misery.

"One night, though, we kissed. But, then, I never saw him again. It's probably because he felt bad about making out with such a failure, but, to be honest, I don't know if the kiss was just a drunken hallucination or something that I made up to put in the journal. Anyway, after I lost my best friend, I just sank into a deeper and deeper depression, drinking all my money away and avoiding everyone else in my life. I stopped going to class, but I killed myself before I could even fail out."

Rowan stopped to gauge Casey's reaction. His human partner was a few shades paler and at a loss for words. When Casey didn't say anything, Rowan resumed his story.

"You know what happened after that. I was raised from the dead in a ritual—don't be like that, you didn't know what you were doing—and now I have to fight for my life every week because of it. But, I've come to understand that I don't even mind all of the fighting because I'm alive, in a way. I got a second chance, which is something that barely anyone else gets. Also, I have you. You are an amazing person, and you showed your true colors after that shooter was taken out."

When the shooting had stopped, Casey did his best to comfort the survivors. Alex had disappeared, but Casey had found Rowan and helped other people find the loved ones that they were separated from. It took all the strength he had not to break down in despair, a fight that unfortunately lasted for days afterward.

"You knew that the best thing for you to do was to help the other people that were there, even if it meant that you couldn't focus on finding Charlie. You put others above yourself in that moment, and I really respected that.

"Now, you have one more person to help. Well, if you could still even call me a person. But, without you, I'm a sitting duck out there. The only reason I won all of our past fights was because you were augmenting my strength. Without you, I would have been dead for sure. The Wrath proved it. When this all started, I was jealous of you for getting all of the attention while I had to put my life on the line. Now I know that you are risking just as much as I am. We're in this together, you and me. The convention was terrible, but I know we can bounce back."

Rowan exhaled, having said all that he could. He had tried to be inspiring, but Casey's attitude didn't seem to change. Casey laid back on the couch and closed his eyes. Then, he began sobbing uncontrollably. Rowan yelped and embraced him, but Casey did not stop crying. Rowan held him tighter, and Casey wrapped his arms around his sc'ermin.

"It's just... it's just that I just got him. I used to love him so much and then I had to push it all down because I thought he would never love me back. But, then, when he told me he did, the feelings came flooding back and I was power-less over them. They just consumed me. And I let them consume me, I let them wash over me and through me and I loved him so much. But then he was taken away from me because of this fucking ritual that I didn't even know what it was about when I read it. And I'm so stupid! I'm so stupid because, yeah, maybe he never would have admitted his love to me if I didn't have you to spread feelings of Lust... but at least I would still have him in my life."

"It's not your fault," Rowan said. "It's this fucked up world we live in full of demons and dark magic."

"And it's not your fault, either," Casey said. "You didn't ask for this, you just wanted to die on your own. That was your choice. And I ripped you away from peace and brought you back into this shithole for absolutely no reason. Because I didn't even know! I didn't even know what I was doing and it eats at me every time I see you standing there and drinking your chemicals because I know that I fucked you over and now you're stuck with me and now I don't even have Charlie to comfort me anymore."

Rowan hugged Casey tighter and said, "Listen, I don't want you to get the wrong idea. From what I read in my journal, I was a terribly sad person. And, yeah, maybe I did make the choice to kill myself, but my hand was forced be-cause my depression was so strong. Now that I'm here, and now that I have you as a friend, I'm glad that you did the ritual. I get another chance at life and it's all thanks to you. Sure, now I have to fight literal demons instead of the ones in my head, but I'm so much happier now than I was back then. And I know this because, now, I can *tell* that I even *am* happy. Back then, I definitely had *zero* happiness. So I can compare how I was back then and how I am now and know that I am better off than I was, and I couldn't have even had the opportunity to realize this if it wasn't for you."

Casey buried his head in Rowan's shoulder and let out a muffled, "Do you really mean that?"

Rowan nuzzled his head against Casey's and said, "I really do. Casey, you saved my life, you didn't ruin it. Without you, I would be rotting in a coffin, bloated from the river. I wouldn't have been able to work through my pain to get to where I am today. Sure, it seems like we just lost everything. But there is always more to come. We can work harder to make sure that nothing like this ever happens again, because next time we'll be ready. We still have Fix, and he can give us intel. As long as we choose our battles we can never lose."

Casey pulled back and looked his sc'ermin in the eyes. Rowan had wild hair on his head and face, and his square jaw hinted at the sharp teeth in his mouth. His black tail lolled off the side of the couch, and Casey could feel the tips of his black fingernails on his back. But, when Casey looked into his eyes, all he could see was love and compassion, shrouded slightly by the ambiguity of Casey's coming response.

Casey could tell that Rowan genuinely loved him for the second chance at life that he had received. And it was true. Without Casey, Rowan would be dead, truly dead. Casey did this to him, but it wasn't a bad thing. Rowan accepted him, and Casey realized that he had chosen his own lot in life, whether he was aware of it at the time or not. It was time to act, to use their powers for good.

"I think you should find Steve," Casey said. "I think it would give you some closure to see how he is doing now that you've left him."

"I think that's a good idea," Rowan said. "But I don't know where to find him."

"You can probably check the university records to find his name, if you know what year he is. I'm sure the administrators wouldn't mind if you poked around on one of their computers."

Rowan smiled devilishly with his fangs and said, "No, I don't think they would." He stroked Casey's hair and said, "Are you good?"

"I'm pretty far from good," Casey said, "But, I also feel better. Thanks, Rowan. You really mean a lot to me. I felt so guilty before, and I still do. But at least I know you're happy."

"I am," Rowan said. "And, I want you to be, too. It'll take time, but you'll get back into the swing of things."

"I hope so," Casey said. "Whenever our next challenge appears, we'll be ready. Whether I know it or not."

CHAPTER 25

FINDING STEVE WAS surprisingly easy. Although his last name was never revealed in the journal, Rowan had noted a particular sociology class that they had taken together, along with the name of the professor. When Rowan strolled into the administration building at their old university, he was able to use a computer that someone had left open in their office. He sipped from a red can of gasoline as he searched for the enrollment list, his long nails *tap tap tapping* the keys.

And, suddenly, there he was. His name was Steve Pirelli, and he had indeed taken a class with Rowan in his past life. Rowan winced when he saw his own incomplete grade in the system. He didn't snoop any more into his academic performance. He already knew that his time at school was behind him and would not affect him whatsoever, at least after he closed this last loose end.

When he got the name, all he had to do next was access the student directory that was available to administrators and advisors. There, he found Steve's address.

Rowan wrote down the pertinent information on a sticky note and left the university, never to return to within those walls.

⟡

???-???-????: The movie that you auditioned for fell through. The heads didn't think that it would be a good idea to continue in case the attack was directed at them. Pity, because Alex told me how magnetic your performance was.

Casey stared at his wall, alone in his apartment. He could hear the screams of the convention goers in his head, and he could see their bodies on the floor. A pillow was propped up behind him, but he could feel it quaking as bullets were fired into it, over and over.

???-???-????: Thankfully, I sent Alex along with you. I don't know what would have happened if he wasn't there. Alex is a good fighter, and he does whatever I say. I can have him escort you wherever you want, if you want to feel safe.

Casey heard the shots getting louder as the attacker approached him. He could not hear her steps over the screaming, or, maybe, each step she took was another scream from the mouth of a terrified cosplayer. Either way, Casey was shaking in his bed. He pulled the blanket around him, but it did not do much good.

???-???-????: I know that you're reading these messages, Casey. I know everything. You should answer me so that this doesn't happen again. You might be in over your head here, but I can save you. Just listen to me, talk to me, and this will all be okay.

◦✦═◦ ◦═✦◦

Rowan was able to find Steve's house with ease once he had the address. He lived on a main road in a duplex apartment. Steve left the door unlocked, and Rowan could have waltzed in to have a look around. When he got to the front door, he grasped the doorknob and held it as he became washed in apprehension.

Rowan did not know if he was ready to see his past love. He did not know if it would do anything to help him. Maybe he should have left it in his past life, something that he overcame to move to the next one.

Except, he did not overcome it. He succumbed to the lure of suicide, leaving a loose end behind in the world. Rowan had a unique chance to find out how his actions affected others, but, now that he was so close to discovering the answer, he was afraid of the truth.

Rowan wanted Steve to be okay, to have moved on with his life, but at the same time he wanted Steve to feel his absence, to make it seem as if there was a point to their friendship. Rowan struggled with the question of which answer he wanted.

Rowan removed his hand from the doorknob when he felt it turn.

The door opened and Steve was in front of him. Instantly, Rowan felt a vibrational energy between them that seemed to solidify into a solid field around Steve. Paradoxically, the area between them felt empty enough that Rowan could have reached out and touched him with no resistance.

Rowan's reaction was to move out of Steve's way as he exited the house and walked towards the street. He followed close behind him and noticed his easy gait and the way Steve carried himself. He seemed so tall, but that was because he stood at his full height and carried the weight of the atmosphere effortlessly on his shoulders. Steve looked around as he made his journey down the street, occasionally waving at people across the way or shaking hands and giving hugs to friends that he passed. Steve did not linger for long. There was somewhere he had to be.

That place was a coffee shop a few blocks away from Steve's apartment. There was a woman there who hugged him, a deeper embrace than the others. Steve looked into the woman's eyes and they kissed each other on the lips. Rowan watched with curiosity. There was no mention in the journal about Steve being a in a relationship.

Rowan felt elation at the fact that his friend had found love, but his stomach also felt empty as if he had not eaten in days. He took a swig from the gasoline that he had been refilling since the attack at the convention center to fill himself up. As he drank, a budding awareness took hold in his spirit, one of a tempered passion, a respect for others, and the collision and consequences of the bubbling aspects of the universe.

⊶⚎⚏⊷

???-???-????: If you don't answer, I'll have to send Alex down to check on you. I hate seeing you like this, and I do see you. I know everything there is to know, Casey. I know that you made a mistake bringing Charlie along to the convention. You fell in love with him, didn't you? Zephiscestra saw your love as getting in the way of her plan. You killed for Lust, and Charlie was killed for Love. In this world, opposites keep us in balance. When you cross too far in any direction, a correction must be made. I can help you to walk the line so that this won't happen again.

Casey could not help but read the messages from Fix, but he was too hurt and confused to answer. If Fix knew that something was going to happen, then why did he let Casey go to the convention?

He must have known, otherwise he would not have sent an armed guard along. If that was the case, and Fix wanted me to be protected, then he could have at least told me about the danger instead of being secretive about it.

Casey mulled over his thoughts while Fix continued to text him. The messages got more frantic as they came, with Fix afraid that Casey was angry at him. It almost sounded like they were going through a breakup. Casey already lost his boyfriend, and he did not want to lose his only guide to the supernatural as well. He finally decided to answer. When he picked up his phone, though, he got a call from an unknown number. A different number than Fix's.

⊷═◉═⊶

Rowan's finger was about an inch from Steve's cheek. He wanted to reach out and touch him, to fall into the smooth water of his skin, but something stopped him. Something about the way Steve looked at the woman made Rowan understand that Steve was his own person with his own wants and desires. He knew that people were individuals, but he finally was able to internalize that facet of existence and become comfortable with it.

By touching him, Rowan could not make Steve remember him. He could only increase his feelings of Lust for those around him. If they were to touch, Steve would probably jump over the table and start making love to his date right there outside the coffee shop. No matter how badly Rowan had wished to see his friend naked in his past life, he presently felt no wish to manipulate Steve's emotions. The best thing to do would be to leave. Now that Rowan had closure, now that he was sure that his friend had moved on, there was no reason to stay.

The budding awareness in Rowan quivered as if it had just been doused with a nourishing dew.

Steve pulled out his phone and typed in the password. Rowan could not help but look at the password. Steve checked a message and slipped the phone back into his bag, and Rowan did not fight his own hand when it crept in after it.

⊷═◉═⊶

"Hello?" Casey answered the phone tentatively, half expecting a crazed fan who would blame him for the shooting. He had already blocked so many numbers, and he knew that many more people with fresh phones could have gotten his contact information.

Ugh, who is this, now?

The voice on the other end answered his question.

"Casey Benton? This is Amy Whittaker. I'm a Junior Executive for Extraspace Records. Have you heard of us?"

Amy was delighted to hear that he had.

"I'm calling to let you know that our Executive Producer has taken an interest in you. He's heard some of your covers on your channel and wants you to come into the office to discuss some business opportunities."

Casey rolled over in the bed and put his arm over his eyes. "Sorry, I just don't think that I'm up to it. I was there during the mass shooting that just happened in L.A. and I need to take it easy for a while."

"That's just it, Casey," Amy said. "We are calling because of the shooting, too. Our producer saw you on the news, and he saw your sc'ermin, too."

Casey's blood ran cold, and he almost shattered his phone against the wall as if they did not already know where he was. When he recognized his own fear, Zephiscestra noticed it, as well. The Goddess enacted the next step in Her plan of the transformation of Casey Benton.

Indeed, the world is balanced by opposing forces. Casey had Indulged in the desires which had been fulfilled by Zephiscestra, and each and every interaction with fans had pulled the strings of his heart into the direction of joy. Now, She swung the pendulum in the other direction.

Casey felt a surge of anger, an anger that he had never known. It came with a lack of inhibition, a lack of awareness of negative consequences that allowed his spirit to move towards revenge, unobstructed by reason and unhindered by fear.

Casey gritted his teeth and said, "It was you. You were the ones who sent that shooter."

⊷⊷◉ ◉⊶⊶

Rowan entered the password to Steve's phone. A picture of a dog was set as the background. The messages app had several notifications on the icon, and Rowan pressed it open.

He scrolled through the many texts that Steve had received over the past few weeks until he found what he was looking for. His heart beat rapidly in his chest when he saw his own name in the list. There was a smiley face emoticon next to it.

Rowan could feel his pulse through his fingers when he opened their history. The only messages were on the right side of the phone, meaning that Steve had sent them. The most recent messages were sentimental and loving, as if Steve had been texting his brother or close relative. The messages were for Steve alone, and they spoke of forgiveness. As Rowan scrolled back in time, the texts became more frantic and confused, and Rowan felt tears behind his eyes for the first time that he could ever remember.

Rowan went back to the present and read the last message a few times, then smiled and put the phone back into Steve's bag.

Everything was the way it should be. Steve had lost a friend but found a lover. The only thing holding him back from delving into the depths of the woman with him was the memory of someone who used to hold him so dear.

The budding awareness blossomed into a material Love, a force with direction, attraction, and polarity. The secrets of discretion, of combination, of keeping to a path and moving forward into the wilderness. He unlocked a drive within him that knew when to stop and when to go, knew what turns to take and how to remain within the boundaries of success.

Could this awareness come from god? From Zephiscestra? It doesn't feel like Her, though...

Rowan stepped behind Steve and, while he was looking at his girlfriend, put his hands on both of his shoulders. He could feel Steve tense up as if he were a serpent coiled tightly around a field mouse that had been dead for days.

An energy flowed through them, one that Rowan did not completely understand bet knew how to use. Rowan felt his awareness merge with Steve's. He felt his emotions surge higher, and he found that he was in control of the surge. When the timing felt right, Rowan eased the surge and felt his emotions soften and expand. Before he could feel them evaporate, he surged again to bountiful, energetic life.

When Rowan opened his eyes, Steve grabbed the woman's hand and almost dragged her away, back towards the direction of his apartment.

Rowan watched them go with a smile on his face. He could not make Steve forget about him, but he could help him remember the people that he was with. Steve had a life to live, and Rowan was fine with giving it a jumpstart. It was the least that he could do for his closest friend, after all. For a moment, Rowan fancied the thought that Steve was picturing him in his mind. He felt that emotion surge, and then, with confidence, let it evaporate harmlessly.

Rowan laughed to himself as the image disappeared.

The two were separated by life and death itself. But, for a fleeting moment, Rowan felt human.

CHAPTER 26

SEVERAL DAYS PASSED before Casey and Rowan could meet with the Executive Producer. The Junior Executive had confirmed that her boss had planned the attack, although she said that no more information would be revealed unless Casey and his sc'ermin flew to the head office of their production company. She set a non-negotiable date for when they could meet, Casey bought an airline ticket that night.

Fix had been silent since the night Casey received the phone call. Under Zephiscestra's renewed influence, Casey was too determined to even worry about Fix's whereabouts, and he became too confident in his own movements to yearn for anyone else's guidance.

While Fix initially appeared to have his best interests in mind, the mysterious contact's most recent messages had turned aggressive and controlling. Either way, Casey wasn't thinking about him. He wanted nothing more than to meet the Executive Producer and attack him directly. They could die, but Casey wanted to let the Executive Producer know how much of a monster he was.

Casey was seething during the flight, and Rowan sat in the only empty seat that he could find. The pair didn't speak during their travel. Casey navigated through the terminals and taxis and with Rowan at his heels. Through Zephiscestra's insidious influence, Casey's fans didn't try to communicate with him. Casey, in his drive, didn't notice the lack of fanfare. Rowan pondered it but figured that they were simply lucky enough to travel unhindered by people who would only incur Casey's palpable anger.

Finally, Casey arrived at the building of the record head. The immense skyscraper was a pillar of mirrored windows, giving the illusion of recursion with regards to the adjacent buildings on the city block. When they entered the lobby, they saw that the floor was a sea of black glass. In fact, pretty much everything was made of black glass in the building, all planes and edges, from the front desk to the pots that held jagged plants.

The receptionist, a timid man, gave Casey a visitor's badge. A burly woman escorted them to the elevator and entered the chamber with them. Casey and Rowan remained silent. Rowan could have sworn that the woman gave him a once-over, but he had no way of knowing how many people had completed the ritual in the company.

They got halfway up the building before they had to take another elevator to the top. The second lift raised them with meteoric speed, gauged by the pits in their stomachs and the rapidly climbing numbers on the digital display. Rowan's apprehension mounted as the time to the top grew shorter. Casey, on the other hand, clenched his jaw tighter and tighter with his increasing anger. They both could not wait to see the Executive Producer, but each had different reasons. Rowan wanted to see what they were up against, and Casey wanted to see the scum that killed his boyfriend.

Suddenly, the walls of the elevator fell beneath them, the floor kept rising, and then the world spread out before them. The penthouse office overlooked the metropolitan area, and no other building reached higher into the sky. The office was immense and made entirely of black glass, like the rest of the building that they had seen.

There was nothing on the black floor—which spread in a perfect unbroken square to the windows—except for a red-walled cube in the direct center. The cube was about the size of a normal executive office.

As they approached the cube, they could see a man who sat facing them, his red-tinted eyes glowering in mirth. The burly woman beckoned them ever forward, and Casey and Rowan followed her to the devil's den.

Before Casey knew it, he was inside of the red room. The glass panes had slithered open, rippling like liquid, and somehow sucked him in. He felt a strange moment of ecstasy when he passed through the walls, a feeling tinged by primal aversion, but it faded when he saw his enemy.

The Executive Producer appeared even more bloodthirsty up close. A name-plate on his desk read "Noah Larkin." The man laughed when the burly woman pushed them down into the two chairs facing the desk, and he laughed even harder when Casey tried to tell him to fuck off.

"This?" Larkin gestured his upturned, open palms towards Casey and Rowan. "This is the slaughterhouse that A'devios was sending our brothers and sisters into? Into the teeth of Tarwick, the Black Hellhound. How he ripped our siblings to shreds and murdered a few humans as well."

Casey's head whipped around towards Rowan. Casey, who was grieving the death of a human he loved, glowered at Rowan with immediate hatred.

"The Sloth's human," Rowan said. "No one innocent."

Larkin said, "Your old servant here didn't tell you that? You boys are green. I watched the way you cried when Scorn crashed your little audition."

The woman restrained Casey's shoulders when he tried to leap from his chair and vault over the Larkin's desk. "You know nothing of death. Do you, boy?"

"I saw them all die," Casey screamed. "Every one of them, I saw them die. Because of you. Why did you do it? To kill me? You have me right here. Just try to end it."

The hair on the back of Rowan's neck bristled as he sensed Casey's anger, and he readied himself for a fight. He had taken on mutated sc'ermin already, and the Executive Producer did not seem to have one with him.

"You think I need a sc'ermin to take you on?" Casey's eyes betrayed his doubt, and the Executive sat back in his chair in victory. He interlaced his fingers and said, "There is magic that you don't know anything about, isn't there? I have a list of incantations that could make your blood boil, drive you insane, or outright kill you. I don't need my sc'ermin. They're good tools, but I can deal with you through words instead of claws. Not that there's much difference."

Rowan, in a moment of clarity, asked the question that was on his mind. "Who is this A'devios? We've never heard of them before."

"Oh, you've heard of him, maybe just not by that name. He's your contact, the one who has been texting you this whole time and giving you information. He didn't tell you as much as he told us, though."

The pit in Casey's stomach gained new depths, and the confusion was clearly displayed on his face.

"Do you mean Fix?"

Rowan put a hand on Casey's arm to hold back his admission, but the information was already out.

"That's what he's calling himself, then," Larkin said. "Well, in any rate, he's in hiding now. Your friend *Fix* was the leader of our commune called Capital Vice. It's a group of Zealots and sc'ermin living together and getting stronger until the day when we meet Zephiscestra. We Indulge in our sins, making our sc'ermin stronger and squashing any upstarts that won't agree to join us. We are remarkably close to our goddess, and She speaks to us frequently.

"Well, one of our members received a vision of our former figurehead's treason against his own people. It was hard to believe at first, but it lined up with the events that have been taking place.

"Not too long ago, A'devios told us of a sc'ervice, which is a human and their sc'ermin, who he had reached out to and who rejected his message. He sent a sc'ervice of our own, Ravage and his partner, Elliot, to dispose of them. Ravage died, and we heard about the ferocity with which you killed him. Then, Paul and De Lailla proposed a battle with you. The chivalry should have fed their Pride, but your little fans cyber bullied them to their demise."

Larkin chuckled with grim hatred.

"Who would have thought that in this ancient game of life after death, a few posts on social media could hold so much power. Also, don't forget that we found Ms. Bertie Jasper with her head caved in while she was in her apartment. She was a hag, but she was a good source of revenue for us. You took that away."

"So, that *was* who you killed," Casey said.

"You didn't see what she did to her baby," Rowan said. "Smothered it in its sleep,"

Larkin said. "Probably just sat on it, truth be told. But, it's no matter now. You've killed enough of our siblings. I was going to kill you outright, but I don't think that you are really much trouble after all. You pulled some swift maneuvers by bolstering your power, but that won't happen anymore. At least, not until I want it to.

"You see, you'll be working for me now. A'devios is gone. I rallied some powerful members of Capital Vice and we drove him and his sc'ermin out. Now, *I'm* in charge of the commune. You'll be my puppet from now on and you'll do as I say."

"What the fuck would you have me do, then," Casey asked, the rage palpable in his voice.

"Unfortunately, I think you'll enjoy it," Larkin said. "Your Lust for fame will be sated, but I'll make a killing off you. I'm going to produce your album, which, with both of our powers combined, will make untold millions. You'll get stronger, sure, but I will hold all of the cards. You'll have all the creative freedom you want, but that's as much freedom as you're going to get. You'll be staying here, on this floor, and you won't be leaving unless I say so."

"I'll die before I let you keep me locked up," Casey said.

"I don't think so," Larkin said. "Don't worry about getting cabin fever, though. I'm hosting a party at my mansion in three days. I've been planning the unveiling of my new artist, so you'll have to be there. Of course, you'll be heavily guarded, so don't even think about trying anything funny. You'll get up on stage, perform a song, and then you'll come right back to this floor to write more music. It'll be fun. You get your moment in the spotlight, just like you wanted, and I will make a ton of money. It's a win-win, to be sure."

"If you think I'll do anything for a murderous monster like you, you're out of your fucking mind."

"You don't have a choice, Casey," Larkin said. "I know who your little friends are, and I know where your family lives. I have an army of sc'ermin under my direct control, as well as a commune of Zealots who will follow my every word. You're outmatched, Casey. I've been in the game for years, and you've only just started. I've forgotten more about Zephiscestra than you will ever know. She blesses me daily, and it looks like She has turned her back on you. Now, time to show you to your quarters."

Larkin waved his hand and, suddenly, four sc'ermin stood beside them. They were each at least six feet tall and were covered in rough scales. Their fangs jutted out from their mouths and sharp, curled horns adorned their heads like crowns. They stared down at Casey and Rowan with their claws out and ready.

"Bring Casey to the southwest corner, and bring Rowan to the northeast," Larkin said. "Mel," he said, speaking to the burly woman, "Raise the walls and provide sleeping rolls. Also, bring Casey a felt tipped pen and a pad of paper. Nothing else."

The scaly sc'ermin growled their acknowledgement and laid their hands on Casey and Rowan. Casey tried to struggle, but the large sc'ermin could manhandle him with ease. Rowan, stronger and more durable, had his shoulders and sides pierced with long claws to deny his escape. Larkin smiled and waved them away. They were led out of the red office, and again Casey felt the ecstasy that was brought about by passing through the wall.

The enemy sc'ermin separated them and brought them to opposite corners of the floor. Casey tried to turn his head to look at Rowan, to cry out and tell him to fight them. The grip on him was too forceful, and the claws were too near his throat. One combative move and he would be dead in an instant.

Rowan was too far away to reach him even if he was not being held captive by two sc'ermin himself. When they got to the corner of the floor, the two sc'ermin pushed Casey to the ground. They snarled and pointed their claws at him, and Casey backed up against the window. With the skyline at his back, Casey watched as two blue walls of light materialized around him, trapping him in his prison. The scaly sc'ermin laughed a hideous, gravely cackle and then left him alone.

There was no sign of the burly woman, Mel, as of yet, but Casey knew she would be back with his things. They would be the only things he would be allowed for the next few days. A pen and paper, to do Larkin's work for him.

Casey curled his knees to his chest and fought back the tears that were already flowing. He gnashed his teeth with rage at Larkin, at Fix—A'devios—and at the insurmountable army of sc'ermin that were waiting for him at the mansion. He bit his lip until it bled, dug his fingernails into his legs, and ground his feet into the floor. No matter what he did, it was of no use against his frustration.

Rowan was on the other side of the room, about a million miles away. Their captor lie between them. Zephiscestra was somewhere above them, but Casey wanted nothing to do with Her. She had gotten them into this mess with Her cruel sense righteousness. Still, Casey would not curse Her name. During his time in Indulgence, Casey didn't curse at her with any conviction, due both to fear of Her power and to an enjoyment of Her benefits. Still, he had wished that She wasn't around.

Now, Casey struggled with his acceptance of Her, because all he wanted now was for Her to act against Larkin in ways that only She could.

CHAPTER 27

CASEY SAT CROSS legged on a white pedestal, surrounded by darkness. He could not see his own body, but the pedestal was somehow illuminated by a light source that only touched its surface. The cool stone did not reflect anything but seemed to contain the essence of light. Casey looked at the black shape of his hand. He could only see it as a contrast to the white of the pedestal. When he held it into the air, it disappeared.

"Casey, do not be afraid." The voice came from nowhere and everywhere, outside of his head and inside of it. Casey looked around but saw nothing. "It is I, A'devios. You knew me as Fix, but that charade has been ended. I have come to set you free."

"This is a dream," Casey said. He suddenly remembered that he went to sleep on the floor of the blue walled cell.

"You are asleep, but this is no dream," A'devios said. "We are within a fractal of the Black Jewel of reality, a solid space that contains the energy of the universe. We are far, far away from the detection of Noah Larkin, here."

"I don't understand what you are saying," Casey said, but he was suddenly aware that he was contained in something solid. Although he could move freely, he could feel contact at each point of his skin, even his eyes. Casey suddenly felt claustrophobic and afraid, and he began to hyperventilate.

"No need to breathe, Casey. There is no air here. Long ago, great cracks formed in reality, and within those cracks exist the matter that you understand as your universe. We are in a different place, now, where the others can't reach us."

"Is Zephiscestra here? Is this Her domain?"

"Zephiscestra exists on the surface of what we know as reality. I call this ultimate reality the Black Jewel. We are not in Her domain, but in a different part of creation. Her domain is vacuum taught against the angles and planes of the edges of reality, features of the Black Jewel itself. ."

Casey remembered Larkin's office with its flat, black, empty floor. "Larkin modelled his building after that space."

"That is correct," A'devios said. "Larkin fancies himself close to Her. He builds his army of sc'ermin for the day he may present them to Her as a dowry. You see, that is the essence of the ritual that you performed the night that Rowan died. The words are vows with which you propose your life to Zephiscestra, and your sc'ermin is the offering with which you seal the words. When you die, you will have a chance to set your gifts at Her altar and pray that She accepts them. Everyone has their wish to be fulfilled on earth, and then there is the desire that they wish to be fulfilled in the afterlife. Larkin wishes to meet Zephiscestra as an equal. Others don't think that far ahead."

"Why are you telling me this? Why did you bring me here? Why—Why did you lie to me?"

Casey remembered what Larkin had told him in his office, how A'devios was the leader of a death cult and how he had sent his followers to attack him and Rowan. Yet, he also warned them of the coming danger.

"You led them to us. You led us into danger. I don't want to listen to a thing that you have to say. You have brought nothing but pain to me, and now you want to confuse me. You are a terrible person. I don't want to know how many people you have killed to get to where you are."

"It is true that I killed many," A'devios said. "And it is true that I kept you ignorant. However, I needed to trick the other Zealots to keep you alive. Once I became aware of you, I knew that I had to keep you safe. But we live in a dangerous world, and steps had to be taken to rid us of our enemies while keeping ourselves alive. But, now is the time that I shed light on your predicament. Don't forget that you read the incantation yourself. I did lead the initiative to circulate the incantation online, but I had no part in your personal ritual. Once you pledged yourself to Zephiscestra, I took my own interest in you. Now, hush while I explain what you must do next."

"I'm not going to listen to you," Casey said. "Let me go, now."

"You know not the power you hold over me," A'devios said, "But I won't release you back into your prison until I tell you how to get out of it."

Casey shook his head in shock but allowed himself to listen to A'devios, only for the sake of escape from his prison. "What do you have to say?"

"Larkin is going to hold a party to show you off in two days. Once you are there, you must seek his daughter, Lexie. Once you find her, you must ask her to bring you to Larkin's dungeon. When you reach it—"

"To the dungeon?" Casey was incredulous. "You must think I'm an idiot to believe you. You're trying to lead me down there to get killed."

"If I wanted you dead, I should only picture it in my mind and it would be," A'devios said.

"Why don't you picture the death of Larkin, then," Casey asked.

"He's too powerful," A'devios said, "And he is too favorable to Zephiscestra. I have a device that allows me to channel a thought of death and make it a reality, but only if She also wills it. So far, She won't allow Larkin to die so easily."

"What is in the dungeon that will allow me to kill him?"

"Larkin creates his sc'ermin in his dungeon, and he has many, many sc'ermin. Down there is also a vault where he keeps his most valuable possessions. Larkin kills for Greed, and he kills for Greed every time without fail. Where adoration makes you stronger, material wealth gives him his power. You must destroy his treasure trove to bring him to his knees. He has an army of sc'ermin with him, but, if you weaken them, Rowan can help take them out."

"How do you know that this daughter will bring me to the dungeon?"

"Lexie is an independent force," A'devios said. "She and her sc'ermin are incredibly powerful. I can say without a shred of doubt that they are the most powerful sc'ervice to currently exist. She's grown from birth at Capital Vice, although she doesn't understand truly how much more powerful she is compared to everyone else there. From the time of her birth to now, her awareness of her standing in reality has been harnessed by her father and the others who now lead the commune. Everything she has based her understanding on has been merely shadows playing for her against the cave wall. She has never been allowed to understand others for what they really are, compared to her. I've recently helped her see the truth. Lexie will want to take down her father who has exploited her endlessly for her entire life. She is a bit entangled in the commune, so she will need your help to do this. This, I know to be true."

"Okay," Casey said, "But, how do I know that Rowan will be strong enough to defeat the weakened sc'ermin? Shouldn't I augment his power as well?"

"A fine idea, and one that I thought of myself. There will be a video camera in the dungeon waiting for you, one that connects to the internet. Film yourself destroying Larkin's wealth to bolster Rowan's abilities. That being said, Lexie's sc'ermin will really be the one who will do the heavy lifting. Indulging for Rowan's sake will keep him alive."

Casey mulled over the plan in his mind. It seemed as if it could work, if what A'devios was saying was true. If not, Casey would be walking into his own grave. The other option was to remain prisoner and slave to Larkin for the rest of his life until the Executive Producer decided to kill him. There really was no choice but to trust A'devios, even if it was the last thing he did.

"Okay, I'll agree to do this," Casey said. "But, here's the thing. I don't want Larkin dead. I want all of his sc'ermin to be destroyed so that he is left on Earth, confused and afraid. I want him to fear material things for the rest of his life and crawl to Zephiscestra a shell of a man. I want him to die penniless and imprisoned, too scared to even trade a biscuit for an extra cigarette."

Casey could not see it, but he could feel A'devios' joy. The enveloping surface surrounding him took on a sort of black warmth, moist and steaming.

"Men plan, and Zephiscestra laughs," A'devios said. "You continue to surprise me, Casey. Thank you for believing in me."

"I don't believe in you," Casey said. "I don't see myself surviving any other way. By the way, where will you be during all of this? You say you have so much power, but you didn't mention showing up to help me."

"Oh, I will be on the grounds of the mansion that night," A'devios said. "Larkin thinks me gone forever, but, in his arrogance, he forgets that his mansion used to be mine, long ago. I can sneak into the dungeon and meet you there."

"Will you use your sc'ermin to fight with Rowan?"

"My own sc'ermin are known to Capital Vice. I will have to travel alone to evade detection."

"Ah, but you do have sc'ermin. Multiple."

"I have amassed many sc'ermin over the last century or so, yes," A'devios said.

The last century. Could it be? How could this man live for a hundred years?
Casey struggled with the realization.

There was magic that could kill, could there be magic that could make someone live forever? Maybe he could not die unless Zephiscestra allowed it, and he was so vital to Her plans that She kept him alive past a normal human lifespan.

The conscious thought of Zephiscestra's power overwhelmed his senses until even the white pedestal disappeared from his awareness. The Goddess could do anything She wished in dimensional space from her throne on the outskirts of reality. Casey kicked himself for not understanding that Zephiscestra, this mysterious deity, had complete control over death. And, if She were the master of death, wouldn't She be able to master life as well?

Countless possibilities ran through Casey's mind, and he was gripped with a fear that he had never known. Even Scorn's Wrath could not put this type of terror into him. An active shooter was a nightmare to his generation, but Zephiscestra was an ancient, cosmic horror that pervaded every inch of the universe and expanded to what lay beyond its edges. With all of the uncertainty about Zephiscestra, Casey had one burning question at the forefront of his mind as well.

"A'devios, who are you, really? I've never seen you before, but I've heard your voice. I've seen your words, and your followers. You are real, incarnate, but there is a sort of ethereal aura about you. Are you even human?"

A'devios laughed, and Casey felt the encompassing surface pulse against his skin. There was a caress at his cheek. Thin, invisible fingers reached for his loins. Casey covered himself with his hands and A'devios whimpered in perverted playfulness.

"I cannot harm you, Casey, but not because I am physically unable. I have lived for over a hundred years, and I am stronger than ever. I tell you this next truth because I love you. As much as I have torn my soul and sold it to sin, I have found that I have the capacity for love, and that love is for you alone. Yes, I know that you have an eminence of Lust about you, but it's different than that.

"You see, many, many years ago, I was crippled in a horse-riding accident. My body was broken, but my mind remained sharp. I had no use of my legs, so I was confined to a bed for several months. I was lucky enough to have been born into wealth, and I converted my estate's library into my bedchambers. During that time, I read all that I could and gained a thirst for knowledge that could never be quenched. I learned so much from books, about life and about the world, but I couldn't leave my home to see any of it with my own eyes. I wished to walk, to run, to frolic through the streets of every city on earth, but still I remained bedridden.

"One day, a priest came to my home and said that he could cure me. This man had been exiled from his church after claims that he was practicing dark magic. He told me all of this, yet I was unafraid of him. He said that if he uttered a few words I would be able to walk again.

"Well, he said the words. But, as you can guess, he then tried to kill me. There was a struggle, as I could still move my upper body and torso. He was a frail man, to say the least, and must have chosen me because he thought that I would be easy prey. I cried out for my butler, who thwarted the priest's plot and had him imprisoned. As he was being dragged from my chambers, the man shouted that I must die to walk again.

"My attacker was found dead in the morning, but his words to me lived on. He left his papers in my room when he was captured, and I ordered a servant to hide them until I had a chance to read them. I found the incantation that he read right before he tried to kill me. I read myself read the words aloud. Then, I stabbed myself in the neck with a letter opener. When I awoke, I walked out of the house and never returned."

A'devios let the moment sink in. Casey closed his eyes and let whatever feelings arose wash over him.

"Say you will conquer Larkin with me, Casey. Together, we can rule this world."

The darkness around him began to lift, and Casey was able to see the city come into view. He was afraid, but his Lust for revenge was stronger.

Casey had made up his mind. He would take Larkin down.

CHAPTER 28

ROWAN STARED AT the three scaly sc'ermin through hazy eyes. Each of them wore gold jewelry around their necks, arms, and hands. One of them had a tiara perched between the horns of its head. They paced back and forth in front of his blue walled cell, licking the edges of their mouths with forked tongues.

The party at Larkin's mansion was the next day. A'devios had come to Rowan in a vision and told him of the plan. Casey was already on board, not that he had a choice.

Rowan wondered if he would have agreed to the proposed course of action if Charlie had not died. Of course, they wouldn't have even met Larkin if they had avoided the shooting at the convention, so it only made sense that Casey would choose this path. Rowan deeply sensed the vengeance that was building inside of Casey. It made him uneasy.

Rowan was now aware of how Casey must have felt when Rowan was unleashing his anger and frustration only a few weeks before. He hated to see his human partner so taut with hatred. The vibrations seeped into his psyche and made him want to fight the cause of the unrest.

If what A'devios said was true, Rowan would get a chance to kill his captors. If the plan went smoothly, Rowan's powers would be heightened while the enemy sc'ermin would be at their most vulnerable. Rowan eyed the jewels that adorned the sc'ermin in front of him. Precious metals were valuable to humans, but, to Larkin's sc'ermin, they meant the difference between life and death. If they were sacrificed for Greed, even an earring could give them the edge that they needed to kill him.

Rowan came to the realization that the scaly sc'ermin only wore the jewelry when Larkin was out of the office. So, they did not expect to lose the fight with Larkin there.

Could he really kill us with a word? Do they think that I would try to escape?

Such a thing would be impossible. The blue walls of the cell were impenetrable, and when Rowan had tried to put his hands on them, he found that he could not even touch them. His body was repelled by an invisible force that surrounded the walls, and even trying to lean against the surface made him slip down to the floor.

Larkin's sc'ermin could open up the walls, though, and it was three against one. Casey did not have access to social media, so there was no chance of boosting his power at the time. He did not think they would try to kill him, though. No, they must keep him alive so that Casey would be able to generate profits for Larkin. Without Rowan, Casey would forget everything about Zephiscestra and sc'ermin and fear fame itself. Then, he would be no use to the Executive Producer.

Yes, the sc'ermin would keep him alive. But they might have their fun with him first.

Rowan was not sure if he could trust A'devios. Their contact had been caught in a lie, one that endangered their lives. Rowan wasn't sure if A'devios could offer anything that could truly help them.

But then, in his vision, A'devios told him something to slake Rowan's own thirst for the nature of his reality, something that affected everyone in the universe.

In the beginning, the only existence was of Zephiscestra, although She didn't have a name because there was no Other to refer to Her. She was everything that there was and contained all aspects of everything. She wanted to make something beautiful, so She used the only material She owned: Herself.

Zephiscestra took all of her favorite parts and put them together. She formed those substances into an immaculate Black Jewel, a piece of perfect creation. All life as anyone had known it existed within the Jewel, and their goddess was all that was not.

With the best parts of Her removed, She formed into a hideous shape made up of her worst features. The Jewel was so beautiful that it was all that She could think about.

Zephiscestra held the Black Jewel in great regard. It was the most wondrous thing that She had ever seen, not only because it was the only other thing in existence, but because it was perfect.

The substance that filled the Jewel was the essence of Love, and what was left behind in Zephiscestra was a façade of this concept. Zephiscestra took on the forms of Lust for unfulfilling relations with her creation, Vainglory for proximity to perfection, Envy of Her very creation, Wrath for Her separation from Love, Gluttony for Her desire's attention, Sloth in the comfort of Her desire, and Greed for all of it for Herself.

The Jewel was without those things. Soon, Zephiscestra, in an attempt to join fully with the life in the Jewel, tried to enter the Jewel and live within it. However, she could not mingle with the immaculate material. Her force created great cracks in the Jewel. Fragments of its perfection floated in the fissures, and those weaker fragments were subjected to Zephiscestra's control. While all matter was made up of the Jewel, Zephiscestra's force pervaded and influenced it. She, and the sc'ermin that were made to be her servants, were mere shadows of perfection.

Rowan contemplated this story for as long as he could. He knew that he must have felt love in his past life, but he wasn't sure if the blossoming awareness that he had discovered when he found Steve was the same. He wondered if, by connecting to his past life, he was somehow regaining the ability to love, to connect more fully with the Black Jewel, with perfection. He further wondered whether fighting other sc'ermin would allow him to continue down his path of love, or if it would bring him ever closer to Zephiscestra.

There was too much to think about. The revelation of the structure of the universe, coupled with the newfound knowledge of their goddess, still did not protect him from his immediate enemies. There were three sc'ermin surrounding his cell, and an army waiting at Larkin's mansion.

I might be able to take them.

He remembered the other sc'ermin that he had killed, demons who were under the tutelage of A'devios himself, yet ultimately betrayed. They knew more about Zephiscestra and Her power, yet Rowan was able to dispatch them handily.

Ravage was the first, an Envy who snuck up on him. Even though Rowan did not see him coming, he was still able to defeat him. The shock of that battle was enough to instill paranoia deep into his heart, so much so that he was willing to take proactive measures against it. Rowan remembered sneaking into the lair of the sleeping Sloth. There was another shock; Rowan killed again, this time a human. However, the execution could have been a favor in the grand scheme of things. This Mrs. So-and-so would get to greet Zephiscestra with a great gift instead of wandering into oblivion, a slave to toil and turmoil.

If a human dies first, they are transported to Zephiscestra to present their offering. If a sc'ermin dies first, the human forgets all about Zephiscestra—and Her many powers—and fears what they made their offering for.

Rowan shivered with the thought of Casey succumbing to the fear of recognition and romantic affections. He would become a true hermit and probably live somewhere out in the woods, away from all social media, technology, and people to give him comfort. He would die alone, ignorant of the cause of his strife.

It was a harrowing thought, but Rowan already knew which path Casey would take—that is, if he was given the opportunity to choose.

The sc'ermin with the tiara motioned to its partners. Rowan read their lipless maws: "He's bored. Let's cut him up a bit." The other two jewel-adorned sc'ermin looked at him hungrily. One of them scampered to the red-walled office in the center of the floor, reaching the perimeter in an instant. He passed through and rummaged around in Larkin's desk until he found what he was looking for.

The walls evaporated. The first thing Rowan looked for was Casey across the floor. Rowan could see his partner who too far away to reach. Now, the only decision was whether to fight back or to endure their torture until they decided to leave him alone.

Could I beat them into submission?

The first claw bit into Rowan's forearm. He recoiled and dodged when the sc'ermin lashed out again. The second was upon him and seized his arms. They were much stronger than him in this state. *They will not kill me. We are too valuable to Larkin. But this is gonna hurt.*

"The sullen hellhound isn't so tough without his partner," one of the sc'ermin hissed. It struck out again with its claws and swiped Rowan across the cheek. Blood trickled down into Rowan's mouth. The sc'ermin punched him in the gut. Rowan doubled over and was struck in the face again. He howled in pain and was struck again.

Rowan looked over at Casey and saw that he was watching the beating.

Casey's hands were not pressed against the translucent blue walls because they would be repelled by the unseen force, but he was standing and facing them. Rowan saw the rage on Casey's face, and he was momentarily terrified. The scaly sc'ermin sealed their fate by attacking him at that moment; Casey was going to kill them all.

As the cuts rained down from fearsome claws, Rowan looked towards the future when he would be at full strength and fighting a weakened enemy. The tables would be turned at that time, and Rowan would have to choose whether or not to let his enemies live. After this exchange, the choice would be easier.

CHAPTER 29

IN THE CENTER of the widest landscape that Casey had ever seen laid Larkin's mansion. All growth had been razed for miles around the estate. In all directions, only the horizon could be seen in the furthest distances on that moonless night.

Casey sat in the back of a large, private limousine with Rowan and two of Larkin's sc'ermin, as well as two other partygoers named Gerald and Janis. Casey wore a tuxedo, Rowan had his usual clothes on, and the lizard-like sc'ermin pair were loaded with jewelry.

Casey also wore a ring, one not owned by him, but one that made him its bestower's slave.

When Casey had put it on, the golden ring with the boundless black jewel sucked on Casey's finger and wrapped black tendrils around his hand. Larkin explained that whatever Indulgence he gained while wearing it would be transferred to its owner.

"Don't try anything bold tonight, kid," Larkin had said. "You'll only make it worse for yourself."

Larkin was noticeably more confident after binding Casey's power, going so far as to allow Rowan out of his cell to accompany him at the party.

He wants me to know that he has complete power over me, even when I have my most powerful weapon at my side.

There was a way around it, but it was going to be tricky. First, they had to find Larkin's daughter, then destroy the loot. Weakening Larkin in such a way could give them a chance to end all of this.

Rowan stared at Casey silently. He watched him chat with Gerald and Janice about normal things in human life. They discussed his goals and how far he had come in just a short amount of time.

It is obvious they don't know about us.

Rowan gauged the distance between the unsuspecting attendees and the sc'ermin with the menacing demeanors. The limousine was spacious, so Larkin's goons could still rough him up without bumping into the anyone else in the limo.

Not that the others would notice the assault, anyway.

Humans out of a sc'ervice did not perceive the monstrosity that fought him in the parking lot of the convention center, even when it knocked them aside. Rowan feared for what would happen to him at the party when he would be surrounded by those things.

Is it true that he has an army? How many could it be? Hundreds?

When their limousine finally got through the inner gates to the main estate and onto the back lawn's driveway, Rowan saw that his hunch was correct.

Mingled with the scores of partygoers were countless sc'ermin that resembled dragons of all shapes. Some prowled on four legs, some hunched their backs under leathery wings, and still others slithered pompously between serving tables and chafing dishes.

Rowan gulped as the enemies approached over the grass towards the car, as if they knew who was inside.

They do know who is inside. They can sense me, they can sense Casey's ring, probably.

They were everywhere, and most of the party did not have a clue. Rowan mused that he would not be able to focus on finding the trove if he were too busy fighting off his captors. He hoped that Lexie Larkin had a plan to allow them to move undetected.

At that point, Gerald and Janice were asking Casey for a private performance, right there in the back seat. Casey was politely turning them down, saying that he needed to save his voice for later in the evening. That got them excited, and then Janice was asking for a selfie and Gerald was leaning in with a smile.

When Casey and Rowan exited the vehicle, they were swarmed by fans and sc'ermin alike. Casey posed with people and made faces for cameras. Rowan tried to make himself small while getting jostled by enemies.

"You killed our best Sloth," one of the lizard-like sc'ermin said, poking him in the back with a yellowed claw.

"Who am I supposed to stare at all day with De Lailla gone," another asked before launching a jewel-encrusted fist into Rowan's stomach. Rowan tried to stay as close as he could to Casey, who was being harassed and tortured in a much different way. The human partygoers showered him with compliments.

Casey did not want to be adored that night. He wanted to be as ferocious and terrifying as Rowan was on his worst day.

Others asked him if he was going to try to ask any celebrities on a date any time soon. They pointed to other famous partygoers and asked Casey, "What do you think?" They offered Casey "opportunities" for risqué photoshoots with other famous people. There were plenty of suggestions that brought Casey's mind back to Charlie and the fate that he had to suffer to bring Casey here.

Charlie's memory acted as the guiding line that pulled Casey towards his goal. Mustering all of the courage that he could to remain as polite and unassuming as possible, Casey broke away from the throngs of distractors and went in search of Larkin's daughter.

This meant that he had to leave Rowan on his own, since the scaly sc'ermin were still all around him.

I'm sorry you have to endure this torture, but it's almost a blessing that the sc'ermin are paying more attention to you than to me.

While the humans had a myriad of entertainment options available to them, Rowan was the main attraction for Larkins legion of undead sc'ermin. Casey would have had no chance of making it to the Executive Producer's hoard with those multitudinous yellow eyes on him, but the enemy sc'ermin did not seem to pay much attention to him on his own. With the small amount of privacy that had carved out for himself, Casey made his way across the black stone of the pool deck and into Larkin's mansion.

The floors of the estate were made of black marble with deep red veins that seemed to pump intravenous blood throughout the halls. The walls were a soulless gray that seemed to suck the life out of the various conversations of attendees, who consisted of women in sleek dresses and men in sharp suits.

A woman approached Casey with a tall glass in her hand. She kissed Casey on each cheek and introduced herself as Susan Elberton, a model who worked for one of Larkin's offshoot corporations.

"You must be Casey Benton," she said. "Obviously, our reputations precede us. I've been following you online for quite some time, now. Of course, I haven't officially 'followed' your profile, yet. I wanted us to meet in person and livestream us hitting those buttons on each other's pages."

Casey could have dismissed the idea as an insecure starlet's attempt to gain popularity, but, with the siphoning ring on his finger, he had to suspect a higher, ulterior motive.

"Just, before we do this… I have to ask. Did Larkin tell you to come and find me?"

Susan squealed with delight at the notion that she was in cahoots with someone as powerful as the executive producer. She allowed her eyes to go wide with surprise and gripped Casey's bicep.

"Well, you must know that Noah and I talk a great deal. Since you are one of the main guests of honor at this party, and since I am such a staple of his catalog, he asked me to show you around and take as many pictures as possible. He also said to tag you in each post so that you get, and I quote, "Maximum exposure.""

The pit in Casey's stomach churned.

Larkin obviously wanted to steal Casey's power from him and augment his own sc'ermin's abilities so that there would be no chance for Rowan to try anything besides huddling in a corner. Casey decided to try to get as far away from the woman as possible before she made Larkin any stronger.

"That's okay, Susan," Casey said. "Truth be told, I really just wanted tonight to be a fun experience without having to worry about work."

"You've got it all wrong," Susan said. "Nights like these are what people like us live for. If you don't think that this type of work is fun, I suggest that you find another industry."

Susan mistook Casey's aversion for him weighing his career options and delegating how much importance a few photos with her would have on his future.

"But," she continued, "If you want to hang around with us big-guns then you should stop being a pussy and pose for a selfie."

Casey was taken aback, but the sudden harshness of Susan's words made it easier for him to deny her outright.

"If you're that desperate for a picture, maybe you should find another internet star. This place is crawling with them." After he said it, Casey felt a brief pang of remorse for treating Susan so heartlessly, but he was reminded of why he had to focus on his mission when she gave her rebuttal.

"I get that you don't like me, you fucking asshole," Susan said, "so just scurry off like the little rat that you are and do some marketing with someone else. I really only started talking to you because Noah told me to. And, do not think you're special when you start getting notifications from other celebrities around here. Noah told all of us to make you feel welcome and give you all of the shout outs that your shallow body can take. You are not important to us, though. We're just playing along so that Noah will pay us more."

Susan kept going with her tirade, but Casey had stopped listening. He drew back from her and tapped another partygoer on the shoulder. Susan fumed when Casey asked them to check his social media page for him. Susan flipped him a middle finger and stormed off, but the sight of his page was what made him break out in a cold sweat.

Casey's social media page had garnered hundred of thousands of hits in the last thirty minutes. Celebrities of all kinds on Larkin's payroll were posting his username on their accounts, and several people that he did not even know were wildly famous had posted selfies with him from minutes before.

The implication was obvious: He and Rowan were going to have a dangerous night.

⋆⇒◎⇐⋆

Outside, Rowan was doing just that. Larkin's sc'ermin surrounded him again and sent taunts and blows his way. They admonished him for killing their comrades. Some chided him by thanking him for elevating their master to the head of the Capital Vice, but they struck him with their fists and sliced him with their claws all the same.

After an agonizing amount of torment, Rowan simply ran. He got the idea in his head that, if he could just get a moment to himself, he could recover his strength and make it through the night. His awareness became touched by something foreign, something immaterial but undeniable. His perceptions became augmented by something that was unknown, yet something that he felt he could trust. The glimmering gold on the dull scales of the enemy, the carelessness of the drunken partygoers, and the danger of simply waiting for Casey to act all jumped into focus for him. The layout of the estate was laid out before him, not visually, but he could feel a path of least resistance that led him somewhere safe.

Rowan took a serpentine route away from the main event and around to the side of the mansion where intricate hedge-animals basked in the moonlight.

Rowan crept through the hedge-animals, and suddenly the foreign presence in his awareness flickered and disappeared.

Fuck, was this a trap? But I was so sure... No, I made it here without any other the other's following me, somehow. This all must be part of it.

As Rowan crept through the bushes, he tried to bolster his confidence in whatever had led him there. The fact that he was alone was a good indicator that he was on the right path.

Yet, his confidence wavered when, turning a corner, he stumbled upon a lone sc'ermin devouring a partygoer. Rowan grunted his disbelief, and Larkin's dragon-like sc'ermin's pointed ears shivered. It whipped around to pounce at Rowan, not realizing or caring who it was attacking.

In the moments of the sc'ermin's advance, Rowan readied himself for combat. Before they could connect, in a startling instant, scales erupted from the space where the assailant's head used to be. Rowan's eyes widened as he watched the sc'ermin's lifeless, headless body drop to the grass.

Then, the foreign force touched his awareness again, and Rowan looked up to a materializing, feminine form. The form became visible to him, her appearance breaching the space of the air around her as if she were surfacing from below water.

The unknown sc'ermin that appeared before him was dressed in skintight black clothes and had jet black skin. Her forehead was protruded in a rounded bulge, and her hands were shaped like two razor sharp fins. She also had black dorsal fin that curved down her spine. Rowan stood, mouth agape, his own fangs glowing in the starry night, and could only listen as the mysterious sc'ermin "spoke" to him with words that seemed to be his own thoughts.

"Rowan Tarwick, my name is Euphene. I'm here to help."

When Euphene spoke, her mouth moved along with the words that materialized in Rowan's mind. Rowan saw that her teeth were sharp enough to pierce through skin and wide enough to crush bone.

For a moment, Rowan worried that she was trying to trick him into trusting her, that she wanted to lower his guard in order to kill him.

Would she even need my guard to be lowered? Surely, she could kill me instantly if she wanted to.

His fears were then heightened when two of Larkin's sc'ermin came slithering through the hedge-animals, and then he was set at ease when his enemies paid no attention to Rowan or his new ally. Apparently, the foes couldn't perceive them, nor could they see headless sc'ermin and it's half-eaten prey.

"When you became able to see me, I didn't make myself visible," Euphene said, and emotions of trust were transferred to Rowan along with the words that seemed to already be a part of him. "I made you turn transparent with my abilities."

"How is that possible?" Rowan spoke with physical words, and he watched with apprehension as Larkin's sc'ermin continued on their path to slither away.

Euphene smiled and said, "Those blessed by Zephiscestra have powers that you haven't begun to fathom. I'll tell you everything that I can before hell breaks loose."

CHAPTER 30

CASEY CREPT DOWN an ornate hallway, the walls on each side adorned with rows of painted portraits.

He walked past merchant princes, invincible knights, and wealthy mercenaries on his quest to find Larkin's daughter. A'devios had said that she would be inside of the house, but Casey did not see her among the hubbub of the party. He made his way through the hall with increasing anticipation until he heard voices around a corner. Walking as quietly as he could, Casey poked his head around the bend and saw the person he sought to find along with the villain he was hoping to decimate.

"Ah, speak of the devil," Larkin said, as if it were a secret joke between them. "I was just speaking to my daughter, Lexie, about you. You seem to be the star of the night. Everyone is posting about you. You must be immensely proud to have all of your work pay off."

"Can it, Larkin," Casey said, unable to control his rage.

Larkin laughed and said, "Still upset about your little boyfriend? Don't worry, I have a surprise for you later. Actually, he should be showing up at any moment."

Casey's vision blackened when he pictured Charlie as a sc'ermin. "Don't tell me that you have Charlie under your control."

Larkin laughed cruelly and said, "If only I were so devious. No, the convention center wasn't a prime place for me to perform an incantation, although that prospect would have tasted so sweet. I missed out on that slaughter, but do not think that I would throw such an elaborate event, rife with wealth and notoriety, if I didn't have another plan up my sleeves.

"You see, Casey, you are going to help me perform the largest sacrifice in the last century. I have over a hundred prisoners in the catacombs beneath these grounds, all huddled in rooms that are rigged with nerve gas. Did you think that I would have siphoned so much power from you just to keep me safe? From *you?* You are an insect in a world of wolves, and I am the alpha. At the climax of the night, when you perform your little song, the deadly nerve gas will go off and I will gain a legion for my army of sc'ermin. You'll be under my control forever, so get used to it."

Casey bit the inside of his cheek in anger and said, "You'll never get away with it."

"It's hardly unprecedented," Larkin said, moving down the hall to a portrait of an ancient Roman man with laurels in his hair. "Take Augustus, here, for instance. He was a consul, a military dictator, who conquered new lands. In battle, he ordered his men to take as many prisoners as possible and then slit their throats by the scores on the killing fields. Your friend A'devios told me that, at the height of Augustus' power, he controlled over a thousand sc'ermin that gave his soldiers unparalleled martial prowess."

Larkin walked further down the hall, followed by Casey and Lexie, and stopped in front of a painting that depicted a sea captain. "This man was named Edward Clack, and he commanded the SS Keltus, a great frigate in World War II. He recited Zephiscestra's incantation aboard his vessel, which was rigged with explosives. Not one to go down with the ship, Clack escaped the war to live as the sole monarch of several small southern countries. He ruled with an iron fist, and liked to parade through the villages and personally take whatever he wanted. I, however, will rule the world behind the scenes, leading the people into an age of production that will put the Industrial Revolution to shame."

"Daddy, do you really mean to tell him your master plot in its entirety?"

Casey got a look at Lexie for the first time. A woman in her mid-twenties, Lexie was tall with unbothered, formidable posture. Her hair was thick and strong, a blended blonde that turned black at the sheared tip of the fringe that hung above her shoulder. Her skin was smooth and impenetrable, and it gave the perception of a matte friction whose durability lay in the fact that it existed without question. Lexie's clothes fit to her form. Her body was deceptively muscular; the subtle contours of her arms and legs were firm and hard, and the control with which her stance balanced with her trained knowledge that she was not going to strike anyone in that moment conveyed a sense of safety that could be mistaken for submissiveness in the eyes of arrogance.

Lexie spoke with full intention of who would and wouldn't understand her. Casey implicitly knew that she was sending her father away by making him believe that she was working alongside him. Lexie didn't need to wink or nudge him for this understanding to be conveyed. The meaning of her words directed to each individual hit their ears precisely as she intended.

Indeed, Larkin was shaded from her true intentions. He felt that his implicit beliefs about her were being affirmed: she deferred to him and would follow through with his plan. According to Noah Larkin, Lexie's sc'ermin was supposed to be apprehending Rowan at that very moment. With his present understanding of Euphene and all of the work that he and the other elite Zealots of Capital Vice had put into her, *into themselves,* he believed that his plan was already working flawlessly.

This was the peak of Larkin's triumph. Inside of himself, he basked in the glory of success. His deepest desire had always been the amassment of physical objects in all shapes and forms. He easily extended that desire towards sc'ermin, which morphed his view of other humans into raw materials which existed to be refined for his benefit.

At that level of power, he was well within the sights of the Zephiscestra, the ruler of his entire reality. Larkin could feel Her Favor surrounding him like an aura.

The Favor was power flowing from Casey in a barely perceptible iridescence of the light between them. There was another beam of light coming from Rowan, far out in the distance. That beam was being shared among Larkin's many sc'ermin on the mansion's grounds. On earth, at that moment, Larkin's estate was the primary focal point of Zephiscestra, and She pushed against the outside edges of that matter in every direction from the quantum points in physical space. Her pressure from the outside of physical space vibrated the matter that surrounded and consisted them, and Noah Larkin resonated with those vibrations in a way that only he could find such a pleasure.

Larkin noted that he could, indeed, get used to that.

Lexie resonated with the Favor as well, although she remained more levelheaded than her father. Over the course of her life, she and her sc'ermin had

grinded their teeth on the whetstone of hundreds of sc'erva, which were offerings from her father.

Noah Larkin and the others had force fed the inky hearts to Euphene for
decades since Lexie first learned how to speak. Lexie was close to the goddess
Zephiscestra in her own right and was able to wield the benefits effectively.
Only very recently was she able to align those benefits more closely to her true
will.

Casey, his strength stolen, could feel none of it. He stood, numb and filled
with rage, without any deeper knowledge of the supernatural happenings around
him.

Larkin knew this and pitied him for his ignorance. Larkin decided that, with
his victory seemingly secured, he needed to ready himself for his great sacrifice.

Noah Larkin looked at his daughter with performative, smug superiority
and said, "Lexie, darling, why don't you show Casey to your room before he
performs. I know how much you like him, and it would help Daddy out a great
deal."

Lexie's smile conveyed obedience to her father. "Of course, Daddy, anything
for you." For good measure, she added, "And, don't forget about the sacrifices
that you promised to give to Euphene."

"Daughter, after tonight, you and I will possess power that we have only
ever dreamed of before. Now, go and take care of business. I have a little errand
to run before the show."

With that, Larkin left Casey and Lexie alone in the hallway.

Casey, his rage unsatisfied, was about to find out whether he was right to
trust A'devios. Whatever Lexie did next would change the course of everything.

She turned to him and said, "Okay, let's tear this fucker down."

⊹⊱◈⊰⊹

Outside, Rowan and Euphene walked amongst partygoers and sc'ermin alike
without anyone noticing.

Rowan was reminded of the first days after his unholy resurrection, when
he didn't know why other humans couldn't see him. Back then, he often became
frustrated at the loneliness that came with invisibility. After days in Larkin's cell

with only mean-spirited sc'ermin to keep him company, Rowan was thankful to fade back into obscurity.

"We're not actually invisible," Euphene was saying. "Light is still bouncing off of us, it just doesn't register in the others' minds. It's just one of the things that I can do, one of the things that no other sc'ermin capable of alone. Of course, it came with a price."

"How many sc'ermin did you have to kill to gain that power?"

Euphene clicked her tongue and said, "I've eaten the sc'erva of many. Other sc'ermin have eaten many sc'erva as well, but not nearly as much as I have." She stared into the distance at a massive, beastly serpent that was coiled around a manicured tree. "When we consume sc'erva, our bodies become more durable, we have a faster reaction time, and we can generally move more easily in combat. For a special ability like this one, I only had to have the realization to ask for it. Zephiscestra smiles on the strong, and with Her Favor you can do anything you wish. Although, I don't believe that we possess these abilities ourselves. Zephiscestra lowers Her hand to earth and imparts Her will for our benefit."

"All I have to do is ask Her?" Rowan thought back to the budding awareness that he felt while he was with Steve. The ability to guide and control his passive influence over humans was definitely special, and perhaps it was similar to Euphene's ability to control the perceptions of others.

But I've not eaten as many sc'erva as her... But if all it takes is the realization to ask... But did I ask?

The possibilities and potential of this information flooded Rowan' mind. The notion of growing more powerful alongside a sc'ermin that he could call a friend was certainly enticing.

"Well, you do have to eat a lot of sc'erva to get to that level. I was just making a point."

Rowan's awe didn't fade. "What else can you do?"

"I have asked the goddess for one other gift. Well, I have asked her for many things, but if a gift suits you well enough, the goddess will begin to offer it exclusively. She likes to see you in her garments all of the time. Our goddess can be called sentimental, on a good day."

Euphene gazed knowingly into the space around them. Rowan waited patiently for her to continue.

"With just a thought, I could make any one of my enemies' head explode. Their head, or any part of their body, really. The head is just the most satisfying."

"Why don't you just kill them all while we're invisible, then?"

"I've dreamt of it, but we can't do it now. Lexie is tethered by her father. If his precious sc'ermin started dropping, he would be the first to recognize the betrayal. He idealizes his daughter, but his possessions are dearer to his heart."

"What do you mean when you say that she is tethered?"

Euphene smiled ruefully. "Zephiscestra has bestowed certain gifts upon the earth, physical pieces of the Black Jewel that surrounds us and makes up our reality. These artifacts can be used by anyone, regardless of Favor. Of course, Divine Favor outweighs the splendor of the pieces, but they allow humans to share in the power that sc'ermin enjoy.

"Lexie has had pieces of the Black Jewel embedded in her body since the day she was born. Those pieces have counterparts that are embedded into the bodies of Larkin and other high-raking members of the commune where A'devios gathered Zealots and sc'ermin together. If they are activated, some of those pieces can cripple Lexie and I. The most impactful would send her straight to non-dimensional space. The Zealots that hold the pieces would have to sacrifice a great deal to activate them. But that would just be a failsafe to their plan."

Euphene gritted her teeth. "Noah kills for Greed, mainly for money, which he believes brings power. He kills with the same voracity with which he collects dollars, and he has amassed hundreds of sacrifices over the years. When Lexie was growing up, he would kidnap people and turn them into sc'ermin. Then, he would restrain them and have me consume their hearts. I became much stronger because of it, which is why I look like I do now. I also developed an even stronger hatred for Noah, which he mistakes for wariness of his superiority. Due to the pieces that bind us, we weren't able to become fully aware of how we were being controlled. A'devios, though, just recently disposed of the pieces that were within him. He gave us recognition of where we really are, what we are really doing, and what we *could* be doing. I don't trust him completely, but the fact that I can even have misgivings about him points to the fact that my will has been freed."

Rowan didn't trust either of them, fully. But he could not deny that they both fed his thirst for knowledge of his nature and the nature of his reality. From his present state of imperceptibility, he felt like he could observe the world around him, and the revelations acted as the intoxicant that he had craved for so long. For a moment, he felt warm, safe, and detached from the troubles that surrounded him.

Digesting his thoughts with mellow satisfaction, he didn't have the where-withal to question how short-lived this pleasure would be.

CHAPTER 31

Lexie Larkin's heels clicked down the drab stone maze beneath the mansion. They passed door after door of old, thick wood that bore no windows.

Muffled cries could be heard coming from behind the doors, and Casey had the inkling to save whoever was behind them.

"Don't bother," Lexie said. "Most of them are long dead. They're sacrifices that refused to follow my father."

"And the others?" Lexie grimaced. "Kidnap victims, fresh for the night. I'll call the cops after my father is dead. Let the humans take care of each other."

"Is there anything to tie you to the kidnappings and the murders that have taken place here over the years?"

Now that he had a human ally, Casey worried about her safety.

Lexie laughed away insanity and said, "Oh, there's a whole host of evidence that my father stacked up against me as leverage so that I wouldn't betray him. Don't mind me, I have a safe house to lie low for a while until Euphene and I figure out what to do next."

They twisted and turned down the circuitous hallways, their shoes echoing ominously off of the dull walls. Eventually, the doors grew more and more sparse, with more spaced in between them, and the moaning ceased all together.

The stone was more weathered at the end of the labyrinth, and parts of the floor seemed to be stained with the remnants of blood that was solemnly washed away after regular application.

Casey and Lexie reached a metal doorway, large and imposing, made of a shiny black material. While the rest of the doors grew more decrepit as they sank further into the catacombs, this door was well maintained and even seemed newly installed.

Lexie procured a small object from somewhere in her dress. It was an idol carved from a single jewel in the shape of an alligator with ram's horns. She held it up to the door and it glowed a luminous black light. Suddenly, without Lexie otherwise touching its surface, the door opened silently.

Casey peered through the portal and could not believe what he saw. Inside was a cavernous room carved directly into the rock of the earth. Piled throughout were stacks of money in all types of colors and denominations. Some of it was paper, millions of dollars' worth, but there were also bars of silver and gold, as well as priceless antique furniture. A few chairs appeared to be the ancient thrones of powerful monarchs of the past. Brown paper rectangles that must have been the masterpieces of dead artists were resting along the curved walls of the room, and marble busts and statues circled the keep from the time of antiquity.

None of the wealth and riches had as much of an impact on Casey as what lay in the center of the room. There was a large basin made of glittering gems in the shape of a toad with its mouth wide open. Dangling above the great bowl, upside-down and unconscious, were ten men strung up by their ankles with a rope attached to the ceiling.

Casey looked around for the person who could have done this—and then he saw him.

Fix—A'devios—stood on twelve legs next to the door. In four hands held above his head, A'devios held a large idol shaped like an ox with the wings of a bird and fins like a fish. A'devios' forehead and bald scalp were covered with human eyes of every color. Some of the eyes that were gazing up at the idol shot forth to look at Casey and Lexie.

The idol glowed with impressive black light and Lexie screamed. Two of A'devios' arms shattered, their meat flying a few inches away from the bone before evaporating into black embers. A'devios needed to regain his stance when two of his legs exploded in a similar fashion.

Then, as the idol above his head phased out of existence, black minerals shot up her legs from a base that materialized on the floor under her feet, and soon she was completely encased, frozen in place. Casey stood rooted to the ground in fear as the basin began to glow as well. The men above it regained consciousness and tipped their heads back, screaming, as their blood poured from their mouths and was collected by the hungry toad. When their lives were spent, their empty husks fell one by one into the dark pool without a single splash or ripple. Their bodies disappeared into the shallow basin and were gone forever.

⊷⇒◉⇐⊶

Rowan did not directly identify their invisibility wearing off. He and Euphene still remained as visible to himself as before. But he observed Euphene step into a combat stance and the scaly sc'ermin turn their heads in surprise.

Larkin's sc'ermin were aware of Euphene's ability and noted that she and Rowan materialized together.

Euphene sent a thought to Rowan's head. Her telepathic words came with warm understanding. In his mind's eye, Rowan could understand that the thought that she sent him was a dense, complex seed that he wouldn't be able to fully understand in the time being. Euphene, with her years of preparation, was able to decipher all of the seed in an instant, then transfer the actionable information to Rowan.

"It seems Zephiscestra wishes that we hasten our plans. She is rescinding my gift of invisibility and bestowing upon me another."

Their minds connected, Rowan was amazed and afraid of the mental paths that Euphene could take while riding the fickle waves of Zephiscestra's will. Through Euphene, he could understand that the goddess worked Her will in a single direction. Every seeming reversal of motivation that sent them careening through their emotional rollercoaster appeared as a straight line from a higher, divine perspective.

Larkin's sc'ermin quickly realized that their ally had gone rogue. After a moment of recognition, the enemy was upon them.

They came from everywhere, weaving through celebrities and servants to descend on their position. One of the sc'ermin pounced at Rowan, claws and teeth bared. There was a series of clicks and the air seemed to whine, then the foe's torso shattered, splattering Rowan with thick black blood.

Before he could make a move, strange sounds engulfed him, muffled, as if he were suddenly underwater. Dozens of sc'ermin exploded around the lawn, staining the immaculate linens of the party with each volley of clicks.

Rowan looked at Euphene, who was sending her attacks in every direction.

One of their opponents got too close to her and she sheared him in half with her razor-sharp fin.

A loud thought intruded his head. "Don't just stand there," Euphene communicated. "Defend yourself!"

⊶⩵⊙⩵⊷

A tendril of black smoke wisped out of the concoction from within the basin. The tendril snaked towards Casey, who shouted for help and almost passed out from fright. Undeterred, the smoke wrapped itself around Casey's finger and the ring that Larkin had placed there. The ring melted, and Casey felt a sense of wellbeing and strength that was totally out of place considering the blisters that were appearing on his skin.

⊶⩵⊙⩵⊷

Rowan licked his lips and the world came to focus in an instant. There were dozens of them running at him with breakneck speed. Rowan saw the hunger in their eyes, and his heart pounded in his chest.

Rowan took a last look at the oblivious partygoers who were becoming increasingly coated in inky blood. He was not sure why, but his strength suddenly returned to him. It was as if heavy chains had been loosened from his wrists. He bared his teeth, crouched his knees, and joined the fray.

⊶⩵⊙⩵⊷

A'devios spoke. "Ah, Casey. You are much more lovely in person. I must say, you are absolutely glowing."

The spider's voice was the most terrible thing that Casey had ever heard, gravelly and noxious, and it reminded him of rocks falling on a casket.

A'devios continued, saying, "I've waited so long to meet you, but—and you must understand—I've been very shy. That's a new feeling for me, one that I haven't experienced in over a century. However, I am so glad to finally meet you."

Casey's wits returned to him and he said, "Fix, what the fuck did you just do?"

A'devios tittered and said, "No need for my alias, Casey. The cat is already out of the bag. My former followers know that I was helping you kill them. I can never return to Capital Vice. You might as well use my real name. I would love to hear that word on your lips."

Casey gnashed his teeth. "Why did you kill Lexie? Why did you kill those men? That was never part of the plan."

"I knew you wouldn't like it, and that's why I never told you. However, if you are to be a true Zealot for Zephiscestra, you must learn to deal with a little violence. That is how our goddess operates, after all."

Casey fumed, the pressure in his head building and seeming to solidify the spaces in his brain.

"Lexie isn't dead, as you can see if you look closely. In fact, I'm *protecting* her."

Casey whipped his head toward Lexie and saw that what the spider said was true. Lexie's eyes were rolling in her head and her mouth was open in a wild scream. She was completely trapped in the translucent jewel encasement, but she was very much alive.

A'devios said, "Her body has been, well… booby-trapped, for lack of a better phrase. Myself, along with her father and a few other Zealots, implanted her with very small, yet very powerful idols. Those idols allowed us to control her and keep her true power in check. Now, though, I need her sc'ermin to kill as many of her father's sc'ermin as possible. He would be able to cut her off if it weren't for my protection.

"As for the men, that should be obvious, my love. Larkin was stealing your power and making you weak. I so hated to see you in such a state of depression that I chose to set you free. You can't fault me for helping you."

Casey shook his head in disgust. He knew that he needed A'devios' help to destroy Noah Larkin, and he would *still* cooperate, but he wouldn't play politics with his words. "You know nothing about me," he said. "You're a monster."

"You wound me, Casey," A'devios said. "Now you know why I waited so long to reveal myself to you. But, I thought that you would be drawn to *power.* I mean, *look* at me. I said that I recited Zephiscestra's incantation and then sacrificed myself two hundred years ago. I became my own sc'ermin, and I have been evolving ever since. I performed the ritual in order to walk and see the world, and I have been everywhere on earth, as well as places beyond. Do not be afraid. This is what true power looks like. Surely, you must be impressed."

Casey narrowed his eyes and scowled. "Impressed? I'm horrified. But it's not just your appearance that disturbs me. It's the fact that you can murder ten men without batting an eye, and then act like it was nothing."

A'devios frowned deeply. "Zephiscestra is the true name of justice, and all I do is through Her will. You can gain Her favor as well if you follow me. We can make a new community of Zealots, and you will lead them with me."

"You say you love me," Casey said. "If that's true, you'll end this with me and let Lexie go."

"It's not that simple," A'devios said. "I wasn't sure that I was even capable of love anymore, but then you showed up. I'm too powerful for Lust energy to affect me so strongly, and yet I want us to share in carnal relations more than anything else in the world. If it's true love, so be it. If your Lust is that strong, I am fine with it as well. It would mean that you are a powerful Zealot, and that is what I crave most of all. I want to see you grow old, and when you die, I will follow you to our goddess's kingdom and meet Her with you at my side. You made me realize that my time has grown too long on this planet, and you have given me an ultimatum to meet with my destiny."

"You've lost your mind if you think I'll do anything for you," Casey said. He couldn't believe what was happening. He could take down Larkin with A'devios' help, but he would only be trading one captor for another.

The world seemed to spin as A'devios kept talking. "You don't really have a choice," he said. "I could control your mind if I wanted to, but you'll follow my orders willingly. We are going to set fire to this room and everything in it, and I will film you so that Rowan and Lexie's sc'ermin can wipe out Larkin's sc'ermin, just like we planned. You have your song prepared?"

Casey's eyes shifted as he nodded.

"Good. I have set up a grand piano for you to use. We will do this now."

Casey was sweating, and the cave wasn't even on fire yet. He was determined to see this part of the plan through. But, since he was still unsure of what would come next, he decided to chide A'devios once more. "And if I refuse?"

A'devios looked at him as if he were a petulant child. "Then, Rowan will die, and you will lose your memory of him, as well as develop an intense phobia of all types of personal recognition. I wouldn't be surprised if you became terrified of technology as well, since you have been exploiting social media since this all began. Larkin knows that you have been freed from his curse, and his sc'ermin are already descending upon us. Give him the strength he needs now, or it's all over for you both."

"Why didn't you use your statue to kill Larkin instead of getting rid of the ring? Wouldn't the curse have been rendered useless?"

"First, you would still be under his spell. Your power would simply go to the surface of the Black Jewel in Zephiscestra's palace. Second, that idol was meant to lift enchantments, not to kill people. However..."

A'devios reached into a fold of his cloak and revealed a scepter that was about a foot long. It was a slender rod, made from a single mineral like the other artifacts. The wand was chiseled into the shape of a dove, tiny wings outstretched at the tip, with tentacles forming the shaft and handle.

"*This* idol can kill, but, either way, Larkin is too favored by our goddess for it to have any effect. The power of these objects come from sc'ermin who reside in Her Palace, but any blessing they give must be approved by Her. I sacrificed many of my own prisoners while you were locked in Larkin's cell, yet he remained alive. The only way to get to him is a traditional battle of strength. That is why you must sing. There is no other possible course of action."

Casey considered his options and found that there were few. His only choice was to follow A'devios' lead. He could set Lexie free, augment Rowan's strength, and bring Larkin to his knees, all with one song. It pained Casey to abide by the will of the murderous creature before him, but until this was all over, he had to follow A'devios' rules. Larkin was the more immediate threat to Rowan aboveground, who was now surely fighting for both of their lives.

Really, there was no time to mull over a decision.

Without another word, Casey strode through the vault and up to the piano. He took a seat on the bench, scraping the stone floor, causing the vault to screech.

Casey recited the lyrics in his head. He had an idea for what the melody would sound like, and that would have to be enough. He practiced with his fingers while A'devios walked around the room with another idol in his hand. Soon, the room was alight.

A'devios gave Casey a small lion-like idol to protect him from the flames, then began filming.

CHAPTER 32

"My lips were still warm,"

Hundreds of thousands of people watched Casey sing into the microphone that A'devios, now off-screen, had prepared for him.

Rowan, with unprecedented power, clamped down on a sc'ermin's rough, slender bicep until he completely closed his jaw. He spit the scales out of his mouth and dodged under a brutally fast swing that left its sender reeling. Rowan ran forward and tackled a dragon that was six feet tall to the ground.

"My nerves were a storm,"

Paper of all kinds of worth blackened and curled in the magical red flames. Landscapes were lost in their melting frames of gold. Dead presidents passed again in waves of light.

Rowan punched into the tall sc'ermin through the soft underbelly and reached through his ribcage for the heart. When he freed it from the body, he tore into it with his teeth. With all of the power flowing through his veins from Casey's Indulgence, the maneuver was fairly easy.

"I saw the outlines of the dead,"

The massive piano played Casey's gentle melody to locations encapsulating the globe. Casey's own eyes were closed as countless onlookers sat enraptured by the bright, flickering light on his face.

A smaller sc'ermin jumped on Rowan's back and slipped his claws between his ribs. Rowan felt his torso being stretched in the instant before his load lightened in a shower of scales.

Euphene, thanks to A'devios' protection, was still the most powerful sc'ermin on the battlefield. She far surpassed Rowan in unaided strength, and, for the first time in her life, was shielded from the dampeners of Capital Vice.

"While the night before, I shared their bed."

A'devios reveled in his triumph. He was not unlike Larkin in that he had amassed a lot of power in his life. Consequently, he had gone mad from it. The centuries hadn't been kind to the Zealot in terms of the integrity of his subconscious. After years of preparing himself for his goddess through building physical power, he had lost the ability to feel Zephiscestra's true will. A'devios had no idea that he would be leaving his home dimension that night, forever.

A clock struck 11:00 PM and collapsed in a fiery heap on the floor. Casey's livestream reached two hundred and twenty-four thousand comments in a matter of seconds.

Anti-Capitalists were divided on the content, one side praising an abstract idea of a world without currency, the other side lamenting the gross waste of resources.

"And my baby's passed on,"

Euphene realized that the gain of her power meant that someone was augmenting her strength. However, it was more power than she had expected to receive that night. She telepathically reached out to Lexie, but the sc'ervice couldn't connect their thoughts. A potent thought entered Rowan's mind: "We have to get to the catacombs."

Finely aged wines burst from their bottles and sizzled on the hot floor. Their corks burnt to ash and blew around the room in the turbulent air patterns. Alcoholics Anonymous members cited passages from The Big Book, but connoisseurs wept into their glasses.

"While he's fighting on the lawn,"

Casey's voice was elevated above the raging fire wreaking havoc in the cave. The idol that A'devios had given him worked like a charm; the flames circled him but left him a wide berth. Casey felt the inferno's warmth and carried his voice as far as he could, all around the world.

Elsewhere, Larkin felt the loss of his power immediately. He was alerted to the activity on Casey's social media pages, and found the livestream instantly. Larkin recognized his treasure trove beneath the crackling fury and sweltering heat. He fingered the nooses that he kept in a bracelet around his wrist, then started for the vault.

"I'm just an empty shell,"

Rowan pounded through his enemy's weak spots, making holes where their sternums once protected their precious hearts. He pulled out as many sc'erva as he could and swallowed them hastily. Euphene eliminated all threats that escaped Rowan's decisive blows. Rowan felt his torso elongate as he consumed the hearts. His arms stretched until it was easier to put them on the ground, then Rowan was running on all fours and pouncing on his foes. Euphene had never seen a transformation more rapid and complete. She was in such a state of awe that she sent a sc'ermin through the wall of the mansion instead of decimating his body outright.

"Consumed by things from Hell,"

Rowan's hands became paws and his jaws proved ever more lethal. He could sense aspects of objects that he couldn't see with his eyes, wandering spectral hallways on the trail of Casey's scent. He shot through the hole that Euphene made in the wall of the mansion. He smelled the Indulgence emanating from his master and chased the sensation.

War bonds curled and cracked in the chaos and twisted through the air like smoking jets. Deeds to thousands of acres of land were razed into dust, their cremains drifting throughout the desolate atmosphere.

"And I need to pull my weight, for all the demons that we ate,"

Larkin was transported through the earth by idols like fish in the shape of clouds. He was dropped at the doorway to the vault. Larkin pressed his key-ring onto the door, but the gate wouldn't budge. He realized that A'devios must be involved, which meant that many Favors would protect them.

A'devios held the camera with a steadily trembling hand, giving the cinematography a more natural look. He felt Larkin's presence outside the vault and, with one of his remaining hands, clutched the idol that he might use to sacrifice Lexie, if he could sense that Zephiscestra would allow her father's life to end. In the heat of his triumph, A'devios didn't consider that Larkin could breach his defenses.

"And my secrets keep me sick, but I know what makes you tick."

With Euphene obliterating holes into the walls and floors of the mansion in a straight shot to the vault, Rowan barreled as fast as he could towards Casey. Any enemies in his way fell in heaps on his warpath, but Euphene told him that they were running out of time. Rowan bared his fangs and pressed on, never considering the scenario where he didn't save Casey.

A grotesque sc'ermin pressed its body against the vault door while another handed Larkin a knife-like crowbar. Larkin stabbed the tool into his sc'ermin's back, oozing black blood onto the metal and stone of the floor. Larkin removed the tool from his sc'ermin and wedged it into the doorframe. The blood on the crowbar started to boil, and the tip of the pry began to glow.

"Please baby, show me the way. I can see your love in the light of the blaze."

The camera shut off as the doors opened.

Larkin entered the vault. He was accompanied by four highly developed sc'ermin that had the appearance of ancient dragons of myth. Two of the sc'ermin had nooses around their necks, the ends of which culminated in a bracelet around Larkin's wrist.

Casey stopped playing the piano. The trails of sad notes drowned quietly in the roaring inferno consuming Larkin's hoard.

A'devios let the camera clatter to the floor. He had a faraway look in his eyes, and he seemed to be praying.

"End of the line," Larkin said, sweating. "You've taken a lot from me tonight, but not more than I can recover by making a more sacrifices. Unfortunately, I'll have to kill you all first. Even you, Lexie, my sweet daughter."

The bracelet on Larkin's wrist glowed and then detached itself and rose high into the air, bringing the lengths of rope with them. The nooses tightened and the sc'ermin were lifted off of their feet by their necks. Their yellow eyes bulged out of their sockets before they were sent to their goddess in non-dimensional space.

A'devios looked at Casey knowingly and said, "Next time we meet, we will be employed in the court of Zephiscestra. I look forward to fighting by your side, my love."

Larkin's sc'ermin fell lifelessly to the ashen floor.

The ropes that had bound them shot towards A'devios. His arms and legs were mercilessly restrained by expanding, looping cords, then the ropes began to pull him apart. A'devios screamed in bizarre ecstasy as he was ripped limb from limb, the gifts he received from Zephiscestra collecting on the stone floor in a puddle of black and red blood.

A'devios was taken to the goddess when he was just a torso and a head. His more mutated appendages and features evaporated in a cloud of gold, and his already decaying human form shriveled and stiffened. The scepter shaped like a dove rolled in between Casey and the corpse.

Larkin laughed as Casey scrambled for the scepter. "Go ahead, Casey. Try to kill me. A'devios couldn't do it with that idol, or else I would already be dead. I could feel his futile efforts to end me during these past few days. Your supposed savior made countless, fruitless sacrifices. You don't even have anyone to use as an offering for our goddess. Pick it up, and give it your best shot."

Rowan and Euphene bolted through the catacombs until they could see the vault. About a dozen impassive sc'ermin were blocking the entrance. The foes stared at each other for an instant before Euphene collapsed one of their chest cavities. Rowan growled deeply and charged on all fours.

Casey held the wand and pointed it at Larkin. The Executive Producer didn't have any more idols to hang him with, but the teeth and claws of the scaly sc'ermin could kill him just as effectively. Larkin waited patiently as Casey began to speak.

"Noah Larkin," Casey said. "You are a mass murderer and slave driver. You take pleasure in killing if you stand to gain from it, and you are completely without remorse. Zephiscestra, I call on you now."

Casey had wanted to see Larkin devastated, but not dead. As an abstract, long-term punishment, he had figured that his unending hatred of him would be nourished by the knowledge of Larkin's living torture. However, in that moment, Casey wanted nothing more than for the man in front of him to be erased from the world.

"Zephiscestra, I have nothing to offer you but my own life. Take it in exchange for this man's immediate death."

Larkin laughed. "You hate me so much that you would sacrifice yourself? Sorry to disappoint you, but I'm staying on earth. I can send you to Zephiscestra now. It's not *entirely* what you wanted, but consider it a parting *compromise*."

As Larkin's sc'ermin attacked, the mysterious scepter glowed. Larkin looked down in horror as his feet became encrusted in black gems which rose quickly to cover his entire body.

Casey shrieked when the wand turned its pointed tip at his own heart. The dove's tentacles separated and then formed a geometric pyramid of sharp angles and thin lines.

Euphene shattered several of the sc'ermin in their way, and Rowan mowed down the rest with his fangs. They finally made it through the vault door.

Rowan arrived just in time to see the wand pierce Casey's chest. His human fell to the floor.

Rowan looked back at Euphene, who wore an expression of pity and gratitude. Then, Rowan dissolved in a wave of yellow sparks and golden dust. As he disappeared, the world around him faded and he saw that he was in a trench that was rising in all directions. He saw the smooth surfaces of the Black Jewel covering every line of sight with infinite faces. The Jewel was opaque, but he could sense other trenches hidden behind the solid walls of the universe containing forms of life that he never would have thought possible. Rowan could feel the energy of infinite facets of the great gem which shined on him in brilliant warmth. Then, the outer reaches of the gem glowed in a color that he had never seen before. Rowan realized that there were outer edges to the universe, final waypoints to the space beyond. The Jewel was made of infinite aspects in a finite area. The boundaries of his reality opened up before him, and suddenly he was free.

Larkin's sc'ermin turned to face their encased master. As they watched, a score of glittering daggers materialized in the air around him. The jewels encircled Larkin's form, then plunged into his body.

There was a shower of radiance, and then Euphene and Lexie were alone in the vault. The jewels fell away from Lexie and clattered to the floor. Euphene caught her human before she hit the ground.

"Are you alright? I don't sense any injuries."

"I'm fine," Lexie said, her eyes closed. "Where's my father? A'devios? Where's Casey?"

Euphene shook her head.

"They're gone. They're all gone."

Lexie's eyes fluttered open for a moment until she saw that what Euphene had said was true.

"Then it's all over," Lexie said.

"For now," Euphene said, "until your father tries to take his revenge from the right hand of Zephiscestra. And, on earth, there's still the survivors of Capital Vice. None of them were here, tonight."

Lexie gritted her teeth. "Then, there are certain steps we must take."

The fire still raged around them as they picked up Casey's body. Euphene held him in her strong arms, and Lexie led her out of the vault, away from their home. Forever.

EPILOGUE

Trevor Greenbrook sat alone in his apartment, putting the final touches on his newest video.

He had an empty feeling in his stomach, and he wasn't able to get comfortable in his favorite chair. He couldn't stop thinking about the news articles that he obsessively read over the past few days.

Noah Larkin, the famous producer, was found stabbed to death in his home. Even more terrifying were the mass graves found on his property and the literal dungeons he kept beneath his mansion.

Trevor shuddered at the thought of the prisoners the police had found down there. The main suspect of the murder was someone that Trevor had been interested in, before all of this came to light.

Casey Benton had been missing since he filmed himself destroying untold millions of dollars' worth of Larkin's property.

It was too much for Trevor to bear. A few nights before the slaying, Larkin had contacted him with a business deal. Although Trevor usually kept his distance from labels in order to retain full creative freedom, he was enticed at Larkin's offer. If the contract were signed, Trevor would have gotten to work very closely with Casey as part of a team.

It had certainly piqued his interest. Trevor had already been paying attention to the rising star.

However, before he could agree to anything with Larkin, Trevor had gotten a call from a mysterious man with a heavily modulated voice who basically told him everything that was just then appearing on the news. He threatened Trevor's life if he chose to go along with anything that Larkin offered, as well as speaking about anything from their phone call.

Trevor got up from his chair and stood in front of his window, wondering what it all meant. Suddenly, there was a knock on his door. He opened it and gasped at the form standing in his hallway.

Lexie pushed the door open wider and stepped inside the apartment.

"Hi, Trevor," she said, brandishing a long, sharp jewel. "I need you to read something for me, and then we're going to take a little trip."

Made in the USA
Middletown, DE
01 August 2022

70347296R00146